MAKING WAY

a novel

Theo Dorgan

NEW ISLAND

MAKING WAY
First published 2013
by New Island
2 Brookside
Dundrum Road
Dublin 14

www.newisland.ie

PRINT ISBN: 978-1-84840-224-9
EPUB ISBN: 978-1-84840-225-6
MOBI ISBN: 978-1-84840-226.3

Typeset by JVR Creative India
Cover design by Andrew Brown
Printed by Bell & Bain Ltd., Glasgow

New Island received financial assistance from
The Arts Council (An Comhairle Ealaíon), Dublin, Ireland

10 9 8 7 6 5 4 3 2 1

For Pat & Raffaela
στην Ορτυγία ξεκίνησε

1

A fishing boat stuttered past outside, coming home with nightfall; the yacht rocked gently, her transom dipping once, twice to the worn concrete quay. Tom Harrington glanced over his shoulder, a reflex, checking the shorelines, then turned back to the woman smiling at him across the cockpit. She raised her glass, a silent salute. It was her boat, after all, her varnished hull that might have scraped.

The evening plumped itself over Ortigia, a soft dusk settling on the bay outside, a more velvety dark coming to roost in the spaces between the tall trees, between the trees and the high stone wall behind them. Under the old streetlights, as their ancestors had done for hundreds of years, the people paraded slowly the long walk away and back.

Tom bent to the ice-bucket between their nearly touching feet and poured them both the last of the dry white wine. She leaned in to touch foreheads as he filled the glasses, a warm, companionable gesture. Soon, he knew, she would raise an eyebrow, her head tilted to one side, and he would take her hand, allowing her to lead him below.

Just then, as the glow warmed him, content that his instinct had been good, that this matter-of-fact young skipper desired him, he looked up at the quay again. A tall, bony young woman was sauntering past, part of the evening flow. She glanced at him without breaking stride, a flick of a look, no more. For a second, two, he met and, unaccountably, held her eye.

He felt a momentary discomfort, a fleeting thing, a quick stab of unease, easily smothered. He brushed it away as his new-found companion drained her glass, looked to her moorings and then back at him. It's time, he understood her to mean, and he smiled back at her. She raised an eyebrow.

Four boats further along the ancient quay, the young woman stopped.

She did not look back, but stood there a long time, pale in her black linen shift, her bare arms folded, looking down into the cockpit of Tom's boat. When she turned away and walked on, she did not look back.

2

Dawn, and the quay was deserted. Tom stepped carefully ashore, bent to the line, coiling the free end from long habit before tossing it on board. His back ached, and a spasm made him cough as he straightened. The Frenchwoman stared at him gravely, seeing through the moment, a brief trouble in her thoughts. Then she smiled, turning away, raised a hand in farewell, her other hand reaching blindly for the throttle. A cough of blue smoke from the engine exhaust as her boat nosed out, her attention on the fishing boats coming and going nearby. As she brought the wheel over she turned and called: "See you, Tom, don't know where, don't know when. Fair winds."

A sailor's farewell.

Tom stood there a moment longer. He hadn't asked where she was bound, and there was sense in that: why would he want to know?

They'd sailed in together two nights ago, which is to say they'd arrived at more or less the same time, two single-handers standing off the long quay in the purple dusk, watching and pondering, choosing a berth. He'd waved her in ahead of him; she'd smiled, and in that moment each acknowledged a transitory bond, birds of passage recognising each other. That she was maybe twenty years younger than him had bothered neither — each had recognised in the other the settled calm of the habitual solitary sailor, the seasoned willingness to take each day as it came, each small adventure as it presented itself.

Cordiality. Tom savoured the unbidden word as he walked the short distance to his own boat. Amity. *Amitié.* He glanced seaward, and saw she was already far down channel. A moment of melancholy squeezed his breath as he hauled his boat's stern in, crouching to step aboard. How many more such moments would there be?

Prompted obscurely, he looked back over his shoulder as he ducked to go below, already drawn into the familiar smells of home. He stood in the half-dark, his momentum having carried him down, and considered what he'd seen: the girl from the night before, still in her black dress, regarding him coldly (it seemed to him) from her seat at a café table. After a moment he climbed back up again, and looked across at the line of shaded tables. All were deserted, each standing in a pool of water that was already drying into the rising heat, each with four chairs tipped forward to let the water run off.

Tom knew what it was to have fate touch his neck, to feel that sudden cold spread up the back of his skull. He was perhaps not paying attention now, but soon he would remember that sudden chill, that click when your real life breaks through the daily fog.

3

He hadn't meant to sleep; he'd simply stretched out a moment on the starboard bunk in the saloon. He felt old and stiff when he woke, his khaki shorts twisted around his scrotum, his sandals uncomfortable, his neck sore. I need a shower, he thought, smelling himself as he sat up, rubbing the back of his head. What time is it? Dark in the cabin, the sun on the bow, so it must be late afternoon, the hatch looking aft a brilliant shield of light. Christ, I must have been worn out. In the head, under the warm water from the black bag hoist to the mast spreaders, he took stock. Where would she be by now, he wondered, Christine? Heading south, the wind, what, south east, what there was of it? She'd be tacking to keep offshore, maybe thinking about abandoning her vague plan to make for Tunisia. He soaped himself, allowing his hands to evoke memories of last night, feeling the middle-aged weight of himself in the heavy stomach, the padded shoulders. She might change her mind, he thought, take the wind for prompt and make off for Bari on a long reach, then up into the Ionian's late-summer winds. Something to play with. Where after all, liveaboard vagabond, did she have to be if not where she chose to be? One place as good as the next.

He knew he was already forgetting her, as she would by now be forgetting him. There had been other Christines over the years, might be again. One way or the other he was mildly grateful, detached, expecting little, content with what came his way. Restored to his habitual self, he was whistling as he dressed, considering practical matters of food, supplies, the small jobs that always need to be done on a boat.

Wincing suddenly, he lifted the lid of the chart table, reached into the back for his tablets, shook two into his palm and replaced the bottle.

Swallowing water, he climbed the companionway and stepped out on deck.

He didn't see her at first. The German boat to port had slipped away while he slept. There was a charter boat coming in on his starboard side: fenders out, he saw, four people on deck, coming nice and slow. No bother. He turned to the quayside and there she was, legs dangling to the slapping water a metre below, toes turned in, one sandal dangling. Painted nails, long legs, her knees covered by her white sundress. She was holding a straw hat in her hands, a man's hat he thought, irrelevantly, in an oddly formal pose.

"Good afternoon, Captain", she said. He was oddly disorientated. Partly because of her tone, steady and low, something else there too, and partly by the shock of her clear blue eyes under short-cropped jet-black hair. Bony face, he thought. Voice and look confused him, he wasn't quite sure to what he was answering when he nodded, coughed and managed a lame "Good afternoon to you" in reply. Was that a faint hint of mockery in her brief smile? She said nothing more. She sat there, waiting. Something familiar in her face, her poise, the feel of the moment. He felt far away, and then he felt ice on the back of his neck.

He stepped forward, stretched out a hand. "Come aboard, won't you? May I offer you a drink?" Pleased with his own laconic playfulness. She regarded him coolly, unfolded with surprising speed and grace, dusted the back of her frock and stepped onto the after deck, her fingers laid firmly in his upturned palm. She sat, put her hat in place with both hands, looked up at him with shaded eyes. Waiting. He felt himself steady, calm flooding through him. Like someone taking a deep breath after a cold shower, towelled dry, eyes closed. Her sudden smile seemed to him, was, a sign that she'd understood. He smiled back as warmly, feeling suddenly very comfortable in himself. Sure.

"We've met", he said.

"We haven't", she said, still smiling.

"A gin and tonic?" he asked.

"A gin and tonic", she said, and turned to watch as the incoming boat glanced softly off their fenders.

He handed her a glass, a broad tumbler; the blue of the gin, faint bubbles, ice bobbing around a thin slice of lemon. She stood to take it, each looking at the evening light in the other's glass. Their heads came up together, time resuming its orderly flow. They chinked.

"*Sláinte*", he said, and "*sláinte mhaith*" she replied.

Tom surprised that he's not surprised.

"This morning…" he said. She turned, motioned with her free hand: he saw the faint stripes where the wet chairs had printed dust across her dress. He looked for perhaps a moment too long at her shapely ass. She pretended not to notice, meant for him to see she was pretending.

"Last night…" he said.

She shrugged and turned away. "No business of mine", she said, but that wasn't what he'd meant, and when she saw that he'd meant the look that had passed between them she nodded once, and saw that he'd understood.

4

"You must be hungry", she said eventually. They'd sat there for a long time, watching the crowds brush past, up and down the long promenade under the tall, thick trees in their burden of dusty leaf, under the yellow streetlamps, under the stone walls giving back the heat of the day as it faded.

I am, he realised, as if the words had triggered the thing itself, hunger suddenly raw and overpowering in him. He dipped below for a light sweater, paused, rummaged out another, this one smaller, more delicate, a pale blue. She took it without a word, looked at him thoughtfully, took a quick sniff at the faded perfume. Tom shrugged, she let it go, let him see she was letting it go.

"It's clean", he offered, uncertain for a moment — and meant to go on to say that it suited her eyes, but then saw with sudden clarity that they were past banalities. He couldn't quite see how this had happened, and for a moment he was puzzled, his head lowered, his shoulders hunched.

"It does", she said, expressionless, reaching a hand down from the quay.

"It does what?"

"It goes with my eyes. Good, huh?"

She stood beside him, considering gravely, her lips moving a little as if debating with herself. Finally she set off down the long promenade, leading the way at an easy pace. He caught up in two strides.

"How long have you been here?" he asked presently, ducking aside as a small boy barrelled past on a bicycle, his father calling after him, the child pedalling as fast as he could and laughing ... laughing.

"I'd say that was you when you were his age", she said, as they watched the father break into a run.

"And what were you like?"

She thought about this for a moment or two, looking around her as they walked.

"Like … her." She pointed, selecting a small, dark girl who walked between grandparents, composed, watching the passing crowd with detached curiosity. He looked past the child's mask of assumed solemnity, saw the pent-up vitality in her eyes for a moment, the active intelligence, restrained by precocious will. In training, he understood. Training herself.

"They don't know what they have on their hands", he said, watching the grandparents go by.

She looked at him sidelong without breaking her easy stride. "No indeed, they do not. Do you find that easy?"

Find what, he was going to ask, and then thought better of it. "Sure."

"Could you do that from the start? I mean *see* people?"

"You know the way you mask it, and then after a while you start losing it, and it only comes back occasionally?"

"Yes", she said, "and then one day it comes back and you accept it and you know it's back to stay?"

They stopped for a moment. They looked at each other. They walked on.

He was thinking about Christine. How she'd come down along the quay to take his sternline, had looked in his eyes when she tossed the end back to him, stood there a moment, searching his face then said "Come by tomorrow, I need to sleep now. What's your name?"

At the Fountain of Arethusa they turned left, climbing against a tide of young people on foot and on noisy scooters, of sauntering tourists enjoying the cool of evening, locals out for a stroll or bustling by on some business or other. The Piazza di Duomo opened out before them, flagstones still warm underfoot, baroque palaces and merchants' houses to right and left of them, the Duomo itself up ahead on the right, facing a scribble of bright-coloured awnings.

Suddenly Tom was decisive. "Right then", he said, "I think a prosecco at the Café di Duomo, yes? Then fish? There's a good place…"

She swept her hat off with a gay flourish that was only slightly mocking. "Yes, my Captain, whatever you say, my Captain."

Seated, a hand to her cheek, legs swept decorously together to one side, she leaned in towards him in a pose of breathless adoration. "This is killing them", she said, motioning with a flick of her eyes to a table of soberly dressed older men nearby. "The older one's a judge, the younger ones are lawyers", she said, "and they can't figure out what a *principessa* like me sees in a salty old reprobate."

"Old? Old? What do you mean 'old'? I'll have you know…" — hamming it up, enjoying the bluster — "and how do you know they're lawyers? They might own the shops, work in pharmacies…"

"They're lawyers", she said, "and I know how old you are."

He let that pass, leaning back to look at her frankly.

"I won't sleep with you, you know", she said then, watching the retreating waitress carefully, "but you knew that anyway."

He did, he knew that, had known it the night before when their eyes met. He looked at her steadily now, feeling the seriousness that had materialised between them. He, too, looked after the waitress and she laughed. "She won't sleep with you either; you're way too old for her." And then she grew still, looking directly into his eyes. She took his hand between hers. Tom wondered at how cold her hands were, then thought no, not cold: cool.

"I'm getting cold", she said then, drawing the cardigan from her lap, draping it over her shoulders, settling the hat on her head the wrong way round.

"Thirties look, right? Cardie, cloche, ingenuous expression?"

"Come on then, and by the way, don't you think it's time?" Pushing back his chair. A scraping noise on the flagstones, heads turning towards them.

"What? Oh, names. You're Tom, right? I'm Clare Hogan." She stuck her hand out as they rose. He took it, briefly, to the puzzlement of the lawyers.

"You're some *ingénue*." Tom wondering how she knew his name. A small prickle of doubt.

"That's right, a hungry *ingénue*. Tipperary, since you were about to ask. Originally."

"Originally?" Tom settling with the waitress, overtipping by just enough to get a nod.

"See you, *Tom*, don't know where, don't know when" — her accent perfect, the broad Provencal vowels — "that's how I know. You were wondering. Relax."

Then, stage Russian accent this time, leaning towards him as they started walking, "I. Am. Not. Assassin."

"So ... originally? And then?"

"Oh, good schools, Trinity, you know. I live in Dublin." Then, forestalling further questions, she took his upper arm in both her hands, allowing him to mock drag her up the Piazza.

In the street after, he thought she was going to kiss him, and she thought he was going to kiss her — and that would have been the end of that, both realised. Instead, with no awkwardness at all she buttoned up the cardigan, set her hat right way around and said: "OK, I have to be getting back to my hotel." And she was gone.

Tom didn't look after her, set his mind against thinking about her, let his feet carry him down through the winding lanes and steep-stepped streets back to the boat. He sat for a long time on the foredeck, one hand flat on the cool teak planking, one gripping the forestay, his feet dangling either side of a stanchion. When he rose to go below, hearing the crew from the boat beside him making their way along the quay, he registered with little surprise that he had no recollection of whatever it was he had been thinking about. He swallowed two painkillers, stripped, washed and climbed between the sheets of his bunk, still without conscious thought. He dreamed all night, deep, slow dreams, but when he woke he had no memory of those dreams.

5

Clare woke from a composed sleep, lying on her back, hands loosely clasped across her bare belly, the sheet in a tangle around her waist. She lay a moment with her eyes closed, then opened them smoothly, lay there a moment longer, gaze unfocussed.

Right then.

She showered, packed her washbag, took a last look at the bathroom and closed the door. Next, she selected her clothes for the day — pants, cut-off blue jeans, white T-shirt and, after a moment's thought, boat shoes; she packed her bag, gave the room a last look-over and left without looking back. Ordinarily she would feel a moment's inexplicable nostalgia leaving behind any room she'd slept in, even if only for a night. Not today.

To her right as she left the hotel, the bridge back into Siracusa proper. Ortigia, that island city within a city, had a pulse of its own; she had felt this when she'd arrived, had settled into that pulse in the week she had been here, walking the narrow streets, coming out of the shade from time to time into sudden, blaring sunlight. A place of secrets, she thought, of old families long-established, a place where everyone knew everyone else, knew everything there was to know about everyone else. She climbed to the Piazza Archimedes, and hesitated. Which way? Shorter to turn right, but she chose the way ahead, to the Piazza di Duomo.

She disliked the baroque façade of the Duomo, she decided finally, standing there, the bag at her feet, giving it one final inspection. Too fussy, too full of itself and of the architect's smug pride. Hmmph!

She smiled at her own ... bossiness, was it?

The books made rather a point of the fact that a temple to Athene had stood on this site; that columns of the temple had been incorporated into the fabric of the church. Clare tried to imagine that temple now, turning slowly on her heel, subtracting the high, ornate buildings, seeing as it came into focus the wooded hill, the fall down the north face to the city walls, the big harbour beyond.

Inside, she sat demurely before the statue of the Virgin, gathering herself, her thoughts, her forces. She closed her eyes.

When she opened them, minutes later, an old woman was looking at her, close, black clothed from headscarf to thick stockings, time-worn shoes. Leaning on an elegant stick, she stared at Clare, nothing hostile in that look, in those shrewd, measuring eyes. Clare looked directly into that considering gaze, and after a long moment each smiled, woman to woman. The old one reached forward, pinched Clare's right cheek between thumb and forefinger, patted her head.

Crossing the Piazza with a firm stride, Clare passed by two men who had stopped to look frankly, inquisitively, at her. *"Buon giorno, gli Avvocati"* she said as she strode by, seeing them begin to bridle, not looking back, acknowledging the wink from last night's waitress with a grave nod.

6

Early as Clare had woken, Tom had woken earlier, resolved. He'd filled up his water tanks, been to the bustling market for fruit and vegetables, the supermarket for other provisions, the harbour office to pay his dues. Everything stowed away, he was thinking about Clare as he tidied his lines, unhooked and stowed the sail cover, ran some basic engine checks, hosed down the deck and cockpit.

Parting, the night before, he'd been on the point of asking: will we see each other tomorrow? When he'd realised, simply, there was no need to ask. Now, shaving carefully, he wondered about this. Women liked Tom, he knew this, and he liked women. He often felt, with men, that he was acting some tedious part, some cartoon version of being a man. Not with women. Some men, he amended the thought, some men. It was true, he had some good male friends, and he asked himself, as the thought jinked away from him, what those men had in common. They didn't bluster, he decided, they were brave, mostly; brave in their feelings, he amended this, forceful *and* tactful. And they liked women, and women liked them. Women, a sardonic young nephew had informed him recently, are the *beta* version. He'd been ready to explain this, in the lordly way of young techies, been disconcerted when Tom had laughed and punched him on the shoulder, told him there was hope for him yet. Remembering this now, Tom laughed again, thinking of Clare with true appreciation. Not a word wasted, the phrase came unbidden, not a word wasted. Then, finally, clarity at last as he held his head under the cold tap: What is this about? What next?

He had a sudden, searing urge to see her. Now. "Come on", he muttered, shoving his feet into deck shoes, tugging a T-shirt over his head, "come on." Then, "steady now lad, steady, steady." He felt something that was not quite an erotic electricity course through him, a charge from the mains. He stopped, puzzled, on the first step of the companion way. Last night, when she'd said "I won't sleep with you, you know", he'd known it was true, known that as an absolute fact, a decision that would not be revisited. It had been plain between them, acknowledged, understood. He thought it strange now, head down, that he hadn't felt even a moment's disappointment. Tom had always been at ease with women, had laughed outright in recognition, years before, when he'd read that phrase in Kerouac's last sad book, "I am a great natural bedfellow." Now, thinking of Clare, he realised he did not desire this desirable and obviously very *interested* young woman. Not exactly. But she excited something in him. As if looking at a cinematic image, he saw himself suddenly in a room long ago, arguing to a group of friends that Freud had got it back to front. The sex instinct shaped by the larger life instinct, appetite. As abruptly as the image appeared, it dissolved. Park that thought, Tom, he told himself, park that thought. Come on, come on.

And of course there she was, in the café across from him, cradling an espresso, the small red-banded white cup in one hand, the other hand raised, palm towards him, fingers twinkling.

When he didn't respond she looked, for just a moment, disconcerted.

Walking across to her, taking his time, Tom saw the waiter in his doorway, watching all this with interest. He signalled to him with thumb and forefinger opening away from each other, a lift of his chin, a nod.

"Well, well" she murmured, rising to take his kiss on one cheek, the other, "Master and Commander!"

Tom looked at her haughtily, pulling a chair around so that they sat side by side.

"Behave yourself, woman" he rasped, "steady now."

She spluttered, giggled, surprising them both.

"Jasus" she said, broad Dublin, when she'd stopped coughing, "did Christine come back last night or wha'? Mister testosterone himself!"

The waiter put Tom's large Americano before him, palming a handful of wrapped biscuits to Clare, beaming when *la signora* flashed him a radiant smile.

Tom looked at her shoes.

"You're going sailing", he said.

"I am indeed."

"With me."

She looked at him, held his look.

"Fate", she said. "You know how it is." A pause, then: "But…"

"I know, I know" he said, "you won't sleep with me."

"Well, you might look as if you regret that?"

Tom turned, pushed back, looked her frankly up and down.

"You're very beautiful", he said, "you are. And we click. But it is how it is." He thought for a moment, and added: "It is how it's going to be, right?"

That silence around them. That particular silence.

The waiter brought her bag. He watched them walk to the boat, he watched them go below. His thoughts were very far away.

7

They stood in the saloon, looking around them. The galley to port, U-shaped. Clare touched the cooker, it swung; gimballed she thought. To starboard, chart table, an array of instruments on the console above it. She counted them off: radar, GPS, radio, wind speed, depth … all present and correct, she thought. Two long settees either side, door in the forward bulkhead open to show head to port, hanging locker to starboard, a spacious double cabin in the bow. "Yours if you like", he said, gesturing. She nodded. "I like to sleep in the saloon", he said then. She nodded again. Plenty of storage, she thought, everything squared away. Shipshape.

"What is she?" Clare asked, following him up on deck now. "Cheoy Lee, built in Hong Kong 1960. Thirty-six footer. Teak all the way, solid. Bronze fastenings, Oregon pine mast and boom." He was proud of his boat, she saw, noting his tone of satisfaction. Shy, almost. Slab reefing, she noted. Modified for single-handing. Good winches, too, big enough for the job. "Long keeler?" "Yes", he said, looking at her, seeing how relaxed she was, and attentive. They went forward on deck. "Cutter rig", she murmured, testing the inner forestay.

"How much sailing have you done?" he asked her then. "Pretty much coastal, really. Out of Dublin. On and off. One trip to Cornwall. Around to Baltimore. That sort of thing."

"Nice lines", she said, looking back from the bow at the long coachroof, the big, sturdy wheel in its deep cockpit, the short afterdeck.

Tom made a hand gesture as if to say, all yours if you like. She smiled and said "I'll stow my gear."

When she came back up, the engine was running. Tom had been ashore, run the sternlines though the mooring rings and led the ends back aboard.

"Right, then", he said, "here's what we'll do. You slip the sternlines, here, one at a time. Then you go forward. I'll bring the anchor in as we go out, with this" — a small hand-held control on the end of a cable. "You watch it come in, call back to me if it doesn't come smooth, OK? Watch yourself as it comes home, right? When it's set in the roller, there's a short length of line by the winch. Tie off the shank of the anchor with that, yes?"

"To stop it moving about, I know." Matter-of-fact.

"Keep an eye on that gobshite on the jetski, yeah?"

"Can't shoot 'em eh?"

"No. More's the pity. Hang on." He disappeared below, re-emerged with a glass of whiskey, handed it to her. Waited.

"You testing me?" She stepped to the stern, and poured the whiskey into the oily water, watching it disperse.

"To Poseidon", she said, turning to face his grin. "To Poseidon", he answered, pleased. Then, "ready when you are."

Out they went, then, neat and steady, the anchor coming obediently home. She swayed back the deck to stand beside him as he cleared the harbour mouth. The great bulk of Castello Maniace looming to port, then swinging astern.

"You haven't asked", he said.

"I haven't."

The boat heeled suddenly, a catspaw out of the south east.

Tom narrowed his eyes. "Won't be much, but we might as well get the main up. Here, take the wheel, keep her on this heading."

She stepped in silently, letting her fingers feel the helm as a live thing.

Up at the mast, hauling the big sail up hand over hand, Tom looked back at the fortified island as it fell away from them, thinking I wouldn't like to sail in here under guns. Or ballistae for that matter.

"What?" she asked, as he came back to stand beside her, considering the shape of the sail, hardening in the mainsheet.

"What? Oh, what was I thinking up there?"

"Yeah?"

"I was thinking" he said, embarrassed, "that the sea dissolves the weight of history."

"Well now, isn't that very profound."

Not mocking, indulgent, becoming serious.

"Is that why you spend so much time out here on the boat?"

Tom, suspicious: "Who says I do?"

"The log", she said, having kept him waiting for his answer.

Tom glanced through the hatch, no log on the chart table. She saw him look.

"I put it back. What're the tablets for?"

She saw in his face that she'd gone too far. Flinched.

"I'm sorry, that was wrong of me. Could you take the wheel, please, I need…" — she ducked below.

The damnable thing was, he'd forgotten the tablets today, hadn't felt the need for them until she mentioned them. Now he could feel the need growing, something suddenly wakened that wanted immediate satisfaction. Well fuck it anyway, he thought, and hooked a short length of line from the coaming to the wheel. Keep us on line a minute, he thought, if the wind holds up. Might as well put the kettle on too.

He cursed, letting the chart table lid down on his finger, looked forward involuntarily. She'd come out of the head, was standing there looking at him.

"Tom, I'm sorry, that was none of my business."

He couldn't understand why she should be so distressed.

"Ah look it, I don't know why I reacted like that. They're … they're painkillers, right?" Motioning vaguely towards his chest, brushing the matter away.

"Here, the kettle's going to boil. Make some tea, woman! You can bring it up to me."

"Aye aye, Cap'n", she said, half to herself, with a tentative smile at his retreating back.

They sat on the windward side, motorsailing, shoulders touching. The burnt land slipped by, dipping and rising in time to the swell. Inshore, small boats chugged back and forth, impassive fishermen hunkered down in some of them, sports boats and speedboats breaking the day open with their noise.

"You haven't asked me where we're going", Tom said presently, the mainsheet slack in his hands.

Clare stretched, yawned. "Don't mind, really. Malta?"

She was elaborately not looking at him, felt him stiffen.

"Now how in the hell …? Oh, I get it. The chart under the log book."

"Give the man a cigar. "

"Listen", he said, serious now, "you turn this boat upside down, inside out, OK? Everything about it you need to know, you ask me, or you look for yourself. I don't suppose you're a diesel mechanic?"

"Nope, sounds sweet to me though."

"Ah never a problem, well hardly ever, but you never know, and me and engines don't always get along, you know?"

"Right then", brisk, "if we tack now we'll make in nicely to Lido Arenella. What would you say to anchoring off and swimming ashore for lunch? You can swim, can't you?"

"A cold Moretti and frutti di mare? Sounds good to me."

"How long have you been here, anyway?"

"A week, eight days."

"And...?"

"How much time do I have? Oh weeks yet, as much as I want, really."

And she went below to change.

"What's that?"

"That, my dear, is a piece of genius." Tom was packing towels, shorts and T-shirt, keys and a wallet in a plastic crate. "Now, suppose you don't feel like eating lunch in that rather fetching swimsuit? You pack, whatever, in this, I seal the lid, attach it like so with this here bungee cord to this here piece of polystyrene and ... off we go."

"What a practical man you are, Mr Harrington. And here's me with only this."

She waved a small Ziploc bag in his face, yesterday's sundress squeezed tight and small with a flat purse.

'And if, say, you wanted to bring back beer?" he asked.

She considered this. "A draw?"

"A draw", he agreed.

Two small boys watched them come out of the water, carrying the float between them.

She nudged Tom. He recognised the cycling boy from the evening before. His older brother was bending to have something whispered in his ear. "Probably pirates," he answered the younger one in a penetrating whisper, "and that's their treasure chest. Let's follow them."

"No children, Tom?" she asked him gently, as they climbed the steps to the restaurant, elaborately not noticing their breathless shadows. His stride lengthened. "You look sad, that's all. Never mind."

They dozed after lunch; both woke at the same time, wordlessly picked up the float and made their way down into the water.

"No beer," she said, "and we never even changed."

"We have beer anyway."

"I know."

"We'll have that wind on the nose until we clear the point, then we have to come around to the south west, maybe 225 degrees, no make that 220. About four hours, OK, maybe less? We'll get a land breeze when the sun starts going down, soon now. Might be able to switch the engine off then, get the staysail up, right? Think you can handle things while I get some sleep? I feel pretty tired."

"I can handle it. Want me to run the jenny out when the wind picks up? If the wind picks up?"

Not sure what to say, Tom hesitated. On the one hand, she'd hardly have offered if she didn't know what she was doing, and the big jenny would make a difference to the ride, for sure. On the other hand, and he felt suddenly cold and uncertain when he thought of it — what did he really know about this woman?

All this sparring, flirting, whatever it was had been fun up to now, but Tom was always more sober on a boat than on land. No, he thought, make that distrustful. Positive distrust he called it, explaining the concept to people he was teaching to sail: trust everything, trust nothing. The good ones got it.

"No," he said finally, "call me when you think it's time for a sail change."

Hands on the wheel, staring ahead, she nodded. He could tell she was unhappy about something, could feel irritation stir in himself. God's sake, he was only being sensible, pretty standard stuff with new crew until you had their measure.

She stole a glance at him as he went below without another word. Grey in the face, she thought, something wrong there. She heard him lift the lid of the chart table, let it fall with a bang.

Girl, she thought, what have you got yourself into? Then she gave herself over to the boat, into the long rhythm of it all.

8

Dusk was violet, a great canopy of it, horizontal smoky red bands over the land to the west, when she heard him stir.

"New moon", he called up.

"Turn over some silver in your pocket", she yelled back. "Quick."

"My mother used to say that, when you'd see the new moon through glass. For luck."

His tousled head sticking out the hatch, his good humour back.

"Jesus, woman, are you not cold?"

"A little bit, I suppose. Here, take the wheel and I'll get a fleece."

"Christ, I never thought of that", he said when she re-appeared. "What'll we do if the weather turns bad? You won't have the gear."

"Well, I have some light waterproofs, jacket and trousers. I can layer up beneath them, right?"

"You have some … what possessed you…?"

Something flashed across her face as she turned away; something he couldn't put his finger on.

"Look, I'm funny OK? Be prepared and all that? One time, years ago, this time of year, in Majorca, there were summer storms so bad yachts were washed up on the coast highway! Stuff doesn't take up much space, it's light…."

Defensive. Uneasy? Maybe just embarrassed. Tom thought of teasing her, to lighten the atmosphere, decided to let it go.

"Right, then, land breeze is here, bit fresher than I expected, let's get that jenny out. He stood and watched, waiting to see what she'd do. Good woman, he thought, as she flaked down the coiled lazy sheet so that it could run free. Next, uncleat the furling line, flake that down. One turn on the port-side winch and she began to haul, steadily, evenly, looking forward to check that the big sail was running out free, flicking a glance at the lazy line, make sure it wasn't snagging.

"All of it, you think?" she asked.

"Yep."

Two more turns on the drum now, she reached for the winch handle, began to wind. When the sheet was taut she fed the tail into the self-tailer, jerked it tight. She coiled the end of the lazy sheet then, draping it over its winch, did the same with the furling line, tucking it into its hand-made canvas pocket. Nice stitching, she noticed. Wonder who did that. Satisfied, she sat on the windward seat, leaning back against the slight increase in heel, her elbow tucked over the coaming to hold herself in place. Tom cut the engine, and looked at her curiously. You're pretty fit, he thought, hardly out of breath.

"Tai Chi", she said, still looking forward, frowning at the mainsail. Tom let the mainsheet out a fraction and the boat, coming into balance, found her groove. She turned to look at him, and they both burst out laughing.

Back to mindreading.

For a long time they just gave themselves to the wind and the onrush, the sky going dark now, stars coming out.

"Want some soup?" she asked, shaking herself out of reverie.

"Safety switch for the gas is on the left above the cooker. Chicken is good, in the …"

"… locker beneath the pot store. I know."

Tom shook his head, unsurprised and bemused, as she vaulted below.

9

Night at sea is so utterly different from night at land that Tom had often struggled to explain the difference to people who could not make the comparison for themselves. Think of it as a kind of subtraction. On land you have always the sense of being surrounded by people. Even if you can't see lights, way out in the country, you know there are houses there. You see cars going by, their lights at least. You feel the solidity of things around you. At sea, at night, even in rough weather, pitch dark, big seas, big winds, you feel surrounded by ... emptiness. Water below you, all the way down. Air around and above you, all the way up. The boat starts to feel like an extension of yourself; you sense everything that's happening to it as if you're being touched by whatever touches the boat. What you can't see you feel or smell, a weird kind of intimacy, as if you had feelers all over you, reaching everywhere on the boat. Even on a fully crewed boat you sense, deep in some part of you, the part that never sleeps, that monitors everything, that you are absolutely alone.

And that this is OK.

Maybe it's to do with buoyancy? Being borne up and dandled? And being sheltered? You can go below, turn off the lights, lie there in the complete dark and you're being borne along, you're being borne up. Safe. For the moment. Moment by moment.

Or, on a clear night, it's how bright the stars are, how vast, going back beyond all imagining in the dark where the stars are set? People say it's like that in the desert. I wouldn't know. I think maybe it's not quite the same. "There's no dust in the sky", he'd say, "that's the first thing, everything is clearer when it's clear out here."

"It's like the world has fallen away", he'd say. "Do you feel, I dunno, isolated?" — someone had once asked. "No," Tom had said, "not isolated exactly. Not like an island, if that's what you mean. An island doesn't move with the sea, it stands out against it. The sea is its enemy. On a boat, the sea is with you, and you're with the sea." "And you, on the boat?" "Same thing, you're part of what little there is. You feel very little, you know? Not small, exactly, little, the way you feel little when you're very young." Children know far more than they are aware of knowing, Tom always thinks, and he values this perception. With children, knowledge is direct and immediate, not processed, not … inflected? Nothing belittling about being little, he often says, trying to prise the perception into someone's mind. Once, very stoned, he'd said that children's awareness grows outward in all directions at the same rate, like a sphere expanding. The one inside who knows stuff doesn't change, it's just that as the information grows and grows and grows, he has more to work with. Now who was that? Who did I say that to? No matter, it was the closest he'd come to explaining — getting nothing more for his insight than a dull uncomprehending "right, man, right. I see what you mean, man."

How many conversations, down the years, in which he'd tried to explain this sense of things, the stripping back to conscious, intelligent innocence?

They're into the night now, Tom and Clare, the land breeze holding steady, a couple of miles off the rocky shore — a faint line to the west against the great overarching bowl of night, the bowl of the sea under their keel. He can *feel* her sleeping down there below, a kind of soft, steady throb in the dark cave. There's a low swell, the sea folded over in silver and navy blue, a faint white bow wave coming back the hull, a fuss of disturbed white water astern. The diesel hums happily at low revs, the big sails are full.

Clare is dreaming of the courts of justice. Behind her, as she paces, stern in a black gown, a file clutched to her chest, a gallery full of strangers. Four men on the bench above and in front of her, cold, stone-hard, each with the face of her father. She drifts close to waking, irritable with the crude obviousness of such a primitive dream, impatient with herself for permitting it, but she's tired, tired, she sinks back again into the deep, into the cold ozone logic of that narrow, recurring world.

The door to the forward cabin is wedged ajar. Tom, warming up the radar, the wheel lashed, feels the change in her mood, a faint arrhythmia, feels the long pulse resume.

Part of him says, coldly, you're judging by her breathing, her movements, her stillness. This is stuff you've learned from being with people. But Tom is at sea, down deeper in himself than when he's on land, he trusts that other sense more, he trusts the watcher inside, the one who knows things there are not words for. Strong, he thinks, she's strong, but there's a fault there somewhere, a twist, something not yet worked out and freed.

Back at the wheel, breathing deep and slow, eyes closed, guiding the ship by feel, he understands that they have a compact of some kind (but he knew that from the start), no, he is beginning to sense the nature of that compact, feel it out there ahead of him in the days and nights to come.

I hope I'm up to it, he says to himself then, I hope I'm up to it.

Then, out loud for the night to hear, he says it again, opening his eyes: "I hope I'm up to it."

Movement below. He leaned forward from his place on the starboard coaming. She was bent over peering at the radar, her cheekbone, left shoulder, sharp in the green light.

She felt his eyes on her, or maybe just heard him shift his weight.

"Hi", she said, "bother you?" She meant that she was naked.

"Nope", he said, "but have to admit you look pretty good."

She had a T-shirt in her hand, and she pulled it over her head, still watching the radar.

"What's that up ahead?"

He ducked his head under the boom, looked forward.

"Isola Capo Passero, remember?"

"Oh yeah, off the tip. We going inside or out?"

"I think we'll stay out to the east, probably going to lose the land breeze now, any minute I'd reckon. If it goes back south east we don't want to be in there between the island and the Cape."

She nodded, still watching the screen.

"What are these?"— pointing.

"Fishing boats, most of 'em, a motor yacht or two. Something big heading towards us, two miles."

"How can you tell?" her voice shifting as she stumbled on one leg, the other, climbing into her jeans.

"Come up here and I'll show you."

"Show me what, big boy?" — the universally parodied salacious tone of the long-dead Mae West.

"Behave", he said. "Look, see there?"

"Uh-huh?"

"You can see red and green, right?"

"Means he's heading towards us."

"Corr-rect. What else do you see?"

The oncoming vessel yawed, blanking her red light. "Huh? Oh I see, two white lights on, it looks like, masts?"

"Also corr-rect. Two white all-round lights, one at the stern higher than the one in the bow means vessel over fifty metres. Now, you see those cabin lights, how high they go? You see that they're at the back of the ship? Means she's probably a tanker."

"I getcha. You planning on doing much night sailing?"

"Would you like to?"

She looked around her in a long slow sweep, craned back her head to look above her.

"Oh yes", she said, entranced, not having expected to be, "Coffee?"

"I'll make it, here…."

She took the wheel. He pointed out the various boats that he could see, explained that the radar alarm was set, and would sound if anything got closer than a mile.

He looks OK, she thought, full of quiet. She heard him set the kettle on the gas, the click of the lighter, the soft whoosh as the flame caught.

She closed her eyes, heard the water gurgling past, the occasional exhaust pop from the droning diesel, the creak as the boom moved slightly, settled.

Can't hear the wind, she thought. Pity.

Big old trees around the house, the wind through their heavy burdens of leaf in a summer storm, the thin, high note of a gust when the trees were winter bare. In the high attic she'd made her retreat at, what, fifteen, sixteen? The whole floor to herself, how the empty rooms all around her felt, pockets of cold, grey menace on the bad nights, weights of agreeable loneliness on the better nights, pressing in on her, on her lit room under the eaves.

I haven't been lonely for a long time, she thought, opening her eyes and looking carefully all around. How long do we have? I don't have the instinct to start talking, not just yet. What if he does?

She closed her eyes again, breathing deep and slow, willing herself to feel the solidity of her body, her bare feet planted square on the deck, the feel of things coming up through her soles, the buoyancy, the drive onward....

He watched her curiously, unmoving, braced to the slight roll, there on the companionway, a mug in each hand.

Something familiar. Something familiar....

"You going to stand there all night admiring me?"

"Shut your mouth, you cheeky bitch. You're way too thin for my taste anyway. I suppose you'd like a biscuit now with this?"

"We're almost round" he said presently. "Keep her head south for a half hour, bring her to..."

"220 degrees?"

"No, more like 210. I've been thinking. I don't want to cross the mouth of Valletta in the dark if I can help it, too much shipping. Best if we pick up the coast a bit farther east, stooge along tomorrow night, maybe heave to for a couple of hours."

"OK, we're in no hurry anyway, are we?"

Time, it's time. They both feel it, right now, right here.

"Wind's going south east, like I thought", Tom said, breaking the silence, feinting away for a moment. Watchful.

Not a word said, she hauled in the sheet on its smooth-running traveller, centring the main. A quick look around — "Ready about", she said, soft but clear. Then, "tacking."

"Neat, very neat", Tom said, coiling the new lazy sheet, a critical eye on the jenny as it settled to the wind coming over the port side; small things below rattled, settled, finding new niches for themselves.

Clare, knowing from the feel of the moment that the initiative was hers (why had she said that about not being in any hurry?) lined up her thoughts in her head. The case for Clare, she thought. OK.

"I'm a lawyer", she said. "Barrister. I do mainly criminal work." She paused, allowed him to decide against a smart remark, and spoke on into his silence.

"The summer's my own if I want it to be. I travel a lot. The Med, mostly. I'd never been to Sicily, got fascinated by Siracusa — you know, Plato, Archimedes, Normans, Saracens, all that.... I was there a week when I saw you come in. Saw the tricolour", a backwards jerk of the head, "and by the way, isn't that supposed to come down at sunset?"

"It's OK if you just wrap it, I'll set it flying again at sunrise."

"You say so. Where was I? I'm always doing that, interrupting myself. Yes. Saw you hook up with, what's her name, Christine. Ah yes, French Christine. You do that a lot?"

Taking Tom off balance. "Do what?"

"Are we going to be like this?" Sharp.

"You're right, sorry. No, not a lot. Depends."

"On...?"

"Both of us, each of us. She came down from Corsica, travelling alone, happy to get away, be by herself. I'd been in Lefkas, where I base the boat? Much the same, really, coast-hopping quietly down, being by myself. No particular place to go. I caught her eye, she caught my eye, you know how it is?"

He's prodding her now, willing her to jump on.

"You caught my eye, too. Remember."

Not a question, a prompt. Parry, thrust.

"And you caught mine. Not the same thing, though."

"No", she said, "not the same thing."

Silence. They thought about this. She ducked to look under the boom at a fishing boat making across their bows, brought the bow a point right.

He waited. She waited.

"I usually avoid Irish people when I'm moving around", he offered.

"Me too", she nodded.

"So...?"

"So, I saw you come in, waited to see who else was aboard. Saw you were travelling alone. I thought, a man who sails on his own. Interesting. Then I thought maybe you and what's her name were maybe travelling in company, you know?"

"What's her name?" Tom is amused.

"Christine, all right, Christine. Don't go reading things ... oh, OK, you're just playing. OK. Don't, right?"

We'll lose the thread, Tom thought, and knew that they mustn't. He gave her a sober look, said nothing. She looked at him for a while, nodded finally, looked away ahead again.

"This is going to take time. You understand that, don't you?"

Tom's turn to nod.

"So, idle curiosity. I wondered if you might be somebody I knew, somebody I might have met over the years. I thought maybe I'd pass by and have a look, OK? Without you noticing, see? Maybe I'd feel like talking to you, maybe I wouldn't. Don't look like that."

"Like what?"

"Oh for God's sake. You think I was sizing you up as a prospect? Have you looked in a mirror lately?"

"Jesus, girl, easy, easy OK?" Tom feeling a sudden concern that he can't fully understand — part of him thinking: Jesus why would she want to insult me like that? Not really caring about the insult; stung by the sharp cold in her voice.

If he were more alert he'd have seen her blush to the roots of her hair, seen the mortification in her suddenly brimming eyes.

"Oh Tom, I'm sorry, I have no idea what that was about. I'm sorry."

Now what? She's floundering, takes a deep breath, another, knows he's waiting patiently for whatever this is to pass through. Recovered, steady again, she said "You're a good man, Tom. You know that?"

Tom, being wise now and aware of it, said nothing. She cut in under the stern of the small fishing boat, not too close but bearing away a bit so as not to rock him in their wake.

"You believe in fate, Tom?" Holding her breath.

"I had a band called FATE once, a long time ago."

"You're a musician?"

"Go on", said Tom, "finish what you're saying. Me next."

"Look", she said, "you ever see someone and you know immediately you have some business with them? It was like that. It started with, I dunno, idle curiosity, and then, I was walking by and you looked at me and ..." her hands off the wheel, gesturing, knees pressed forward to hold her steady, "... and, well ... here we are."

"All at sea?" he offered.

"Hardly."

"It was a joke."

"I know, I'm laughing, see?" She bared her teeth at him.

"Jesus!"

"I'm a defence lawyer, remember? Practice. Good, though? Were you scared?"

And that, he thinks, is some combination: a warning followed by a deft lightening of the atmosphere.

"Your turn", she said. Openers.

"Well, I'm a musician."

"You said that."

"You knew already."

"What? What!" Ferocious, fire in her eyes.

"You went through the CDs below, like you went through everything else, right? Like I told you to? You would have anyway. I played on a lot of those."

"Of course, of course. You're right. Still, tell me about it, yeah?" — pushing him past the moment, don't let him dwell....

"Keyboards, mostly, a bit of bass. Lately, these past couple of years, I've been mostly producing. That's why I'm here, in a way."

"Huh?"

"I just finished producing an album...". He waits for her to ask whose. She doesn't.

"So, I was pretty exhausted, and pretty well-paid, too, so I thought I'd head out here and bum around for a bit, spend some money on the boat."

"Would I have heard you play, seen you?"

"Seen me, no. Heard me, maybe. I hardly ever play live now, small gigs here and there, obscure places with old pals kind of thing. More for ourselves than anything else. These past, what, twenty years I've been happier doing session work, or producing."

He waits for 'who have you played with?' but she tacks suddenly.

"Nobody special in your life? Married?"

"Married?"

"The ring, Tom, the ring."

He holds his hand out, palm down, looks at it for a moment.

"No" — quietly — "not married, no. And nobody in particular in my life either, since you ask."

"Ah Tom...".

"Sorry, sorry, didn't mean to sound sharp."

The moment passing, he thinks, enough for now. A sudden energy drop. The pain sidling up again. Stiff, suddenly, and slow, he hauls himself to his feet. "You OK here for a while?"

"Pass me my fleece, would you? Ta. No, I'm fine here, enjoying myself. You want a call?"

"Only if something changes. Otherwise I'll wake in a bit."

"Sleep well", she says softly to his backward wave.

That went OK, she thinks, that went OK. She listens for the sound of the chart table opening.

10

He slept through the night, woke with a guilty start. Dragged on some clothes, stumbled aloft. Still on the port tack, he noted, surprised and relieved that the wind hadn't changed. She was curled in one of his jackets in the corner of the cockpit, one eye regarding him blearily, her hands tucked up inside the sleeves. The wheel ticked, responding to a short drop in the wind, ticked again as the wind came back.

"Autopilot", she muttered, slurring a bit. "Found the autopilot, found the volume on the radar alarm, turned it up full. Thought that would be all right. What time is it?"

Too tired to look at her watch.

"Coming up to five, nearly dawn. Jesus I'm sorry, I only meant...".

She waved his explanation away.

"'s all right, I kind of napped on and off. You must have needed it. Look behind you."

They were closing the coast of Malta, still a good bit out, but the low red-brown cliffs were getting clearer with every inch the sun climbed over the horizon.

"You want to grab some sleep?"

"No, no. Coffee. Would you make m' some coffee, Tom, would you?"

Heikell's 'Mediterranean Pilot' lay on the chart table, on top of the Admiralty Chart for Malta, north coast of. A neat pencil line showed their course, a series of small circles like beads on the line, the time of the position-taking in a neat hand.

"Figured out the GPS too", she called down, making the hairs bristle on his neck. She hadn't moved, he could tell from the sound of her voice. How did she ... ah for God's sake, Tom, he told himself, doesn't take a genius to work out what you must be looking at. A pretty good guess, come on.

"Don't need to check the log, so?" Trying to keep it light.

"You know you don't need to, why bother asking?"

And that's me in my place, he thought, turning back to the chart, tracing a finger along the coastline ahead. The kettle whistled.

"You know what?" — unthinking, he'd pulled her in close to him, had an arm around her — "I had a look, right, no shipping lanes over there" — pointing slightly east of their present course, towards a small indent in the approaching coastline — and I thought we could heave-to for a while. What do you think?"

"Oh that all sounds jolly nautical if you ask me, heave-to me hearties … this is nice, you're warm, snuggly" — and Tom wonders if she's been drinking.

"No", she says, reading his mind, "I haven't. I'm … just … fucking … tired."

Her head dropped as if her neck had collapsed. Fast asleep. Her breath on his cheek. He sniffed, he thought delicately. She snapped awake, bumping his nose, "I told you! Don't make me cross!" and was asleep again in a second.

Gently, though he knew she wouldn't wake now, he laid her out on the port seat, just long enough for her to lie at full stretch. He went below for a blanket, his fleece, some cushions; he tucked her in carefully. She made small murmurs, contentment he thought, that's what it sounds like. Quietly he rolled in the jenny, slowly, muting the rasp of the winch. He went forward, attached the staysail halyard, took the sail out of its bag, hanked it on to the inner forestay, quietly, quietly; he attached the clew to its runner, pulled it out to the port rail, fitted the tack to its hook on a short strop and hoisted the sail, hand over hand, quietly, slowly. Satisfied, he made his way back, pausing before stepping down into the cockpit, struck by a sudden tenderness. She'd worked one hand free from under the blanket, had slipped it in between cheek and cushion. She was smiling in her sleep, as children do, and Tom found this, somehow, almost unbearable. He shook himself once, twice. Then he disengaged the auto-pilot and began to feed the bow towards the wind. Just as her nose went through he slowed the turn until the staysail was filling from the port side, the sheeted-in mainsail from the starboard side. Like that, the boat stopped in the water, bobbing gently up and down in the barely notice-able swell, drifting, he knew but couldn't see it, slightly sideways.

Hove-to, he thought, sipping his cooling coffee. A painted ship on a painted sea.

After some thought, he got up and set the spray hood over the companionway, keep her head in shade as the sun climbed over the bow.

He leaned out over the afterdeck, set the flag free, watched it snap in the cool breeze.

Then he lay down himself, his heels tucked in, a cushion under his neck, and slept again.

11

The wind shift woke Tom. "South", he grunted, "good, good." A beam reach to Gozo. Come up a bit, too.

Chin propped on her palm, still lying on her side, she was watching him calmly. Smiled. "Thank you", she said.

Tom grimaced as a stab of pain hit under his ribs. He saw her eyes cloud over, and closed his own. Bad, he thought.

Her hand under his neck, helping him sit up. She handed him two tablets, a glass of water. Alarmed, he tried to bat her hand away.

"Now Tom", she said, chiding as you would a child, "don't be irritable. Don't be silly. We're neither of us stupid."

He waited for her to ask what the matter was, felt half-resentful when she didn't.

"Feel like pushing on?" he asked.

She thought about it. "Yes", she said then, "five minutes, a shower and a change."

Tom fiddled with the sails, slow in himself, squinting against the hot, hard sun.

They were riding softly again when she came back up, their leeward drift arrested. The light made bright plaques of silver in the water around the boat, sending glints in under his half-shut eyelids.

A tray in one hand, she flicked open the leaf of the cockpit table, set down yoghurt, fruit, honey, rolls and orange juice. "Butter", she muttered, "I forgot the butter."

A grey tank top, black cotton shorts, a broad silver bracelet.

Tom gestured to the bracelet: "Loose", he said, "be careful it doesn't snag in anything."

"I will", she said. "I thought of that but I thought I'd make an effort."

"To cheer me up, is it?"

"To cheer you up, you ould lech."

Tom caught his own thought as it formed: I was going to get indignant there, what do you mean, I don't need cheering up.... "You're right, I do need cheering up."

Now, he thought, now she'll ask — the sudden panic of knowing he would tell her, that he would answer any question this woman put to him. He braced himself. Literally, his head rigid, shoulders squared back, barely breathing.

She reached across and patted his cheek: "You do", she said, "Ah Tom, you do. Now, what's the plan, Captain?" Brisk, letting him off.

Christ, he thought, I took on a hand and she's halfway to being an Admiral. Not even a day out.

"There's a place I like on the west side of Gozo, but I thought you might like to take a look at Valletta on the way? Unless of course you've been there before?"

"On my extensive travels, you mean? Was that a dig?"

"Yes", he said, surprised at himself, "Yes, I suppose it was. Don't know why, though."

"Retrospective jealousy. Reflex." Smug, licking honey off her spoon, watching him.

"What?"

"You're jealous of all the men you imagine I've been travelling with, or the men I've met and fucked on my travels. Simple."

A challenge, Tom sees that at once. Sits back, decides to think about this. He has a sense that this conversation has already happened.

He's looking down into a room, at two people sprawled on their backs. Naked, cold, but not cold enough to pull the covers back on. They've been making love, there's rain beating on the high window. Summer rain, the light coming into the room filtered through heavy leaves. Saturday morning, he knows it's a Saturday morning. Himself and ... he can't make out who it is. Oh but he knows her so well, so thoroughly he can't *feel* if he's in his own skin or inside hers. Everything in the room is crystal-sharp, the books on the floor, cigarette packet on her crumpled jeans, her blue-and-black glass necklace beside it, his watch on the inside of his right wrist. She lies still, her hands behind her head, soft tufts of hair in her armpits, her smooth brown belly stretched taut, her breasts almost disappeared. The boy is almost as still, Tom sees, but there's pain in his face.

Then Tom is inside himself (he knows it's himself down there) so very far back. Of course I've had other lovers, she's been saying, and of course he knows that but hasn't thought about it; of course I've had other lovers she's been saying and he is ... miserable. Simply unable to deal with what this makes him feel. Desolate. Desolate.

The boom jolts. Tom, opening his eyes, reaches for the mainsheet. She's there before him.

"Take it easy", she says, "take it easy. It's OK, it's OK."

She climbs around behind him, he can feel the heat of her against his back. He tenses, feeling her fingers dig into his shoulders.

"Ssh, ssh", she says, "let me. Talk to me."

"I was very young, you know? I don't know what I thought I was doing with my life. Drifting. She was a cellist, big head of long, curly brown hair. Huge eyes, the most amazing eyes. Oh Jesus we couldn't keep our hands off each other, nothing we wouldn't try, nowhere we wouldn't do it. We were ..." searching for the word now, hugging himself tight, "... we were ... delirious. I wanted, I wanted...". He takes a deep, cold breath, resolution, clarity — "I wanted to OWN her. Completely and absolutely. Nothing I wouldn't do for her, nothing I wouldn't ... but I wanted to OWN her, d'you understand? I wanted to own her body and soul, past, present and future. Jesus what a fucking fool I was, what a fucking fool...".

"Ah let it go, Tom, let it go. It's gone now, it's a long time gone, Tom, how could you know, how could you know, you were only a child, Tom, only a child."

Her breath on his cheek, her face against his face, bone against bone. Tears pouring down his face. Release. Release.

"Come on", she said then, rapping him on the top of the head with a knuckle. "Up we get, Tom, places to go, work to be done."

She went away forward to sit in the bow, feet dangling over the side, the sun glistening on her red-painted toenails. Looking away towards Malta.

And now Tom remembers who it was, back there a long time ago, he remembers how simply they parted in the end, what she did with her life after. He remembers her funeral. He remembers her sister's face at the graveside, the cold, white disc of her face, how she touched his cheek wordlessly, walking away, and kept on walking.

A line from a poem came back to him: "It has not been what we expected."

Then he thought, is that what I am, jealous? No, the answer immediate and convincing. Not jealous. I'm going to die, he thought, I'm going to die some day and before I go I want to transfer everything I know, everything I feel and know into … into someone. I want to be someone else, I want all this to go on. No, he thought then, something inside of him watching this thought unfolding, feeling the rightness of it, no, that's not it. I want to be everyone I meet, and the bigger the impact they make on me, the more I want to be that person, absolutely — while still being me.

I was always like this, he realised then, wondering at himself, I was always like this, since I was a child; caught between always wanting things to be new and always wanting the moment to go on expanding, expanding….

He ran out of energy, then. Just plain ran out. The thought blew away on the wind, but Tom didn't mind, he let it go.

12

"Fancy a quick stooge in to have a look at Valletta?" Tom, invigorated, bare-chested, hands low for purchase on either side of the wheel. "Getting a bit brisk, now, eh? You like it?"

"Which? A stooge in as you call it or the bit brisk? Ah never mind, only joking. I was never in Valletta" — a level look to see his response, a grin, a nod — "right, so. Let's have a look then."

"OK, get the jenny in, then, leave the staysail where it is. There'll be all manner of yokes running in and out of here, we don't want to ram a fishing boat. Or one of Her Britannic Majesty's warships, God forbid."

She's grunting over the furling line. "Could you come a bit into the wind? Ta. Easier now. You heading for home, Tom? Eventually?" Then, answering his sharp, questioning look: "Atlantic Pilot, Tom, Portugal, Spain and France, it's on the chart table."

"Well yeah, possible. I was thinking about it, sure. Why?"

"You thinking of heading into Gib, then?"

"We could do."

We? Careful now, girl, don't spook the horses. But Tom is too preoccupied, lets it drop.

Small boats whizzing in all directions, a few freighters, a tanker the length of a football pitch, the great slow-moving cliff of a container carrier blotting out the sun as she goes by to port. Clare goes forward without being asked, hanging off the forestay, calling the boats she thinks Tom might miss. Tom standing on until the harbour mouth opens, the engine fired up as he centres the sails, puts the wheel hard down.

To left and right and ahead of them as they enter Grand Harbour, rank upon rank of pink-ochre houses, palaces, churches and castles. The sun-baked deep-bedded stink of history, layers and layers of it, generation piled upon, pressed down into, generation. War, pestilence, greed, armour, fire and blood, Islam out of the burning desert, Christ on his bloody cross, the chimerae and phantoms that have burned in the minds of millions. And the daily lives too, the lines of washing strung between a tenement balcony and a decaying palazzo, children's clothes, bleached, speaking of poverty and resilience, of shopping and cooking, of menial jobs found and lost and found again, of small, sweaty rooms in summer, the cold of winter.

All this in a dizzying blast, funnelled into their faces, overwhelming minds that have been calmed by the sea, carried out and down into some deeper silence.

They look at each other in something not far from panic. She comes back to stand in close as Tom hauls the wheel over savagely, gunning the engine until it over-revs, roaring; she puts a cool hand over his on the wheel, he reaches down, pulls the throttle back until the noise is bearable. An arrowhead of foam at their bow as they sweep back out.

"So that's what you call a stooge, is it?" She prods him in the upper arm.

"No it is not. Stooging is … stooging is kind of the sailing equivalent of hanging around, you know, no particular place to go."

"Chuck Berry!"

"What?"

She makes air guitar shapes, growls "no particular place to go", fingers flying over invisible frets.

"You got that wrong", he laughs. "It's all down here along the bottom frets. Look", and he mimes a solo for her.

"OK Mr Muso, tell me all about it then!" Holding a microphone to his face, fiddling with the recorder hanging from her shoulder on its invisible strap. He raises an eyebrow. "Ah call me old-fashioned, I still prefer the oul' DAT, you know?"

"Well", he says, "if you want broadcast quality", ("I do, I do"), "then we'd better kill this" — he pulls out the engine stopper — "and while we're at it, here's a good breeze, let's get the jenny out again, yeah? We've a way to go yet, she'll fly with all sails set, you'll see."

"You love this boat, don't you? I mean you love it, her, like a person?"

"Ah not like a person, now, but yeah, I suppose I love her. Been good to me, you know?"

"Ah go on out of that. You'd ride her if you could!"

A roar of laughter from Tom at that, he's getting to prize this unexpected ribald streak in her makeup. She winks at him, "Oh I can be a cheeky bitch when it suits me." Broad Dublin again, her way of signalling ... happiness?

She's put her imagined headphones, recorder and microphone down carefully, is speeding though the business of rolling out the great headsail, settling it down, making the small adjustments until he nods to her inquiring look, satisfied.

"Right then, where were we?"

"Well, Clare, you asked me about my influences. Let's see. I suppose I'd have to say Choppin was the earliest."

"Chopin?"

"Nope", deadpan, "Choppin. Watching my father splitting logs for the fire." He waits a beat, then "He had a way, of tapping the log once, twice, then splitting it in one go, right? Then he'd tap the chopping block as he swept that away, pick up the next log, tap that twice ... and so on. You know the sound an axe makes on a big log? And then the rhythm, see? He did things whenever he could to a steady rhythm." Faraway now, looking back down the tunnel: "Digging, setting the table, whatever, he had a great sense of rhythm, my Dad did. Like when, say, he was mixing concrete, some small job about the place? Always the ring of the shovel, the tap, double tap, he'd be listening for the note, the beat."

She sees the surprise on his face, rapt in memory.

"You're serious, aren't you? And you never thought of this before, did you?"

"No", he says, "I didn't. Funny ... but I can see it so clearly. I used to go around the house, the garden, very small, before ever I'd have left the house on my own, you know? Stick in my hand, tapping things, listening to the different sounds, chancing all kinds of rhythms. Sometimes when he'd be, oh, I don't know, chopping I suppose, hammering, whatever, I'd try to keep time with him."

"Did he know you were doing it?"

"Yes! I never thought about that but yes, now that you mention it."

"Ah Tom, you should see your face. Lots of love there, was there?"

His face clouded over for a moment. She held her breath, he shook himself.

"Sorry, just, I miss them sometimes, you wouldn't believe how much."

Stop that now, Tom, he tells himself, let it go. Another time.

And then it hits him, no big deal, that they'll speak of these things later, that there's a space out ahead in this conversation for that part of the story. He looks at her and has again that sensation that she's reading his mind. Go on, her face says, go on. And keep the game going too, Tom.

"Puff The Magic Dragon!" he says, "Wooden Heart! Christ, haven't thought of this in years. That thing, who was it, Jim Reeves? 'Put your sweet lips …'" and he hums it, pleased when Clare joins in, sweet and low.

"Harmony!" he says.

"Convent choir", she says, with a grimace. "Boarding school", she adds, and he catches the sour note, files it away for later.

"So, anyway. My Grandfather bought me a guitar when I was, what, ten? Horrible thing, strings way up off the neck, you know? Cut the fingers off me."

"Was he like, musical? Your Grandfather?"

"Musical? That fella? Well I suppose he'd sing a bit, with a drink in him. Which, I have to say, was rare. My parents didn't drink at all. Nah, he just twigged, somehow, that I was musical. God only knows how. Constant source of surprise to me, that fella. Told me once he'd tried mescaline over in England when he was working in Fords. I wouldn't mind but I was stoned at the time. Could have knocked me down with a … ah but sure that's what he was telling me."

"What? You've lost me."

"That he knew I was stoned of course. Sure we just assumed nobody but us cool young dudes knew anything about the likes of that. God! And getting it up for me, too! See your grass and raise you a psychedelic!!"

"Hello? Tom? Hello? Journalist at work here?"

"Huh? Oh, right. Next door had a piano, lovely woman, a widow, Mrs Callaghan. She taught me to play. Here's the thing, though. You'd expect scales, right? Little bitty pretty piano pieces, right? Not a bit of it. I was cutting her hedge for her one day, snagged a finger or something. She's looking at my fret hand, the grooves them old wire strings were cutting into the fingers, OK? Next day she calls me over. Into the front room, never been in there before. Lovely black upright, the cover back, not a speck of dust. Not like in our house, I can tell you. She was what my mother would call 'A Lady', you know? So, what's propped up on the piano? You'll never guess."

Rapt, now. Away back. She sees the wondering child in his face, reaches past him to correct their course a point or two, he doesn't notice. Moves his hands automatically to the new position.

"'The Pop Songbook', that's what! Could you credit that...? Stuff you'd be hearing on the radio, you know? First thing she did, she taught me to vamp chords with my left hand while she picked out the melody. I was hooked on the spot! Lovely mellow tone, that piano had. And when my legs got long enough to reach the pedals! God the things you could do, working the pedals. By the time I was sixteen that thing was part of me. And she was dead. Heart attack on the steps. Coming home from Mass. God but...."

A sudden fury shaking him.

"The fucking platitudes out of everyone. 'Ah but she had a lovely death, she had, she had.' 'Think of it now, on her way home from Mass!' 'Ah she was a saint, God love her.' 'Oh you can be sure she's in Heaven already.' On and on. As if they knew her. I knew her. I knew her watching her hands moving over the keys, arthritis and all, she had a lovely touch Mrs Callaghan, a lovely touch."

"You were angry by then?"

"You have no idea. At everything, everything!"

"Your first death?"

"Second. My Grandfather, a year before that."

Coming out of the trance now, shaken. The pain again, spasm.

She rubbed the back of his neck, small circles, slow, small circles: "Go below for a bit, Tom, maybe have a nap, hmm?"

He shuffled to the hatch. He didn't ask if she'd be all right. Didn't have to, knew that he didn't have to. "Keep her off the rocks", he said. "I will", she said. "There's a way to go yet."

13

He woke when the engine came on. She knew he would, called down: "Gozo, Tom, coming up."

"OK, keep going, be there in a minute."

In the half dark, lights glinting and flashing in the saloon as the boat dipped and rolled, he sat on the bunk's edge, waited for the flashes of memory to settle down. Why am I letting this happen, he asked himself, why now? There's an obvious answer, but that doesn't interest him, because he knows that 'why?' isn't really the question. 'Why now?' is the question. He'd known this was coming, the roll-call, the revisiting of, the ordering of those memories that make up the narrative of a life. That was to be expected. At a certain age, in certain circumstances, all men do this, he knew. Stocktaking? Not quite that, more like answering to … someone or something. What have you done with this life that has been given to you? Something about 'why now?' that he doesn't want to deal with just at the moment, his attention drawn more to Clare and her part in this 'why now?'

He needs to know more about Clare, he realises, needs to park the big questions and find out more about Clare. On deck, Tom, on deck.

Tom has good sea legs, has always had good balance. His alarm as he feels himself lurch towards the companionway must be showing in his face, he thinks — Clare gives him a hard stare as he comes up. He brushes the moment off, but there's a small knot of unease in him now, a small cramp in his breathing.

"Very well, my dear, where are we then?"

She knows that he knows the answer to this, that he's neither unsure of his whereabouts nor testing her navigation, but she answers him anyway, sensing his need for the normal, the commonplace. She's noted that lurch, though, filed it away for reflection.

"Gozo, Cap'n, Sir, eastern tip of."

"Very good, Ms Hogan, very good. The men not giving any trouble?"

"No Sir, Cap'n Sir, all under control."

"Excellent, excellent. I don't smell coffee?"

But his heart isn't in it, she realises, and by unspoken consent they let it drop.

He asked if the wind had been holding and she said it had; he asked why she hadn't put her on autopilot and she said that she liked standing there at the wheel, thinking her thoughts, feeling the boat talk to her through her hands, through the soles of her feet.

She switched on the autopilot then, and followed him down, sat there, her chin on her hands, watched him make lunch.

"Where are we going then, Tom?"

"West side of the island, a bay I like, not far now. You'll see, you'll like it. Interesting place."

She let a moment pass, asked again: "Where are we going, Tom?"

He stood hunched over the chopping board, braced unnecessarily against the roll of the boat, immobile. He put the board and the half-diced onion into the sink, laid the knife down on the board. Without turning he said, "You know what, I think we might relax shipboard rules. You want a beer?"

He took a long-neck Moretti out of the top-loading fridge, some glasses out of their rack, and sat down at the saloon table opposite her. They watched the foam settle in the glasses, chinked.

"I'm taking the boat home", he said then, "I've always kept her out here since I got her, warm water, places I like to visit. The sailing's not hard, mostly; you get blows but mainly I avoid them. I'm taking her home because ... anyway ... So, Ireland. We're going to Ireland. Howth, in fact, you know Howth, right, you sailed out of there. Yeah, well that's where I'm going, that's where the boat is going...."

"And, what? It's up to me if that's where I'm going? I mean, if I'm going with you?"

"Up to you", Tom nodded.

She looked at him.

"If you want to, that is. Be glad of the company."

"You sure? Solo all the way home, isn't that what you'd planned?"

"I wasn't making a point of it. Tom's big adventure, home from the Med all by his lonesome, not like that. I'm just going home, bringing the boat home. You don't want to come with me?"

Clare kept her head down, thought about what to say next, but Tom spoke again: "Clare, tell me this, what are you doing here?"

She should have answered immediately, should have anticipated the question long before this. She continued to stare down dumbly at the grain on the varnished table. Tom let the question hang there, tilted his head back, his gaze unfocussed.

She said: "I don't know."

He looked at her then, cold and shrewd, his free hand massaging heat into the back of his neck.

"That's not true, Clare."

She started, stung, defensive. He mistook this for anger at being called dishonest.

"Sorry, sorry, that came out a bit harsh. I mean..." suddenly floundering, "... I mean you didn't just walk on board saying 'take me away, mister', did you?"

Firmer ground now, her confidence coming back in a rush: "Swept off my feet by your magnetic personality, you mean?" She looked at him from under her brows, her expression softening him, "I wouldn't entirely discount that, you know. I mean, look at the effect you had on...."

"What's her name", he supplied helpfully, making her hoot unexpectedly. Joyous relief to both of them.

"You're very sexy when you laugh, Tom. I bet all the girls tell you that."

He let that go, knowing how she meant it, feeling a sudden unexpected need to protect her from ... herself? Himself?

"We've become friends very quickly, haven't we, Tom? I'd imagine that comes more easily to you. I like being with you, I'm in no hurry to get back. If you're OK with it, sure, I'll sail back with you — what, three weeks at the outside? I have the time. And sure, look, if we get sick of each other I can bail out along the way — you're not planning to make it all in one go, are you?"

"No", he said, shaking his head, feeling the conversation slipping away from where he'd intuited it was going, not quite sure where that was, or how to get it back on track. The boat heeled to a sudden gust; he waited, alert, then relaxed as she came back on course.

They sat in silence for a while, then Clare asked again, reaching for his hand: "Where are we going, Tom?"

But this time she meant the question for herself.

"It's good down here, isn't it?" Looking around. "All this panelling, cupboards — I mean lockers — mattresses, oil lamp … safe, huh? Feels like a safe place."

Taking her time. Getting there.

"I lived with a guy once, used to beat me occasionally. Know what I mean, he'd, I don't know, make an occasion of it? We were very young, just out of college, really. IT. He was early into IT. Pretty rich, now, actually, come to think of it. Not a nerd, though, more the rugger and mountains at dawn type. Bright. I suppose we thought we were in love; I look at it now and I don't know what I thought, really. Big guy, too. Nice flat in Ranelagh, big circle of friends. Don't clench your fists like that, Tom, this was a long time ago, you're not my brother. Let me be, OK? Anyway … anyway every now and then he'd clatter me. Open hand, right? He could have killed me with a punch, I was so scrawny, give him that, he knew that much at least. The funny thing was, I could always see it coming. He'd start, how do I put this, winding in on himself? He thought he was one of those 'new man' types, you know? Talking about his feelings, balancing the macho side of himself? Took me a while of course to see that what feelings he was getting in touch with. To be fair, maybe I wasn't that clued in. But, he'd wind up tighter and tighter, I'd feel it coming, he'd feel it coming and then, wham, some night we'd be squabbling about small things, you know, the small things that drive people daft, right? And he'd let a roar out of him, face all twisted up like you wouldn't believe — and he'd smack me.

"Long after, I used to think about how he never left a mark. Funny, huh? You think he'd thought it out? I don't think so, more an instinct thing probably, but you can't be sure about those things, can you?

"So anyway, there I am, Ms Ferocious Barrister in the making and this, this fucker gives me a slap whenever he feels like it? And I keep taking it? Forgiving him?"

Tom is afraid she'll crush the glass between her hands, prises it gently out of her grip. She gives no sign that she notices.

"So of course, eventually, I left him. Walked out one Saturday afternoon in the clothes I was standing up in. Just like that. Didn't even know I was going to do it, to be honest. Just up and walked out. Taxi to the airport, credit card, Lanzarote. Bam! Just like that. Came home a week later, I sent some of his friends round for my stuff, his friends mind; subtle, hah? Never heard from him again. Can you believe that? He never once, not once, even picked up the phone."

All this time staring sightlessly past Tom's shoulder. Now she looks at him, asking a question with her eyes.

"That could have been me, once", he says.

"No, Tom, no. You know that, I see that. A man who's going to hit a woman, I can tell him a mile off. That's a surprising number of men, by the way. More than you think. I'd say that, at the most, you snapped once and hit a woman. And never forgave yourself. Am I right? The look on your face, Tom. Am I right?"

Looking straight at him now, waiting for his answer. Needing his answer.

A long silence. He feels, hypnotised? He feels, it's owed? How did we get to here, he asks himself, and then he puts his head down and he tells her.

"Came home after a few days away, a gig, Manchester it was, she was in bed with Long Tony. What she said after, when I called her on it: 'Don't get so upset', she said, 'it's only Tony.' She just looked at me over his shoulder when I walked in the room, just looked, said nothing. Fucker smirked at me, rolling off her. Bad idea, the smirk. We all knew Tony, you see, all the musos. I'd been in a band with him once. Long skinny cunt, hair down to his scrawny arse, always in leather jeans. Dead eyes, he had. Thought he was God's gift, you know? Fucking lead singer, if you don't mind. What is it with lead singers anyway? We all knew what a cunt he was. Oh full of himself, was our Tony, affected doesn't even begin to describe it. What? Yeah, OK. I remember seeing red, I swear, I saw red, it's true, you do. I grabbed him by the ponytail , scrawny bastard, swung his head into the wall. Lucky the fucking place was so damp, the plaster I mean.... Anyway, he legged it, cowardly fucker, mister fucking macho, and she got mad at me for 'being so violent', about 'shit that doesn't matter.'

"'Doesn't matter?' I said, I remember saying, and I hit her an unmerciful clatter, right across the face, her kneeling up there in bed, sweaty, screaming at me. She went awful quiet then, just rocked back there on her heels, not a tear out of her, head down, and next thing I know I'm vomiting out the window."

He looks up at Clare. She sits there, unmoving. No signals, none at all.

"I went over back to the bed, I was after walking away to the window" — almost dreamy now, lost to the sway of it happening all over again — "I went over to the bed and I kneeled down on the floor in front of her and I hung my head down and I never said a word. Not one word. I saw the sheet flow past my eyes after a while and I knew she was getting cold and wrapping herself up but I never looked up, not once, and I didn't move and she didn't and then it got dark and we stayed there like that until it was all dark and neither of us said a word until she reached out and put her hand under my chin and lifted up my face and looked at me and said, 'You'll never do that again, will you? I don't mean just me, but not to anyone? Ever?' And all I could do was shake my head meaning 'no' and she just looked at me, both of us could hardly breathe, and I just looked at her and it was the saddest thing in the world because we knew nothing could ever be the same again between us."

Silence. A juddering from the boom, a snap as the jenny folded in, cracked open again. She leaned to one side, looked past him, out the porthole: "Just passing the headland, Tom." He raised his palm towards her, saying let it be a while, let it be.

Then he said: "Those women, you know, when Mrs Callaghan died? I forgave them. Took me a long time. What do you do when you run up against the big stuff, life as it actually is? You run for cover, mostly. I learned that. All they were doing, they were trying to understand the world like it had been taught to them. See, I didn't understand then that they believed all that stuff. It was bullshit to me, I was so smart, so cool, so tuned in, right? But it wasn't bullshit to them, it was life and death stuff to them, and what I didn't know was, I wasn't old enough or smart enough to be serious about understanding what the world was like for other people. Whether I thought they were right or wrong. And when I realised that I'd forgiven them I had a mountain to climb before I understood that the point was to forgive me for the way I'd been to them. About them? So yeah, I forgave myself for hitting her, but it took a long time. Too long, maybe; it took the time it took."

And Clare said, almost in a whisper: "And did you forgive her, Tom?"

"The truth? Yes and no. For sleeping with the guy, yeah, sure. That passes, right? I wasn't a complete Neanderthal, you know? But, the funny thing, for a long time I thought she'd ruined something that might have been very special for the two of us, for us both, you know? I mean, I was for going on, she was for going on, we tried to keep it together after that but, somehow, it wasn't … right any more? We were drifting apart, and there was nothing we could do about it. All the good will in the world. Then she drifted off out of London, America it was, and she wrote, once, twice? And I never heard again."

"But you were happy after that, Tom? You met someone who made the difference, yes? You made the life with someone else you thought you'd make with her?"

Tom shook his head, no. All of a sudden he felt that tenderness towards her again. He said, softly, "It's not like that, Clare. It's not like there's a place in your life, an empty place, and someone comes along who fills it, you know? It's not like that at all. I thought once it was maybe something like that, but it's not like that at all."

After a pause, seeing that somehow he had knocked her off track, he said: "Come on up, work to do."

The Cape was behind them to the left, the wind still south.

"What we're going to do now, we're going to tack right back in there, back down inside the Cape, see? There's a bay in there where we're going to anchor for the night. You'll like it, you'll see."

She looked, what, mutinous, biting her upper lip. He considered this, then he said: "Where are we going, Clare? You asked me where are we going? I don't know. I don't know. Looks to me like we're opening boxes for each other, hmm? Who knows, eh? Sometimes you trust your instincts, don't you?"

She's not sure she knows what he means, so much … stuff, clouding around them.

He said: "Something's going on in my life, something's going on in your life. Big pattern, yes, call it, I don't know, fate, for want of a better word."

She nodded, doubtfully.

"Come on, think back now. When you looked at me, and I looked at you, it wasn't man-woman now, was it? You saw that, right? You said so, remember? Well, no harm to you, beautiful as you are" — she dismissed this with an awkward gesture — "beautiful and desirable as you are", he ground on, laying weight on his words now, "and difficult as it may be to believe, you having access to mirrors an' all, it wasn't like that for me, either."

Snagging her sense of humour now, seeing her soften a bit, winding the line in: "So, we have business with each other, that's how I look at it, we knew that, we even talked about it, remember? So, let's see what happens, eh? Let's push on, OK, until it ravels itself out? Yes? Deal?"

She punched him on the arm and she said: "Deal."

"Ready about", he said, disengaging the autohelm, hauling in the mainsheet.

14

Dwejra Bay faces west and north, walled in by high rocky cliffs. The cliffs are battered in winter by immense storms, and carry the battle-scars of centuries. This was a western outpost for the Knights of Malta, grim men themselves, stoic and stubborn, and an unwary soul might be tempted to find correspondence here, the cliffs under the hammer of weather somehow conflated with armoured knights, belaboured in battle, unyielding until ground down.

Sailors are more imaginative, and less romantic. They look at these cliffs, the great rents and fissures, the tumble of huge boulders at their feet, and they grow thoughtful; they see the immense weight and power of the sea, they see that blind thundering fury and, be the day as calm as you like, the sea like glass, they feel a prickle along the nerves, something unwholesome taking root in their blood.

Clare is transfixed by the blue expanse of water, the slash of beach, the high cliffs mounted behind in a giant child's diorama. Tom is uneasy, casting about with the binoculars as they make in, looking for somewhere to anchor.

"What's up?" she asks him, sensing his unease.

"We've had what, since we left Siracusa, south easterlies, southerlies? Around here the *Meltemi*, this time of year, blows seven days out of ten. You know what *Meltemi* is?" She nods, yes. "OK, northerly, right. Seven days out of ten. We'll be exposed here. I kind of allowed for that, but there's a always a fair chance of a day or two...."

He stops, realising he's uneasy, not only for practical reasons but because the conversation they've just walked away from has left him unsettled. He thinks about this for a bit, realises that he's been uneasy for longer than that — but there isn't time for this right now, he agrees with himself.

"OK, would you mind getting the chart from below? Now, see those symbols here?" — pointing at the bottom. "Right, now find the bay on the chart, see what symbols you can see, tells us what kind of holding ground we might find. Try down there, in the south west corner."

She knows this stuff, she's familiar with charts, but she does what he asks, giving him the small comfort that comes with passing on knowledge, the steadiness that can bring at times.

She said, laying a finger on the chart, "Here looks good, sand, gravel. Nothing to snag on."

"Yes, I remember lying there, thereabouts, last time I was in here. Let's get the sails in, then, easier to do this just on the motor."

The chain rattled over, he gave it a burst of reverse to dig in the hook, then, satisfied, killed the engine. Inshore the short surf murmured against the land. Two other boats lay at anchor not far away, he scanned them with the glasses. Nothing Irish, thank God, he muttered to himself under his breath, not feeling particularly sociable, knowing his countrymen would be unable to resist the lure of the tricolour. Clare watched him as he wrapped it carefully around its staff, prodded him in the back: "Don't be drawing rats, eh?"

"Jesus, are you always this…"

"…quick? Oh yes, even as a child, I used to drive my stepfather mad. My mother called it my witch gene."

Stepfather? She saw the question in his eyes, turned away hurriedly. He looked after her thoughtfully as she swung below, calling "You want a fleece, Tom?"

"What's that, then?" she asked him presently, snuggled companionably up to him, coffee in hand.

"Fungus Rock", he said, and waited.

"Oh all right then, be like that. Why. Is. It. Called. Fungus. Rock? Tom, Sir?"

"I was hoping you'd ask me that, child. Long, long ago, when God was a baby and the Knights of Malta were getting Him into arguments where he didn't belong, they owned all you can see as far as the eye can go. You see that tower? They built that tower to protect that rock. You know why? Of course you don't know why. I'll tell you why, shall I? Impotence. Impotence and *cynomorium coccineum*."

He waited again.

"Cyno-what? Impudence?"

"No, child, impotence. Im-pot-ence. I believe it's something affects the aging male. Ouch! Stop prodding me. There's a kind of purplish-reddish yoke grows on that rock, a parasite botanically speaking, lives underground, sticks its head up after the winter rains. Looks uncommonly like a purply cock, I believe. Your Knights used to send packages of it to European monarchs as a gift — how to win friends and influence people, eh?"

"You are not serious?"

"Oh yes I am. Used it for treatments for the blood as well, probably influenced by the colour, you know? Arab physicians set great store by it too, as it happens. And there's a Chinese variant, I believe, used for what they call 'locking the Yang', if I remember rightly. Which I do."

Beginning to believe him, "How do you know all this stuff?"

Ignoring her question: "Fungus Rock, the Grandmaster had the faces of the rock smoothed, it's sixty metres or thereabouts, to stop anyone climbing up and robbing the stuff. Posted guards all round here, built the tower and so on, three years in the galleys for anyone caught stealing the stuff. Serious thing."

If he had a pipe he'd be puffing on it now, she thinks.

"How do I know all this stuff? Looked it up of course. Last time I was here some blowhard of a Yank was full of bullshit about it: mysterious properties, secret visionary drug of the mystical Knights, that kind of shit. Annoyed me so much I went and looked it up the first internet café I landed in."

"Beats me", she said.

Off balance, to her smug satisfaction, he asks "What? What beats you?"

"All this guff about the Knights Templar, Knights of Malta, all that horseshit. Lazy reading, lazy thinking. Hippy bullshit. People should know better."

Said with such vehemence that Tom is startled out of his dozy torpor. "Right", he says, "right", thinking 'what's this now, what's this?' But she lets it go, settles back again beside him.

"Tell me more, Tom" — in a cod little-girl voice.

"The thing is, they've been doing a lot of research on this stuff, there are lab experiments that suggest it inhibits HIV, lowers blood pressure, improves blood flow and so on."

"I'm surprised an oul' fella like you isn't climbing the cliff already! Hey, sunshine, weren't you making lunch back there a while? Bit late now, what do you say we get an early dinner on?"

"I was thinking of getting the dinghy out, thought maybe you'd like a run ashore?"

"Listen to yourself, you're about as convincing as a limp mickey. You're practically asleep as it is. You want to take a nap, or you want to help with the dinner and we'll have an early night?"

"Yeah, you're right, I'll give you a hand with the dinner, we can run ashore in the morning, OK?"

Going below before him, she pauses a moment by the chart table, looks back over her shoulder at him, questioning? "No", he says, "I don't think I need them at the minute." Then he hears what he's said, and she hears it, too, and they deal with the moment in a look, agreeing to say nothing.

"Tell me about the boat, Tom", she says, rattling the dishes in the sink.

"Well, there's a grey water tank for the washing-up water, if that's what you mean?"

"No, that's not what I mean. And, besides, I know that."

"You do, how?"

"Duh, the label on the thingummy, under there."

"Ah sure of course, Detective Hogan."

He's startled when she whips around to glare at him, skin tight over her cheekbones.

"What'd I do now, all I meant was you have the whole boat sussed, OK? It's a good thing, for God's sake."

A long, considering look, then she shrugs, turns back to the sink. "All right, all right, don't get narky with me."

"I'm not getting narky. Jesus, relax will you?"

Thunder in the air out of nowhere; sulphur, static. The boat buffeted sideways by an errant gust.

"Happens pretty easily, huh?" She says, softly, still not looking at him.

"It does", he says, rueful. "Old habits, eh? The habitual, the banal?"

"Not sure I like Kavanagh, to tell you the truth", she says.

Tom is genuinely impressed. Not just that she's caught the reference. Not having meant to quote, surprised by the phrase himself.

"Too much old guff about how the country is superior to the city, how the city is The Fall. Christ but I couldn't wait to get away out of it." Startled herself by her own vehemence: "The boat, Tom, talk to me about the boat."

"Huh? Oh, yeah. Well, you see for yourself, all teak…"

"…No, no, I mean how long have you had her? How did you get her? That sort of thing."

"Oh. Ah I've had her about thirty years now. She wasn't like this when I got her, I can tell you. I've spent a lot of time on this boat, and money. Mostly time, though. She's sound, you know? Needed a new engine, new boom, new sails every now and then, parts, bits and pieces, but mostly what she needed was time spent on her."

"New engine?"

He laughs. "You've probably made a note of the serial number have you? Don't do that with your face, it unnerves me, OK? Joke. Where was I? Bought her in Marseilles, of all places. Someone I, eh, met one time told me about her, thought I might be interested."

She catches the hesitation, homes in.

"Someone you met?"

Tom thinks about his answer, decides what the hell, might as well say it.

"Well, it's like this. Back then, mid seventies, there was a lot of dope floating around, OK? Not like now, all criminal shit now, hate that, don't know where stuff is coming from. Not like now, right, it was a kind of game, us against the straights, OK? That's how we used to talk. Jesus, we were very innocent, weren't we?"

"Innocent? What do you mean? It was illegal, wasn't it?"

"Illegal? You're serious aren't you? Of course there was me forgetting you were a lawyer. Ah forget it, forget it."

"Tom?"

"What?"

"Don't sulk, it doesn't suit you."

"Don't … I'm not …" — and he sees that he is, in fact, sulking.

"God", he says, more to himself than to her, "I still do that. Imagine...." Then, out loud: "OK, OK, guilty as charged. Will I go on?" Nod. "I'll go on."

She's about to say something, but he waves her to silence. Yes, yes, you got the reference.

"Don't pout, it doesn't suit you. And don't glare! So anyway, London, that time, you know, I met a guy, a Dub, I liked him, you know? Bit of a jack the lad. Somebody in the squat knew somebody who knew his sister or something; anyway there was a whiff of the Devil about him, right? Drove the getaway car in a post office job in Cork one time, something like that. Anyway, legged it to London. So we were playing some kind of a gig down in of all places Elephant & Castle, cover versions, pub rock, you know the sort of thing. No, you probably don't. So this guys steps out the back, we're taking a break, sniffs the air and says 'ah Jasus, lads, that stuff is brutal. Here.' And he pulls out a big chunk of Leb, right? The black stuff with the opium grains, you know?"

She's come to sit down across from him, is shaking her head.

"You don't? Ah here, listen, that stuff was dynamite. When we went back in, Finny, the bass player, he went off into a thirteen-minute solo the first number we did. Can you imagine? A thirteen-minute bass solo! It's a wonder we weren't bottled. So, cut a long story short, I became sort of pals with your man the Dub. Come September things had got bad with, you know, she'd headed off to America like I say, I was at a bit of a loose end. Garrett, the Dub, right, he asked me to do a little job for him. Pick up a car in Copenhagen, drive it to Switzerland, Zurich. You with me? So, of course it was a dope run, right? Offered me a good few grand. I said I'd do it, but only if I could check out the load. 'Game ball', says he, 'I'd do the same meself. Have a gander. If you're happy away we go. If you're not, give us a call and I'll get someone else. Fair enough? I'm doing you a favour, you're doing me a favour. We're pals, right?'

"So, I cut my hair, shaved the beard, into Oxfam for some straight clothes and away with me to Copenhagen. A few hairy moments, naturally, getting used to the wrong side of the road and that, but away down with me, nice and easy, stopping off here and there and into Zurich. Not a bother. No cops, no customs, waved through, everybody bored; into Zurich like I say, park the car in a hotel car park, go to bed. Next morning, there's a note under my door, I go down, check the car is gone, fly home, hand the envelope to your man Garrett, he reads the note, walks out of the room (nice place in Shepherd's Bush he had, two bedroom basement flat, nice), walks back in, hands me a brown paper bag stuffed with money and says 'Thanks very much, I have to go now, we might do this again if you're up for it.'"

"Tom, Tom, what kind of a fool are you? Were you, I mean. If…"

"…I know, I know. Look, every morning on the way down, after I'd stopped for a night's kip, right, I'd check the car, make sure it was still only dope in the cases, right? Those days, the cops hadn't much of a clue, to be honest. And the beauty of this was, everyone was looking at stuff coming up out of Morocco through Spain and into England, Germany, right? Or through Marseilles and into France. Who the hell was looking at stuff coming from Denmark to Switzerland of all places, right?"

"You'd have got … if you were caught…."

"Yeah, yeah, look, I just didn't care, probably. Didn't think about that, *wouldn't* think about that, probably. I was in a very odd state of mind that summer, OK? So, the boat, yes. I did a couple of trips for your man, had a nice stash of money by the spring, right? Still gigging a bit, living simply, spending nothing, hardly anything, and one day in Garret's I met this nice young Frenchwoman…."

"Oho!" from Clare; he waves her down.

"Now don't start on that. She was gay, right? Had to tell me, I didn't cop. Gorgeous she was, but no spark, so she saw I didn't get it and told me. Kind of amused, but not mocking or anything. Bit of a witch gene there, too. So she looks at me, long, long look when we're skinning up after dinner and says, 'Tom, what you need, my friend, is a boat. My brother has a boat. If you give him some of the money Garrett has been giving you I will arrange for him to sell you the boat. A very nice boat, Thomas, what do you think of this?' And she sat back an' looked at me as something went pop! in my head and I thought yeah, exactly, I'd love a boat. Remember we hadn't even started smoking that night, I was clear as a bell in my head and I thought: exactly, I'd love a boat. So here we are."

Dark outside now, the boat swinging to its anchor, the new moon riding light and buoyant through the hatch, a faint, musky smell coming off the land, eddying in the cabin. She ruffles his hair.

"Cyno-whatsit", she said.

"Huh?"

"Trade in vegetable substances, Tom, valuable veggies, right? An old story, eh?"

"What happened to Miss Censorious, then?"

"Did I look censorious? Maybe I did. Not about you, though. It's different now, though, Tom, you know? Big-time criminals now, same guys who're dealing all the dope in Dublin are dealing coke, smack, you name it. Cold bloody bastards they are, too. Nothing's clean any more, Tom, nothing. Those days are gone, right?"

"Ah for fuck's sake, wasn't too bloody innocent either in my day, just that we were too bloody stupid or too bloody lazy to suss what the real story was. You know what's weird though? Listen to this now. Years later, not that long ago in fact, I was in Montreux, right, for the Jazz and Blues Festival? Of all things, get this, I was playing with these Danish guys. Nice little combo, tight, you know? Right. So this woman comes up to me after the gig, two o'clock in the morning and she has sunglasses on the top of her head. Short, hard, blonde hair, know what I mean? Small, middle-aged woman, in good shape now, trim I suppose is the word, but hard, hard as anything, you wouldn't feel like reaching out and touching her, know what I mean. She's standing there in front of me, not saying a word and I'm thinking how odd punters can be, you know, repressed and wanting to tell you something at the same time, and she says, softer that I'd expected, the voice took me by surprise, 'Tom', she says, 'you don't remember me', and I didn't, and she shook her head, no change of expression there, and she said, 'do you still have the boat, Tom?' Jesus! Clotilde, I swear, that was her name. 'What did you call it?' she asked me. '*Lon Dubh*', says I, the Irish for blackbird, and you know what she did? Sang me the line, 'take these broken wings and learn to fly' — just like that, soft like, perfect pitch she had, too. The guys are looking at me, curious, packing away the instruments. So we talk for a bit, she tells me she's into property now, in a big way, obviously, I can tell from the rock on her finger, the Patek Philippe, the gold necklace, big, heavy thing but not vulgar, you know? So we talk for a bit and then she just turns to walk away and she says, 'You heard about Garrett, yes?' And I say 'Yes, I heard.' And she looks at me and just nods, and as she walks away she says over her shoulder, 'You play good, Tom, you play good.' And first I thought it was just an ordinary, polite compliment, you know, and then I heard it as more ... more ... like an instruction, you know? With a bit of sadness?

I watched her walk out the door, the bouncers standing back, giving these little stiff nods, and I headed out, and she was getting into this massive Merc, a guy in a cap holding the door. All on her own. And maybe she guessed I was there or not, I don't know. She just turned and looked at me, just looked, and then the guy closed the door and the light went out inside and he got in and drove her away."

"Never trust a hippie, eh?"

"What? What did you say?"

"Ah something my Mam used to say." Some note in her voice he can't process, can't quite grasp. "And she should know." That note again, bent now, something else there. "Garrett, what happened to Garrett? Busted?"

Bleak now. "No, not busted. They found his body in a ditch near Forkhill, you know, South Armagh. Naked. Tortured as well they said. Bullet in the back of the head."

"Oh. He was political?"

"Garrett? He despised politics, that fella. Fucking all the same, he used to say. In power or looking for power, all the same. Said it one night in a pub in Camden Town and I had to wrestle two fellas off him, they were going to kill him, looked like. No, not politics. Just business, I'd say. Maybe he crossed the wrong people, maybe they thought he was muscling in where he had no business, who the fuck can tell? Eh?"

She pushed herself up from the table, stiff. Looking out through the hatch.

"So, Tom, you'd recognise a Patek Philippe? And you wearing a Swatch?"

Giving him an out, here, seeing how suddenly drained he looks, keeping it light. Masking, she hopes, her concern. He says nothing.

"You tell a good story, Tom, you tell a good story." Bending down now to let him see the softness in her eyes.

"Isn't that what we're doing? Telling each other the stories?" Sharp, unexpected.

She straightens again, looking down at him.

"That's it exactly, Tom, that's it exactly, telling each other the stories. Good night, I'm going to crash. Man."

Not mocking, not even teasing. He laughs quietly, and after a second or two so does Clare. Signal received and understood.

On deck, a while later, washing the pills down with a small whiskey (bad idea, he thinks, but what the hell) he feels an unaccountable lightness of spirit. Good luck to us all, he thinks, we did the best we could, and he pours the last of the whiskey over the side, a wordless benediction.

15

She wakes in the half-light before dawn, in that state between waking and dreaming that was always, to this day is, her place of greatest comfort. There's music, soft and low. Nice, she thinks, waking to music, feeling the boat rock gently under her, not rock, she thinks then, pitch. Fore and aft. Hmm…. She scrabbles on the floor for her shorts, brings her iPod up to where she can squint at its tiny screen. Presses shuffle, pops in the ear buds. Sandy Denny, *Who Knows Where The Time Goes?* Oh dear God, she thinks. Perfect. Couldn't be better. A twist in her mouth, a bitter taste. Brilliant, fucking brilliant. Lovely, Mam, fucking lovely. How do you do it…? She reaches a foot from under the covers to push the door closed, just far enough that if he should glance in he won't see the cold, hopeless tears streaming down her face, pooling in her earlobes. A sudden cramp in her foot. She'll have to move God damn it, she might as well get up now — and all she wants is to lie there perfectly still, for it to be dark morning in her cave under the eaves, the wind sighing in the branches, the song to be coming from the kitchen far below as her mother… her mother….

"See this?" he says, oblivious to her face of rage, leaning in over the chart table, tapping some instrument.

"What?' — almost a snarl. He starts, he doesn't look around.

"Navtex. It…"

"…I know what a navtex is." Short. Abrupt.

He turns, is ready to tease her about mornings, sees her face. She sees the look on his, feels ashamed, turns away. She turns back, shrugs, palms upwards, as if to say….

"Yes", he says, sparing her. "Well, it's gone round, the wind, this here says we can expect northerlies in the early afternoon. 'bout twenty to twenty-five knots. Blustery, but not too bad. If you're up for it?"

He waits, she nods, go on.

"Thing is, we can't stay here...."

"Too exposed, yeah."

OK, he thinks, back to finishing my thoughts for me. Better, that's better.

"So either we head back to Malta, let it blow over and head out again, or we go on."

Regaining her composure by the second, waking up inside, stirred by the prospect of ... action? A challenge from outside? She's not sure how to put it to herself, but a wind, she thinks, a good stiff blow would be good.

"What would you do if you were on your own, Tom?"

"Ah I'd push on, I think, it won't be too bad, and we're not that far from Sardinia anyway if it comes to it."

"Sardinia? That's next on the list, is it?"

"Well, yeah. That's what I thought. Oh, shit, I suppose I should have discussed this with you?"

"Tom, Tom, I'm fine. I'm just along for the ride, remember. Stop that! You have a filthy mind!"

"Come here to me", he says, and steps out into the saloon, and she lets him fold her in a hug, her fingers linked in the small of his back. "Better now?"

"Mmm", she says, and it is.

He has the grey, inflatable dinghy over the side, bobbing on the short silvery chop, snatching at its painter. She sees him look doubtfully at the outboard engine clamped to a board on the after rail. Without having to process the thought, she knows he's dispirited at the prospect of lugging the heavy thing about, getting it over the side, getting it back aboard when they return. Failing, she thinks, only a little and he masks it well, but he's failing in himself, or thinks he is. Ice in her stomach.

"You know what?" she says, brisk now. "I'm feeling in need of a bit of exercise. How about I row us in and out, that be OK? In fact, do you think we should let it go, maybe get a move on, out of here?"

"Ah no", he says, "plenty of time yet, and it's worth a look, I promise. OK, we can row I suppose, best if we head in that way" — pointing — "work our way along and be coming from the north on the way back. In case the wind gets up."

She feels obscurely pleased to have gotten away with this little subterfuge, and then realises that, in fact, she is looking forward to the exercise. Go figure, she tells herself, wouldn't it be great if every little white lie turned out to be masking a truth?

Dry bread, spread thickly with soft cheese, an apple, some juice. "I'll make us a proper breakfast when we get back" she says. "No, I will", he says. "Now, here, lifejackets in the dinghy. Ship's rules."

Mock meekly, she accepts hers. "Crotch strap", he says, as she goes to tuck the long strap out of the way. She makes a moue, dissatisfied. "It could ride up over your neck in the water, when it inflates", he says. "Saw it happen once. Not nice." Not true, either, as it happens, he thinks, but he's taking no chances here, not with Clare. The thought stops him. Not with Clare, he repeats to himself, wondering. Her back turned to him now, she senses something in the air, decides not to turn around.

The tower, he tells her, is called the Quawra Tower. "Yes, Tom", she says, bending into her stroke. "That over there", he gestures, "is known as the Azure Window" — a high rock, maybe twenty metres, an arch in fact. "We going in there?" she asks. Seated on the transom, one hand on each tube, ankles crossed, he's looking away over her shoulder; nods, yes. "Why the Azure Window, Tom?" "What colour is the water here?" he replies. "I suppose you could call it azure, Tom, tho' in point of fact..." "...Yes", he says, surprising her by completing her sentence, "azure, strictly speaking, is a term applied only in heraldry." "Well!" She says, "fancy!" As pleased as he is that, for once, it's him anticipating her. "Pull away there, sharpish!" he says, and she sticks her tongue out at him. "Christ", she says softly, coming through the arch, lifting the oars out of the water. Under the cliff the water's a deep, unhealthy black. "Seaweed", he tells her, "gets trapped here, builds up. Wouldn't be surprised if a child could walk on it. Come on, back, head over there, under the Tower."

There's a tunnel through the rock, maybe fifty metres, she listens to the splashing echoing off the dank walls and then they are out into what Tom calls the inland sea; more of a pond, really, green water here, a pebbly shore, small fishing boats drawn up, fishermen tending their nets. "Oh very picturesque", she says, and he grins. "Yeah, yeah, but it's good isn't it?" "Wouldn't imagine they catch much fish", she says. "Ah but they catch a lot of tourists", he says, nodding away, "bring 'em in here, bring 'em back out again, all day long. We're early, you see", waving no, no, at a knot of men who have risen to look across at them. "OK", he says, "let's go back. What would you say to a nice plate of bacon and eggs?" "I'd say, 'hello nice plate of bacon and eggs'", she says, "Jesus, Tom, that's an old one."

All good humour restored.

16

The breakfast things are washed and put away, she's wedging tea towels in between jars, bowls and the like. He's watching approvingly. She lifts the lid of the pot store set in the worktop, sets towels, kitchen cloths among the pots. Looking around her now, hand in the small of her back. "Eh, the fridge", says Tom. "Oh right", she says. Finished, she stands by Tom, they take a good look around, checking that everything movable is stowed away. "Got brained once by a flying can of beans", Tom says. "That explains a lot", she says. Working as a team. Like people who've known each other for years. "I've got all my stuff back in the bag", she says, "except wet weather gear, some warm things just in case." "Good", he says. "In the space under the bunk", she says.

"You know that orange sail under the other bunk?" he asks. "Yeah." "Well, give it the once over and leave it on top of the bunk, would you?" "Stormsail, right?" she nods, "you think we'll need it?" "Nah, almost certainly not." Tom tying off the hanging oil lamp over the table with shock-cord, a length to the grabrail on either side of the saloon. Last look around. Satisfied.

"OK", he says, as she comes up on deck. "Staysail and main, one reef, I'll get that. You start her up; I'll get the anchor first." He takes a good slow look around, sees the other two boats under bare poles heading east as they round the point up above them. Heading for Malta, he thinks. Hmm....

He gets the main up, the anchor comes in, he snugs it down, double lashing the shank. He takes an old glove from his back pocket, stuffs it into the hawse pipe where the chain disappears below deck into its locker. He hears her centre the main, then engage gear. He gets the staysail up, lashed amidships, then works his way around the mast, checks the reefing line is free to run, sets the first reef and drops into the cockpit.

"Neat", she says, then half wishes she hadn't spoken.

All Tom's attention is on the boat, the wind, the sea. For the first time she sees something hard and implacable in him. He looks leaner, too, gathered in and gathered up in himself. Serious, she thinks, he looks serious.

For a moment she feels afraid. Not of Tom, not of the weather to come. An older fear, the fear that whatever's coming, she won't measure up.

"You'll be fine", he says, suddenly, almost abruptly, still watching the set of the sails, and she's almost offended, as if he's being patronizing, and then he says, "This is all good you know, just relax, go with it", and she gets a rush of pure elation, a flush of well-being that has her laughing out loud, thumping the wheel. Still looking ahead, unmoving, Tom smiles to himself.

As if on a dial, steadily, inexorably, the wind backs, backs until it's coming from due north.

"Excellent", says Tom, "bear off a little towards Africa, would you? That's it, that's it. Hold it there. What's the compass?"

She leans back, squints down: "Now? Eh, 'bout 315 to 320 degrees?"

"Grand, keep her around there. Don't be chasing the compass, you understand, just keep the wind coming from about there, off the starboard bow, like now, see? We want more like 340 degrees for Sardinia but we can tack in a while" — making zig-zag motions with his hand — "backwards and forwards over our course, you get it? Course you do. You warm enough?"

He doesn't wait for an answer, is already through the hatch: "I'll get you something anyway, better to be a bit too warm than a bit too cold. I'll make some flasks of tea, yeah?"

In a magazine, once, she saw a boat described as 'long-legged'. She gets it, now, feeling the boat under her feet begin to … lope, is it? A long, confident stride, the bow throwing up small bursts of spray as the head goes down then the surge forward as it comes up again, the pleasant plumping sensation as the stern lifts and falls again. Loping along, she hums to herself, loping along, loping along … and it comes to her that she's happy.

The hair on the back of her neck bristles, her breath bumps. God, when was I last happy, she wonders — but can't be bothered to think about it. "Feck it", she says out loud, enjoying the shape the words make in her mouth, "feck it I can't be bothered. God what a lovely boat."

"You want me to switch on the autopilot?" Tom asks her, grinning up from below.

"How long have you been there?" she demands. "Get away out o' that, Jesus this is brilliant!"

And on they drive, into the afternoon, into the evening, taking turns at the wheel, the wind climbing to twenty knots, gusting twenty-five, the sea more black than blue now, little runs of foam on the swell coming in from ahead, the rocking-horse motion, the power in the sails, the wind in their faces.

A clear night comes on, racing stars, the keen in the wind more audible now in the dark, though it's got no stronger.

"We need to get organised", he says, eventually. "We've about two and half days ahead of us; if it keeps blowing like this it'll take it out of us. What do you feel about four hours on, four hours off? You able for that? I can do longer watches if you like."

She hesitates, not because she doesn't feel able for it, but because all day he's been full of energy and she fears it can't last. She wants to ask him what's wrong, what the tablets are for, but knows she mustn't. She's watched him these past few days, seen the sudden drops in energy, the sudden spasms of pain. Heart? This is what she's settled on, she realises. His age, his lifestyle. Heart.

He wants to say, it's OK, you don't have to worry about me, but he can't. Or is it won't, he wonders?

"Tell you what", he says, "whoever's off watch should sleep in the saloon; unless it comes on to rain, which it probably won't, that way they can be called if, well, if there's a sail change needed, for instance, or some ship acting the maggot. What do you think?"

Dry mouthed, she nods agreement.

"I've put up the lee cloth on the port side for the minute, OK? The low side, easier to sleep on the low side. When we tack, we shift to the other side."

She nods again. All she can think to say is that she'll take the first watch, if that's all right with him?

"It is", he says, and he hands her up her windproof jacket, following a minute later with lifejacket and harness. He shows her how to clip the harness to the D-ring in the cockpit floor. "You'll think it's awkward but it isn't, not really. You'll get used to it in no time. You know why I'm insisting on this, don't you?" "I do", she says, voice steady.

He folds his hand over hers on the wheel. "All this sounds a lot more serious than it is", he says, "you understand?" "I do", she says, reaching to harden in the mainsheet, just a fraction. It doesn't need doing, but she wants to do something to reassure him that he can rely on her.

Below again, he forgets about her instantly. He touches the framed photograph screwed to the instrument console, his fingers exploring the slight salt tackiness of the glass. Must clean that later, he tells himself. In the morning. Must take the tablets. Must get out of these shorts. Track bottoms, comfort in the fabric. Fleece jacket over long-sleeved T-shirt. Sleep under a sheet, might have to go straight on deck. God, I'm tired. Tired.

When she hears him snoring, Clare engages the autopilot. Dragging the harness with her, she steps out on to the afterdeck, the running light white, bright at her feet. She grips the backstay, leans back, follows it to the masthead, see the red-green white of the tricolour light bright and clear. Looks further up, past the masthead dancing in its figure of eight.

There was a ten-acre field behind the house, sloping away down to the river. She remembers a summer's night, she must have been, what, ten? Lying there in the cooling grass, a car going by on the leafy, sunken road the other side of the river, the horses shuffling in the stableyard. The smell of grass, dust, what her mother called honeysuckle, her stepfather called wild woodbine. Her mother was always right about plants, but he would argue with her, tell her she didn't know what she was talking about.

Lying there, the memory so vivid now she forgets entirely where she is, remembering the teacher explaining the earth is a ball whirling at great speed through, what did he call it, the halls of space. Some nameless fear taking hold of her as he spoke. Now, tonight, lying in the short grass, she is looking up at the bright expanse of stars when, suddenly and absolutely, she has a profound sense that she is looking *down*. Down at the stars. Sheer terror, giddiness, terror again, she might fall, she might fall....

The boat lurched, there was a smack as she hit a bigger than usual wave, then the rush of the water coursing back under her, its phosphorescent bustle and swish.

Clare climbed carefully back down into the cockpit, feeling ... cheated? Alert, anyway. Right, girl, she told herself, firmly and not unkindly, just drive the boat. Just drive the boat.

Four hours later, to the minute, she woke him. She scrunched in beside him on the settee, nudging the lee cloth flat as she moved sideways. "Here", she said. "A cup of tea from the thermos. Small drop of milk, homeopathic amount of sugar, right?"

He struggled up blearily, sipped, held the cup away, sighed. "You OK?" she asked him. No answer. "Right", she said, nurse and workmate, "roust yourself there man, time to go to work."

"To rest is not to conquer", he mumbled, swinging his feet to the floor, scrabbling for his shoes.

"What?" she said.

"My old man used to say that to me, dragging me out of bed on a Saturday. 'To rest is not to conquer.' Is it cold up there?" She shook her head, no. "One time, after my mother died, I was coming home from a gig, Saturday morning, bright already. He was still in bed. I brought him up a cup of tea, shook him by the shoulder, right? 'Come on', I said, 'to rest is not to conquer.' Know what he did? He just looked at me, rolled back away from me and said, 'Ah shag it, who wants to conquer?'"

Wide awake now, smacking his hands together: "Good, huh? Caught me there all right. OK, sunshine, you hop in here, beddy byes."

The warm smell of him, the long hollow where he's been lying. She has her own sheet ready to spread over herself but she folds it now, places it under the pillow, pulls the warm sheet over her face, blotting out the light — and then she is falling, falling, relaxed beyond belief, confident someone is going to catch her. Someone....

17

The wind's from the north still, but it's dropped a bit. It's warm in the cockpit, the backwash from the mainsail carried over their heads and off, the spray hood sheltering them. They're lying back on the seats, heads propped by cushions. Tom has his fingers laced behind his head, Clare is fiddling with worry beads in her lap.

"What's it like, Tom, producing albums?"

"What's it like? Different all the time, depends on who you're working with. I like working with singers best. The ones who write their own songs, they've usually worked them out on the guitar or on a piano, but they hear a bigger sound in their heads, fuller, you know? So I try to help them find that sound. If I've worked with them before, especially if I've played with them, it can be a fast process — you get a feel for what they hear in their heads, you understand me? Others, they send me a tape, I think about it, I try to figure out what kind of arrangements will suit the mood of the songs, or maybe they think they have an up-tempo thing and I slow it down, make it darker, find what they're trying not to say. That make sense to you?"

She'd only meant to get him talking, had chosen the subject, she thought, at random. Now she's interested.

"You ever get prima donnas, you ever get resistance?"

"I don't work with prima donnas, simple. Not worth the hassle. People get reputations very fast in the business; if I hear that someone's, what, full of themselves? Sorry, I'm busy, maybe you should get someone else. I don't mean headstrong, now. I mean, I played with Van a bit, on and off, when Georgie was busy doing something else, say. Van's a monster, people say. Not at all. He just knows exactly what he wants and goes for it. Guy like that you can work with very easily."

"Ah come on, even I know Van's a terror to work with."

"That's where you're wrong. Guitar player, once, was asked if he wasn't terrified working with Van, right? He says, 'Not at all. Van nods to me, I play a bit; Van nods to me, I stop. Simple.' That's about right. But, I mean, I never produced Van, he does that for himself."

"But what if the sound you hear isn't the sound they're happy with? What happens then?"

"Well, I try to guide them towards understanding what I'm suggesting, right? We discuss things, we try different things, I mean I do listen to what they're saying but I figure if they've brought me in it's because they have, what, an instinct that I have something they want — even if they don't know what it is they want. Whether or not they know it, in the end they're looking for someone to find … a direction, maybe. Some kind of overall shape. They're looking for, I dunno … guidance."

"So, what, you're the stern but loving father, is that it?"

"Huh? Come again?"

"Nurturing their talents, showing them the way forward, you're the one who knows them better than they know themselves, if only they'd listen to you it'll all come out all right? That's what it sounds like to me."

"Jesus, no, not at all. What makes you think that? Look, it's more like, how do I explain this? OK, you heard of George Martin, produced the Beatles? You've heard of the Beatles I suppose?"

"Come on, Tom, don't be sarcastic."

"Actually I wasn't being, I was trying to lighten things a bit — I thought you were being sarcastic."

Making a point now of not looking at each other. After a while she said, "We've been here before, haven't we? Zero to nuclear in no time at all?" They let that sink in.

"Well", in a neutral tone now, picking his way carefully, "they used to call George Martin the fifth Beatle. You get it?"

She said nothing. He's getting better at understanding the different kinds of silence between them, relaxes.

After a while, she says "My stepfather, you know? He was like that. Always knew best, had this thing he'd do, he'd be leading you on, like, 'Now, Clare, is this what you really want to say here? Might it be that … would it be better if … what if….' You know? As if I didn't know what I wanted, didn't know what I wanted to say, do, whatever…. Jesus! But he knew! Oh he was one step ahead, he'd been round the block, he …

and I wouldn't mind, he had nothing at all to base this on, right? He had this fucking stupid assumption that he knew best — and nothing at all to base it on!"

Rage. Tom, letting the silence happen. Clare, flustered, sitting up and looking around, ahead, behind, anywhere but at Tom.

"Anything out there?" Tom asks, making a point of being mild.

"What? No. Nothing."

"You don't talk to people much about this kind of thing, do you?"

"What makes you say that? You know nothing about me!" He sits up, heavily, turns to face her. She keeps her face turned away from him, acutely conscious that he is looking at her, not wanting him to see what she's thinking.

"Clare, I don't need to see your face to know what you're thinking. You can look at me. Clare, look at me."

"What?"

"That's better. Isn't that better? We can talk about anything, you and I, isn't that the deal? What have we been doing since, since Siracusa? Telling the stories, right? Take a deep breath, now. Seriously, I mean just that, take a deep breath. OK, now another, another...."

Peace in the boat. Not just silence, not just calm. Something hard and serious and tangible. More ions in the air, you might say. A definite ... atmosphere. Charged.

"Clare, we come to a place now and then where everything's in the scales, everything's up for scrutiny, yes? A moment in your life, one of a small series of moments? You grant me this?"

She says "Yes", low but steady again in herself.

"OK. I don't know how you think of it; this is how I think of it: some people, not many, know that human beings, most of them, are asleep most of the time, right? Some of us get a glimpse of this, maybe early on. Maybe something happens that jolts us awake for an instant, maybe somebody teaches us how to wake up, right? Me, I woke up in bed."

Teasing her with this, probing for a reaction. She laughs, not guessing where this is going.

"That's right. I was madly in love with a very curious woman, well maybe not in love, then, infatuated, say infatuated. And one night, just lying there on the pillow, we had our heads real close, just looking into each other's eyes, right. And looking. And looking. I don't like to do that, normally, hold someone's look for too long, but that's what we were doing. She smelled of woodsmoke, I remember that very clearly, and I'm looking into her eyes and then, then I hear her telling me things, things about her life, about life, about what we are, what human beings really are; very strange stuff, Clare, I mean really strange, we'd have said 'trippy' in those days, and it was like tripping, like a very mellow experience on acid, yeah, and her lips aren't moving and there's no sound in the room except the wind rattling the window and her breathing, my breathing, but I'm hearing words distinctly, right, hearing 'em, tasting 'em, seeing them, Clare. I really can't explain this very well. And I get this enormous sense of … being connected. Connected, Clare. Not just to her, not just to her, to everything. Like something just woke up inside me."

The boat heeled, he reached over without looking, let out the mainsheet until the gust had passed, hauled it in again. Looking away inside himself, then, coming to with a bump, looking at Clare.

She hasn't moved. Something disturbing in her silence, her immobility, but he pushes on anyway.

"So, we get ground down, right? Ground down by the day to day, the busyness of things, the noise. The noise, Clare, right, the noise? That's why I bail out, you see, I get myself out here, not always by myself but often, yeah just me and the boat, and I get in touch again, you know?"

"So what you're saying, I think, is that's what we're doing here?"

"You tell me, Clare. You tell me. Telling each other stories, right? Connecting with … whatever. Tell me what you're thinking?"

"Right now? I'm thinking chopped onions, garlic, tomatoes, all drenched in olive oil, bit of pepper, salt, some oregano. And toasted bread, and some of that feta cheese? What do you say, Boss?"

"I say bring it on."

"OK, on its way. And, Tom? I get it, OK? I get it, that was just a blip. You're not a bit like him. I'm still with the programme, don't worry. Something I don't get, though?"

"Huh?"

"Since we've been on this boat, you haven't put on any music. How come?"

"Well, there's a pretty cosmic reason for that."

"Which is?"

"CD player's broke."

"Ah ya bollix!"

Long since, Tom had mastered the difficult art of letting things come to the surface in their own time — and the equally difficult art of knowing when to say stop now, pay attention here, at the exact right moment.

In more than one failed relationship he'd been accused, sometimes in the same argument, of having a propensity for hearing only what he wanted to hear *and* for never letting anything go. Which was, he concedes, fair enough. What had saved him, often, what had saved the *situation* often, was that he had sufficient instinct to slow time and go deeper, behind the immediate moment to what was really prompting the row, the pain, whatever. Not always, he reminded himself, I caused my own fair share of pain down the years, I could be brutal enough, lash out with the best of them. Didn't always know to trust that instinct.

"It's only partly to do with my stepfather, you know" — Clare called from below.

"OK, witch", he called back, "in your own time."

She grinned to herself, not knowing whether she was most pleased with him or with herself. "Coming", she said, "and don't be vulgar now. I'm thinking of marrying this guy, you see."

Whatever he'd been expecting, Tom hadn't expected this. He held himself very still, standing to the wheel, needing the exercise he'd said, and then, getting that level look, admitting, "OK, just because I enjoy it." "Better", she'd said.

She looked at him now, then looked away astern.

"See, he's a good guy, Tom, really. We've been together now, what, going on two years? After that first guy, you know, I turned into a hard bitch. No, that's not fair. Wary, maybe, that's maybe a better way of putting it. Pick a guy up, or let him pick me up, now and then. I'd come and go, you know what I mean? A holiday now and then with some fella who was a bit more sussed than the others but, you know what, Tom? The world is full of boy-men. Toys, parties, *the lads*, like they'd never left school, know what I mean? Not growing up, just getting older — no, not even that, just bigger and louder and, mostly, a bit richer. Oh Jesus, opinions on everything, you know, and not an original thought between the lot of them. I used to think it was just me, you see, never was much of a one for the girlie talk, I had to work this all out mostly by myself. Coke, too, a lot of coke. Full of themselves, I used to think, and hollow all the way through.

"So, then I met Jack. In a bar down by the Four Courts. Friday, the Library on the piss. I'd walked in by myself, I really needed a drink after the day I'd had, defending some scumbag who was lying through his teeth to me, the Guards, the Judge, everyone. Big dealer, we all knew him, wife-beater, cocky as all get out. The thing is, I was pissed off because the Judge had sent him down. The look he gave me when he was remanded for sentencing! And I was pissed off because I'd lost the case. Even knowing I was glad the fucker was going to do some serious time.

"Anyway, I'm looking at a double whiskey, all on my ownio up at the bar, and this guy beside me taps my elbow, looks around at the scrum and back at me and says 'They're all dead, you know, every last one of them. Dead and damned; we are looking at dead souls here.' And before I could say a word, gobsmacked because I could tell he was completely serious, he sighed, shook his head, smiled a kind of sad smile at me and walked away out the door.

"I felt as if someone had thumped me with a hammer. Know what I did, Tom? Know what I did?"

"Well you ran out after him, of course. What else could you do?"

"Dead on, Tom, dead on. I dropped my drink, I mean on the floor, yeah, grabbed my briefcase, my gown, tore out the door … and he was standing there waiting for me. 'I was just coming back in for you', he said, and he gave me his arm and we walked away down the river into town. Like that. That's how I met Jack."

A long pause, and she said: "Do you believe me, Tom?"

He doesn't miss a beat: "Sure how else would someone like you…"

"…Exactly! That's exactly the way I've figured it, too. I was in a dream for weeks, a kind of delirium. Ah look I won't embarrass myself, OK? But, it was like, I'd start a sentence…"

"…And he'd finish it. And the sex of course was only out of this world.…"

"You think I'm going to say no? What kind of fool are you? And, anyway, look, what you were saying there a while back, about looking into some woman's eyes blah blah blah blah and, you know, feeling connected?"

"Blah blah blah now, before it was 'what's her name?' I'm beginning to have my suspicions here...."

"Ah would you ever shag off, I'm being serious, be serious — Jesus, Tom, are you all right? Tom!"

No warning. One minute he's looking at her warmly, next minute he's doubled up. Worst spasm in a long time, fuck, fuck, have to sit down. Holding himself, arms tight around his chest.

She flies down below, grabs a bottle of water out of the sink, the tablets from the chart table. "Here, here, take these, come on try to stand up, I'll help you down. What is it, Tom? Talk to me."

Gone. Amazing. Just ... gone. She watches the colour flood back into his face. He says, very gently but firmly, "Don't hassle me now Clare, let it go, OK, let it go. Everything's fine. Just a weird thing that comes and goes, the Doc has it all under control. Don't be worrying. I'm probably overdoing things a bit, I'll have a sleep now and I'll be right as rain."

It's dark when the smell of cooking wakes him.

"Ha!" she says, turning around, a long shade by the cooker in the red light from the chart table. "It was the smell got ya! You wouldn't believe how pleased I am with myself, a whole meal prepared and not a sound. And they said it couldn't be done!"

"Jesus", he says, "I have to admit, you're some woman for one woman!"

"Amn't I just, though? Me an' the autopilot. Is it your heart, Tom, tell me now. Straight up."

"Middle age", he says, "middle age, the mysteries of. No, Clare, it's not my heart. I'm not going to croak on you out here, OK?"

"Promise?"

Of course she's considered this, and he would be disappointed if she hadn't. When he says 'promise', he means it and she believes it; she hears the truth in his voice, he sees it in her shift of stance, and they are both, for different reasons, inexpressibly relieved.

18

A sky full of stars. They've tacked twice in the past half hour, fol-lowing the uncertain wind, but now it's steadied, a bit of east in it, consistent, and they have full sail out, three big, sculptural shapes, dark against the sky. Every now and then the lee rail dips, the water curling over the toe rail. Tom has his feet on the cockpit table, ankles crossed, fiddling with a bit of rope. Clare, beside him but on the other side of the wheel, is jammed into the short helmsman's bench, calves tensed as she braces herself against the opposite coaming.

"So", he says presently, "Jack, what is he, a suit? Lawyer?"

"Ah, Jack. Jack, Jack, Jack. He's a painter, would you believe? We're walking away down the river and he tells me he'd seen me at an opening in the RHA a few weeks before. Stalked me, he did. Asked someone, they told him I was a barrister and he went ferreting. Said he'd been in court that day. 'Your face was a picture', he said, 'you were so conflicted.' Jesus, I went cold. 'Nah', he said, 'don't worry, only I noticed. Everyone else was either bored or lying — the guards were lying, your client was lying, and sure that Judge is a notorious cross-dresser, a swine of the first order.' Tom, I started laughing, couldn't help myself, and then you know what he did? He turned to me, put his hands on my shoulders and said: 'You were the only one there who was real.' And I looked at him then, that was the first time I really looked at him. The shock of it."

"He's not a flake, is he? Tell me he's not a flake."

"Look at me, Tom."

He sees what she needs him to see. Hands in the air, "OK, he's not a flake."

"Quite right. He's actually a very good painter, and not too bothered about being successful, either. What I mean is, if I told you his real name you'd know it, which is why I'm not going to tell you. I'm just calling him

Jack, OK I'm confusing things here, aren't I? What I'm trying to say is, he is successful but not bothered about it one way or another. He's real, Tom. That's what I'm trying to get across here. Do you get me?"

"No, to be honest. What difference would it make if I knew his real name?"

"Think about it for a minute."

"Well, I might know him? Or I might know his name, think I know something about him? And … you don't want my opinion of him, if I had one I mean?"

"Spot on. He's not here, see? Just you and me and the wide, wide ocean. And that ship over there, fifty metres or more by the cut of her."

"What? Where? Oh, I see. Very good, Clare, very good. Going away east, nothing to bother us. Don't look so smug, I'd have seen it."

"No, I don't want your opinion. Not about anything to do with my life, I mean. What am I saying? It's like, I can hear myself working things out when I talk to you, does that make sense?"

"Yes."

"Yes? Is that all you have to say?"

"What else is there to say?"

"You have children, Tom? Did I ask you that before?"

"You did, and I haven't. Not that I know of, anyway."

"What? What do you mean by that?"

"Jesus, take it easy. What are you, the league for abandoned children? Just one of these sayings childless men get glib with when the subject comes up. A deflection. Reflex, sorry."

"Oh. No, I'm sorry, Tom, I didn't mean to be sharp. You warm enough there?"

He reaches out a hand, she takes it, squeezes.

"I shouldn't have said getting married, don't know why I said that. As long as we're together we've kept on both our places, you know? It's getting daft, now. Half my stuff in his place, half his stuff in mine. We've been drifting towards settling on one place or the other, and then we started thinking lately about maybe buying somewhere between us, let our own places go, right? Not married as such, you get me?"

"Ah, I'm the same myself", said Tom, stirring, making himself more comfortable. "Does he get on with your family, 'Jack', what's his name?"

"Oh very good, Tom, *touché*. Very witty. Family, what family?"

"Your mother, your brothers and sisters?"

"I'm an only child, like you. My mother's dead."

"I never said I'm an only child, did I?"

"You did, Tom, you did of course, ages ago."

"Well ... anyway, your mother's dead? Recently?"

"Yeah, yeah, about three years ago. He died long before that, when I was twenty. He was much older than her."

She sounds tired, Tom thinks, but he can't figure out if it's physical, or if it's something else. "We've plenty of time", he says, "are you getting tired?"

"I suppose I am, maybe I'll get the head down. Aren't we supposed to be on a watch system here?"

"Ah you have to be flexible in this life, but you take four hours if you want to, I'm grand."

She kissed the top of his head, surprising them both, an almost awkward moment. He shifted so that he could watch her. She switched on the radar, and while it was warming up she looked for a long moment at the photograph. Tom held his breath, but she shook her head, he saw her decide to park it, knew she would ask at some stage, was grateful she'd evidently decided not now. "You going to watch me undress, dirty old man?" He grinned, eyes in the back of her head that one. "I might", he said, then let her hear him stand up, stretch, climb out on deck and go forward to check that all was as it should be. When he got back, the red light over the nav table had been switched off. In the green glow from the radar he could make out her shape in the bunk. A small sag in the middle of the lee cloth, her hip above it. Lying on her side. She had her palm under her face again, he saw, and again he felt that tenderness move inside him, something aqueous settling with a slump.

Once, when he was about fourteen, he'd seen his father look at his mother with an unaccountable expression on his face. I wonder if I look like that just now? She had six years to live, that would be it, she'd have only had six years to go. To go. Life's journey. He stands to the wheel, leans over and disengages the autopilot, feeling the boat come alive through his hands. Boats against the current, he thinks, boats against the current.... I wonder if he knew, Dad?

I wonder if *she* knew? The thought hits him with brute force. He thumps himself in the chest. What a fucking fool I am. I never thought of that. What if they both knew? His mother that time asleep in the armchair by the fire, his father looking at her, turning to see Tom looking from one to the other. Come here, he'd motioned, that undemonstrative man, come here, it's all right, come here. Tom closing the geography textbook, coming to sit on the floor beside his father's armchair, the old man ruffling his head like he used to do —Tom suddenly remembers! — when Tom was very small. "Watch this", his father had whispered, dropping a slipper carefully from one foot, reaching across to tickle his mother's one bare foot with a stockinged toe. She made a kind of snuffle, both hands coming up to flutter under her nose, and then her breathing settled to a slow even snore again. Tom nearly choked, trying to hold back the laughter. He'd looked up at his father, that solid, dependable man, at the childlike expression of glee on his face, and for the first time in his life he'd felt the full weight of human tenderness, felt it flow from his father to him, from his father to his sleeping mother, from himself out to them both.

Never mind that the next day, he's remembering this now, too, he'd had a screaming row with his father, no, with them both, about 'that infernal racket' (oh please, such a cliché), the length of his hair (right, he'd turn into a girl of course), the company he was keeping (they're my friends, it's nothing got to do with you), the usual, unavoidable, tedious, adolescent shite.

That moment lost in the rush of … well, life. But not lost, he thinks then, not lost, just buried. And so much of it surfacing now, this past month, these past few days.

He shook himself, feeling the jenny fold in, bore off a bit until it filled again.

He bent to peer at the radar. Nothing. Still, uneasy now, he had a good look around. Nothing. Come on, Tom, he told himself, get with the programme.

What have we got up here, craning his neck, let's see: there's Orion with his belt, there's Cassiopeia, she's wrong about Kavanagh but never mind, there's Castor and Pollux, and there's Venus, my beauty, hanging there under the horn of the moon.

Unthinking, he touches his throat, feeling for something that isn't there. That last night in her cottage in West Cork she'd leaned in to him, her hands behind her back. Coming in through the open window behind her, so vivid now, this, the smell of nettles after rain. In her hair, woodsmoke. She jerked her chin upwards, a small command. He bent his head. He felt the cool chain as she fastened it, felt the light disc tap at the top of his breastbone. He turned it towards the light of the fire. A black quarter moon, black Venus beneath it, on a disc of silver. She'd leaned all the way in then, her hard nipples against his chest, and she'd whispered, "To keep you safe in London town, until I come for you." Static in the air, a kind of vertigo; promises, what is promised us, how we know it when it's there in the air....

It's not true, what he told Clare, that the CD player is broken. Well, that's not the point, really, since these days he mostly listens to music on his iPod. Which is stashed at the bottom of his bag. Which he knows she won't go poking around in. For a mad second or two he considers slipping down below, putting the CD player out of action.

The truth is, he's taking a break from the music just at the minute. Not that it's gone stale on him, but he needs ... silence. That lovely phrase, 'the music of what happens'.

God, he thinks, imagine, after all these years. Then, why did I lie to her, I wonder? He tends the wheel for a bit, watching the wind, wondering if it's going to veer, planning how to tack if he has to without waking her, no bother, done it thousands of times, and it comes to him that there's pressure here in this unlooked-for encounter, this leapfrogging conversation they've gotten into. Time. Time's pressing, he feels, and all of a sudden he sees his father's face, looking down into the coffin at the face of his dead wife, and he is swamped by a grief so profound and total that somewhere in there, drowning, he wonders, *something* wonders, cold and dispassionate, if he will ever surface again.

Clare, lying awake, her eyes closed, is calculating. The Almanac says, what, Valletta to Cagliari 325 miles. Oh-kay. Whatchmacallit bay to tip of Sardinia must be, what, about the same? Yeah. So the log says, the log says we've been making, what, six knots, sometimes a bit more. So, six into 320, six into 320 is ... about fifty-four. Say two days and a bit left over. Did he say where we're going? He didn't, well not exactly. I can feel it, though. He wants to put in somewhere. Right enough, low on meat and vegetables. God I'd love a glass of ice cold milk. Wonder will there be an internet café. Do I want a glass of water? Too much trouble. No. Snug here, eh, Clare? Who was it told me always sleep with your feet to

the bow? Who was that? Why, though? Think, Clare, bit of the old thinking called for … oh, I get it. We slam into a wave, we don't want to slam
our little heads, no sirree bob. Who used to say that? God I don't like
the cut of Tom. Don't care what he says. Still, what do I know? Drama
queen, that's what she used to call me when I'd try to get my own way.
As if. Until I up and left. "Law", she said, remember? "Law! A lot you
know about law." "Precisely", I said. And she laughed out loud and rolled
us another joint. Wonder if Tom has any dope on board. Will I ask him?
Better not, let him offer if he has. Time, my eye, mostly time he says. Bit
of a chancer there, Tom, there's been money spent on this boat. Lovely
motion now, wonder will I get a green light for the bedroom? A bed on
gimbals, wouldn't that be a hoot. Wouldn't….

And the boat runs on into the night, like so many before her, wind in
her sails, granted passage for now.

19

She came up at midnight, he went down, came up again at 4.00 a.m. Nods, a few desultory words, the one going off watch making tea for the one coming on. She woke refreshed, surprised at how rested she felt, called up: "How are we for water?"

"You want to wash some things? We've plenty, we'll be getting more later anyway."

"You got anything not too disgusting that wants washing?"

"Here", he says, dark in the hatchway, tossing her a T-shirt, "catch."

Bare-breasted, water glistening on her arms, she turns to catch it, stops, looks at him. Now, if ever, each thinks, the frank acknowledgement of it in the air. She straightens, faces him squarely.

Time thick in the air.

"We'd blow it, you know?" he says, and she says, "Yes, I know", and they dip inside themselves for an instant, checking for sadness, regret, finding trace elements of both, perhaps, each in their own way, but they let the moment fill and pass and time starts up again, robust and clear.

"Jesus, Tom", sniffing, "have you been wearing this since Ortigia?"

"You didn't notice? Ah sure it's clean dirt. I'm keeping me shorts."

"You can wash them yourself, thank you very much", she says, laughing, turning away, "seems like we both are. Keeping our shorts on."

"If this gets out", he says.

"Don't worry, Tom", cocking her hip at him, "if we meet anyone you know I'll let on that I'm fucked six ways from Sunday."

"You're some wagon…."

"For one wagon, yeah, yeah, get back to work and leave me in peace."

Six ways from Sunday, grinning to himself, six ways from Sunday, where does she get 'em? He's pleased she's in good humour, pleased, too, that his own mood has lightened. Grief is like that, he knows, it obliterates everything in sight, and then it passes — but you have to let it do its work, make its full weight felt. Coming down past Ithaki, what, three weeks ago now? In broad daylight. Ambushed. Out of nowhere. Crushed down in a ball in the cockpit, helpless, moaning in pain. Heart pain, he thinks, making the phrase sombre now. Heart pain, the worst kind of all. His mother's face, the first time he left home. You won't see me again, son. And … he knew it was true but the taxi was at the gate and he looked into her eyes … and Ruth, dear Jesus, Ruth … he feels the vortex beginning to gather round him, the long watches last night reaching out for him again, and makes the effort he's learned to make, long time since, and comes out and up into the bright, clear light of now.

Ithaki! "Hey sunshine!"

"Yes, my lord?"

"Gozo, right? Know what its old name was?"

"I do not."

"Ogygia. Mean anything to you?"

"And, should it?"

"Calypso's island. Where she held poor old Odysseus in thrall for seven long years."

"In thrall, is it?" She's come to the hatch, hair wet, fresh T-shirt, leaning her head on her folded arms. "In thrall, is it? Listen to me, it took him ten years to get home, the reprobate. You think he was in a hurry, do you? He was in my eye. In thrall? Would you go 'way out of that. Sailors!"

He's laughing in delight. "What's it say on your T-shirt?"

She stands back, arches her spine, throwing her chest forward: "If you dare."

"Peaches", he says.

"Mother o' God, I never thought of that", she says, looking down at her breasts. "Aren't we very well read all the same. Right, breakfast."

The wind's almost due east, they're on a broad reach, carving through the water. "You'd think she senses land", Clare says. "All boats do", he says, "coming in from the sea." They're at the chart table, heads together. "OK", he says, "we'll be seeing Sardinia any minute now, I reckon, we've made good time. See, here? That's the mouth of the bay leading up to Cagliari. You in any mood for a big, ugly city?" No, she shakes her head. "Good, 'cos what I mean to do is head off here, west of the entrance and up inside these islands, here." "OK", she says. "The upper one, Isola San

Pietro, that's where we're going. Small town on the east side, Carloforte. Spend the night there, if you're OK with that? Nice place." "I'm in your hands", she says.

Silence. A flick of the erotic between them. Stillness. It passes.

"I like when that happens", she says. "The might-have-been. Not brushing it away. Letting it come and go by itself." Soft and clear.

He sighs, she elbows him sharply: "Ah you're not past it yet, Tom." And when she senses him go cold, still not looking at him, she says "Come on, Tom, we're using it, you know that."

He sits down, looks up at her. Admiration. She colours, dips her head. Shy.

"You're not as smart as you think you are, you know", he says then. Mischief.

"Really?" she says, "And how's that, Tom dear?"

"Because that kettle's been boiling for over a minute now. Make the tea, woman, what ails you?"

Sure enough, the low smudge of Sardinia is there on the bow when she climbs to windward and looks ahead. "Land Ho!' she yells, pointing.

"Bearing?" he calls back, theatrical himself. "No", she simpers, cupping her belly, "sure how could I be, a simple, humble cabin boy?"

He laughs. "There was a lot of that, you know, in the days of sail."

"What? Pregnant cabin boys?"

"No, you idiot, women dressing up as men and taking to the sea."

"Must have been very complicated", she murmurs, standing in beside him.

"Yeah, I mean...." and he glances to the right, where the ghost of the moon is fading from the sky.

"God aren't you a very sensitive man all the same", she says, locking on to his train of thought. "Ah progress, progress. Don't you worry boy, I won't go mad for, oh, about ten days yet."

"Do you? Go mad, I mean?"

"Oh boy do I, tooth and claw, man, tooth and claw."

"Oh."

"Not always, though. Depends. On lots o' things."

"Oh Jesus", he says, "the inscrutable feminine!"

"Ah, God, you know" — she swings down beside him, nudges him along the seat, "I'm being very hard on the poor old bastard."

"Huh? What're you on about?"

"Rory, my stepfather."

"Rory?"

"Rory Patrick Deasy. Gentleman farmer, horse-breeder, married to my mother. God love him, how did he put up with us?"

Tom leans back away from her, puzzled, bangs his head on the spray hood support. "Ouch."

"You should wear a hat", she says, not exactly sympathetically. "Don't look at me like that. I'd better explain. Look, he was a decent enough man, OK? Never raised a hand to me, gave me anything I wanted, within reason, but he couldn't make head nor tail of me. Decent, OK? Big house, Georgian, proper Georgian, 300 acres, good land, too, and he made an OK fist of farming it. Horses were his thing, though, big, square yard at the back of the house, maybe ten to twelve animals there at any one time. He lived for horses. That's why she married him."

He looks at her, bemused. Where is this going?

Exasperated, she makes a gesture as if to sweep hair away from the back of her neck; he realises it hasn't been short for long. She sees his look, holds it, shrugs, yes.

"Suits you", he says. A grunt, but a brief smile to go with it.

"Yes, well. I spent the first five years of my life on a horse ranch in Arizona, did I tell you that? No? Of course I didn't, what am I saying? My mother Sandra, she's English. She'd lived in Ireland for a while, yeah? Then back to England for a bit, sick of the country she always said, but I never believed her; bailed out of London and ended up, what with one thing and another, working on this horse ranch. Broken Arrow, it was called, can you believe that? Bit of a hippy princess, Sandra was. Oh you should have seen her down there, tanned to bejasus, rangy and tough, a great woman for swearing was Sandra, and a laugh that would melt rocks. Navajo jewellery, right, you know the kind, turquoise and silver, blue shirts and denims except for sometimes when she'd go in to town she'd hoke out this long dress, black with blue trim, waisted, full length, faded red embroidered panel at the bust. Never wore a hat in town. Hair back in a long plait, she looked like a squaw, maybe that's the look she was after, who knows. Big into the ethnic thing, our Sandra.

"One time, I remember now, some shithead in a bar *called* her a squaw. Woke up with a crowd around him. First she decked him, big swing from the hip, I told you she was tough. And then the guys from the ranch started in on him. I was terrified, these lovely men, never done making a pet of me, thinking up treats for me, animals suddenly, savage. She tore them off the poor fucker, one at a time. Tongue lashed them, I was sobbing in the corner. They'd have died for her, those guys. I remember her sweeping me up into her arms, smell of beer on her breath but composed, you know, soothing me, over and over, her hand smoothing down my hair...."

Unconsciously, she is mimicking the gesture.

"All the way back in the truck she held me, in close, the heat of her. Twenty-five miles of dust, you never saw such a sky, stars like diamonds on velvet, somebody one night on the porch said that, picking at a guitar. Big moon over the mesa, big bony nose on McQuaid, the charge hand driving. Not a word out of him or her the whole way back."

Sardinia a definite presence now, when he ducks his head under the boom to have a look. He has a good look around while he's at it. Ferries, be ferries maybe.

She waits, hands folded in her lap. He sees a schoolgirl on her best behaviour, eyes downcast, waiting to go on.

"So, I was five then, right? About that. Not long after, we went to a big horse fair, well whatever they're called down there. A day's drive, maybe? Big trailer behind the truck, 'Lone Star', big black stallion. Sold him on to a pilot, of all things. Airline pilot. Anyway, that's where she met him, Rory. Next thing I know we're on our way to Ireland. You know what I'd love, now, Tom, I'd love a cigarette. You got any cigarettes, Tom?"

"Five years."

"Good for you. Yeah, well, anyway, to this day I don't know what really happened. Never trust a hippy. Sandra, well Sandra came of a rich family, didn't I read that somewhere? 'Came of a rich family.' What I mean is, her parents were well-off, Sandra had always had in the back of her mind that they'd leave her money and she'd start in breeding horses. She was even worse than, than Rory, about horses. I don't know, maybe it all just hit her all of a sudden. One minute she's a tough hippy chick, free spirit, running a ranch in Arizona, next thing you know she's back in Ireland, hair bobbed, sweaters and jeans and barbour jackets, riding to hounds, mistress of all she surveys. Guess what happened, Tom?"

"Her father died and left her a whack of money?"

"Pre-cisely. As if everything since she'd left Sevenoaks, you know where that is, right? Everything since she'd left Sevenoaks was just, just … marking time? Play?

"So here I am, this feral child, in deepest Tipperary, God help me, wet, cold, green Tipperary, with a father, of all things, a father God help me! And good old Sandra, drawling, witty, cutting Sandra going distant on me, new accent, new clothes, new attitude.

"And poor Rory, he obviously hadn't given it any thought at all, poor Rory hadn't a clue what to do with me. Not. A. Clue."

"Jesus Christ!" he yells, springing to his feet, a siren blaring from behind. "Out of the way" — he elbows her aside, disengaging the auto-pilot, hauling the wheel over to bear away. How did I not hear that, how the fuck did I not hear that?! A ferry looming up behind, great white cliff over a narrow triangle of blue. He fires up the engine, running it up as fast as he thinks it will take, but then, as if strings had been cut, he subsides. Leans down and pulls out the cut-off toggle. Not as close as he'd thought, not by a mile he thinks, heart still hammering. Why did I think … the noise, just the noise, the shock of it. Clare is pale, still, elbow pressed down on the hand massaging her ribcage. "Ouch", she says. "Mother of divine God", she says.

"I'm sorry", he says. "In the circumstances", she says. The ferry hauls past, a line of passengers on her port upper rail, many of them waving. Neither Clare nor Tom feels much like waving back.

They settle, but not before Tom has gone forward, right into the bow, for a thorough look round. Clare, unprompted, is scanning the horizon behind, slowly, deliberately, with binoculars. "Good girl", he says, and she nods without turning. "My fault entirely", he says. And she shrugs. "Pair of us in it. Will I go on?"

"Please." He stretches an arm towards her, she hesitates, sits, cuddles in.

"So, I'll skip as much as I can here, you can figure it out. School, I must have been more than half-wild, right? You can guess what they made of me. I made no friends. I look back now and I can see that was deliberate. At the time I just felt I was falling through space, you know? Now I can see, well it wasn't long before I saw, that I was hoping that if I … refused it? Refused it all? That things would get back to normal.

I wasn't a stupid child, I knew very well this was real life, whatever that is, but it would be a long time before I accepted it. Do you understand me? Yeah.

"So, that's how things went on until Rory decided I was old enough for boarding school. Oh I was terrible to him, Tom, terrible. I won't say, oh I was a right vicious little bitch in my time, I can tell you. He'd just walk out of the room, you know? He'd look at me with those blank eyes of his, give a little shake of the head, walk away. And Sandra? Well, put it this way, she wasn't bringing me down the pub with the farmhands. There should be a cook in this story, right? The matronly, friendly heart-of-gold substitute mother? Don't make me laugh. Sandra was the cook. Good, too. Always up for trying something new. Someone came in to do the cleaning, one woman after another, I wouldn't bother knowing anything about them, that was me.

"I couldn't for the life of me understand what there was between them, Sandra and Rory. They had a way of being friendly that took no effort at all, but separate bedrooms after a while, and after a while longer, even I could see, all but separate lives. It seemed to suit her, it seemed to suit him, and after they'd shunted me off to school it began to suit me, too. A separate life of my own, I mean.

"You're probably thinking, typical big house lifestyle, right? Rory was the son of a butcher from some town or other in Waterford. Never spoke of his family, not once, not ever. He'd invented this life for himself, you see what I'm saying? His own dream of himself. None of Sandra's relatives ever came to stay, she never went to visit her brother, her sister. Two solitary, contented beings, all they had in common was a passion for horses.

"Then, one year, I was twelve, thirteen, late summer, I'd come in from a long, dusty ramble down by the lake, there she was, Mam, at the kitchen doors, on one of those rush chairs, you know? Smoking away to her heart's content, a big spliff. She just looked at me lazily. I was transfixed, not surprise, nothing like that, but I was transfixed because I recognised the smell, you see? From back in Arizona? We'd sit out on the porch, sundown, one of her beaux as she liked to call them, picking on an old, beat-up guitar, dust in the air, and the good old smell of ganja.

"I don't know what made me say it, but I just out and asked: 'Mum, all those guys back in, you know, was any one of them my Dad?'

"She had a level look, Sandra, a kind of summing-up look. She just looked at me, held my eyes for a long instant and … shook her head. Not a word. Just shook her head. Didn't take her eyes off me. And then she smiled, long, slow smile. And here's the thing, Tom, you still with me here? Here's the thing, you know what I felt just then?"

"Nope."

"Pure happy. Would you believe that? Purely and simply and totally … happy! Amazing!"

"I don't understand. Happy? Because she told you, she told you nothing!"

"No, Tom, dear Tom, you don't understand, it was because I saw Sandra's great secret then. She was there all along. She'd been in there all along, inside this, whatever she was playing at, she was in there all along. And waiting for me to find her."

They've crossed the mouth of the bay by now, a handful of big ships heading into Cagliari, a handful coming out, turning sharp east or west. "We'll cut straight in", Tom says, "ninety degrees across the westbound lanes, then off to port again for the passage between the islands. Stay where you are, I'll get the jenny. And you found her…", he prompted.

She waits till he switches the engine on again, takes time for a look around, settles in behind his shoulder on the helmsman's seat.

"We going round that point, then, up ahead? How long after that?"

"Not long, time enough. If you feel like it.…"

"Oh yeah, grand. So. Turns out, wait'll you hear this, Miss Prim and Proper has a small plantation way back in the woods, always a few plants going, right? Oh never trust a hippy is right. So, picture me when the teenage years hit, right? Boarding school. Good with the books, so in with the teachers, and the swots. Leggy, athletic, in with the hockey crowd if I wanted to be. And a lovely supply of Golden Vale Marvellous for the cool kids. Tom, I never wanted to go home! No, that's not true. I think one or two of the teachers had their doubts about me, you know? Saw something wasn't quite … right. But I'd be torn, you see. Having a fab time up there in the bogs all winter and then … I loved being with her, you see? Well, most of the time. Rory, well Rory could point to the report cards, the odd trophy, I was presentable enough I suppose, and God love him I'd make an effort for him, when we'd be out socially kind of thing. But, no connection. Nada. What I liked was hanging out with Sandra, mucking out, riding out. Going off with her to buy or sell a horse. Funny, that. Buying or selling a horse was something she'd always do without Rory being there. Not that he didn't know about it, now, they'd discuss it until you'd be bored out of your mind with the back and forth of it, but when it came to the day, it was me and Sandra, away with us. Or Rory'd go off on his own and do a deal, he was like that too. Strange. This went on for a few years until, oh I don't know, beginning of my Leaving Cert year. And Sandra began to tipple. Every now and then. Whiskey. Rarely, but often enough, tears before bedtime. Rambling on about 'The old days, man.' Oh the stories she could tell. Like 'One time, German Tim had scored this real mellow acid....' Like, 'The vibe was good, man, nobody minded who slept with who....' 'Whom', I'd say. 'Whom!' But she wouldn't hear me. I'm making this all sound pathetic, aren't I? The thing is, it wasn't. Not like something cynical and bad off the TV. This was, I dunno, a kind of, of slippage? Like she was slipping a gear, slurring a gear, whatever? Her face would change, she'd look younger. Kind of, hopeful? But it scared me, I didn't know why but it scared me. Turns out it should have. Well, Rory died. I'd taken myself off up to the attic by then, room under the eaves, only for my room the whole floor was deserted. Spick and span, mind, we're not talking spooky here. So one morning I'm coming down, a good day, I'd been listening to Mam below in the yard singing along with something, and I hear a crash from Rory's room so I push in the door and there he is, legs in the bathroom, face in the bedroom and I knew the minute I saw him he was dead. Stood there, desperately trying to feel something other than surprise, and Mam's at my shoulder and I look back at her over my shoulder and she has this expression on her face. The minute I see it I know I've the same expression on *my* face, too. Like, that's Rory there on the floor, Rory is dead. One minute he wasn't. Now he is."

Tom's afraid to look at her, afraid he'll see that expression on her face. Doesn't know what he'll think if he sees that expression. Doesn't want to, see it or think about it.

"A year later, I'm in Trinity doing law. Big row about that at first, her screaming about how I'm joining the establishment, man, some shit like that. Didn't last long. She cut back on the drinking. She'd come up to Dublin more than I'd go down, once we went to Paris for a weekend. She actually smuggled in a bit of draw with her, would you believe that? Said she wanted to get high on the Eiffel Tower. So, life went on. I graduated, blah blah, started practising. We drifted apart, of course. Oh nothing major; just, she had her life, I had mine. I'd go down when I could, less often as the years went by, you know yourself, and she'd come to stay with me in Dublin. We'd go on short holidays from time to time. Grand. I never brought anyone down with me, she never asked who I was seeing. Nothing wrong, you understand? We were, we were, hard to explain this, close — but we really hadn't much to do with one another. I presume she had lovers from time to time, a lively woman was Sandra, but we never … And then, she died. Stone dead, baby. Off a horse. Jumping a wall. Out by herself one bright May morning, took it into her head to try this wall and … poof! Gone.

And now Tom turns to look at her, shocked to find she's waiting to meet his look.

"Three years ago?" Flat.

"Three years ago", she agreed, and said nothing for a minute.

"A small bit more, Tom", she said. "A small bit more. So you'll understand."

Tom's bafflement. Rapt in the story, he doesn't see where she's going.

"Ah, Tom, Tom, don't you see? I'm walking away from the graveyard, nobody coming near me, I think in some way they were all a bit afraid of me that morning, neighbours, the crowd who'd come down from college, a few girls from school…. I'm walking away from the graveyard and going around and around in my head is, my mother is dead, I wonder where my father is, my mother is dead, I wonder where my father is. Do you see, Tom? Do you see?"

She steps away from him, in case he tries to embrace her, comfort her. Her back set square against him, she says:

"You get me, Tom? You have something to say, Tom?"

"Look, lots of kids don't have fathers, you know…."

"Jesus, Tom, excuse me, you think I don't know that? Have you been listening to a word I've been saying? This is not about fathers. Oh! Oh, I see."

"You see? You see what? I'm getting kinda lost here, Clare. Help me out, OK?"

Steady and cool now, his gaze level, his voice neutral. But firm.

"I see I haven't explained anything at all, really. I'm sorry, Tom, I'm sorry. I left something out, what a fool I am."

"Clare?"

"Oh, oh, yeah. There was a look she'd get, Sandra? When she'd be reminiscing? Something, I don't know, stricken? And that day, the day of the funeral, walking away from her, it came to me. Whoever he was, wherever he was, this man, my father, that's who she was missing. She would have needed him to be there. That was the wound. It was like, I don't know, a sudden illumination, would you call it that? A complete certainty. I just *knew*."

"I don't know, Clare, I don't know. Too much to process here. Turn coming up."

"What?"

He gestures over his shoulder. "Turn to pass up inside the islands."

For a moment, she has no idea where she is, no idea who he is. She feels, all of a sudden, a deep, visceral anxiety. She looks at Tom with foreboding, doubt. Tom, out of sympathy for reasons he doesn't understand, is both enthralled by her story and repulsed by it. He feels an aversion to Clare now, a kind of bullying impatience. For God's sake get over it, he wants to say. Look what you're missing, look around you. Stop feeling so sorry for yourself. And Clare, sensing this, feels her battle-self coming over her, the tough, combative streak she has nurtured and trained in herself. Who the fuck is he to be judging her? What the hell is she doing, anyway, telling the story of her life to this stranger, this *old* guy she's only barely met?

The truth is, of course, they're both exhausted, but they don't know this. They have forgotten as most people have forgotten, that we tell stories of this kind with the body, we use up the body's resources to feed the journey inward, to give weight and credence and truth to the soul's stories of its journey. Once upon a time this was a known fact. Tom, with his love of sean nós music, should remember this. A sean nós singer, eyes closed, gone deep for the song, will have a friend holding his hand, churning it round and round to give him a way back, to reassure the body that the soul has not left it. And Clare, how many times has she witnessed the utter exhaustion of a witness when her turn or his turn on the stand has finished? How many times has she felt body and soul drained after giving her all to a summing up in front of … a jury of strangers? And she wonders, off to one side of this train of thought, if Tom is a stranger? He is, he isn't.... Yes, she thinks, of course. I'm just exhausted. And Tom, seeing realisation come to light in her face, her abrupt presence to her self, feels a sympathetic pulse in himself, a quickening.

Another step further in, each feels/thinks, no word for this access of knowledge. Nothing is said, but wherever they've been they understand that they've come through it now.

And you, too? Each asks the other, without speaking. And the answer, of course, is yes, yes, me too.

"God", she says, rueful and distracted, "the body, eh?"

"Get your body down here, you, and get that jenny in, would you? Jasus it's hard to get good help nowadays. And you might get the staysail in if you feel up to it? If it's not too much trouble, like?"

Clare beams at him, would hug him if not for a sudden flush of shyness. Somehow, damned if she knows how, he's telling her she's been heard. That moment when, the plane banking, descending, your ears pop. A moment like that, a quick, unmistakable flush of energy in the blood.

Puttering gently up the narrow defile, the afternoon so still that, sheeted in hard as it is, the main is flapping, a disconsolate thing, robbed of its purpose. Swift, silent, Tom drops it, hops up on the coachroof, deftly flakes it down, ties it off. Hops down again.

"Eh, Tom, the bridge?"

Isola San Pietro is linked to Sardinia by a causeway and bridge. It's dead ahead, looming closer and closer.

"Bridge, what bridge?"

"That fucking bridge up ah... ah, feck you and the horse you rode into town on!"

Tom, no other word for it, smirks.

There's a jetty coming up on the port side, below the bridge, a twin row of berths and a hammerhead pontoon on the end of it. Small boats nose to nose on the central gangway, a thin walkway separating each boat from the next on either side. "What do we draw?" she asks, rooting out fenders. "About a metre and a half", he says, "it's deep enough; we'll go alongside on the hammerhead." She sees him begin to feed the wheel to the right, so she knows he's going to circle around, come alongside facing back out the channel. She ties off the fenders on the starboard side, stands there amidships, the stern line in her hand. Glances back once to make sure it's attached inboard, that it's led under and outside the guard-rail. Not a word said between them. He angles the bow in, a light touch of reverse, cuts the engine, begins to slide sideways on. She steps off smartly and, as he spins the wheel to bring the stern right in she drops the line over a cleat, leaning back slightly, letting the cleat take the strain. The instant the boat stops she drops a hitch over the cleat and steps along to where Tom, scrambling forward, has time to hand her the bowline before the bow begins to blow off.

Nothing a sailor likes better than coming alongside without fuss. Tom puts two beers carefully down on deck, steps down to the jetty and walks towards her, popping one can then the other. Anyone else would have hopped down with the beers and then we'd have foam all over us when we opened them; what a stupid reason, she thinks, to have a lump in my throat. When Tom, tapping his can against hers, says "What a team, eh? You're some woman for one woman", he is startled to see tears in her eyes. Startled, and then obscurely but definitely gratified. "Here's to crime", she says, tilts the can back and takes a deep, deep swallow.

20

Shoregoing clothes. They strip, taking turns, they shower, and dress unselfconsciously together in the saloon. Tom in a grey silk shirt, black linen trousers, Clare in the sleeveless black linen shift she'd worn that first night on the quay in Siracusa. Each is thinking about how much time has passed since then. Elements of the stories they've been telling are freefalling through their minds, like rocks in slow motion down a silent slope.

What Clare sees: A strong man in his mid fifties, not quite lean, short beard, short hair. Deep tan, serious blue-green eyes. Capable, she thinks, a capable-looking man. Class, occupation? Couldn't tell. Whatever he does, he's probably a success at it. What Tom sees: A slender and fit young woman, grave, a hint of devilment in the intelligent blue eyes, a fashionable but practical cut, a certain reserve in the demeanour. Elegant, too, a simple, broad silver bangle her only adornment. A hint of, what is it, danger?

Well now, he thinks, danger. Could be — then, no, not danger. A strong will, carefully masked.

What Clare sees also, though she evades the thought, shifts her attention elsewhere, is the *fade* in him, the slight dimming of his internal light.

"The Swatch kind of kills the look", she says. He thinks about it, wiping water off its face by rubbing it on his thigh. "Ah", he says, making a show of coming to a decision, "the oul' Rolex will only tempt 'em to overcharge us."

Arm in arm they stroll down the jetty to the Corso Battellieri, Carloforte rising up from the waterfront in terraces before them. Two old women are watching them critically as they step up into the evening traffic, eyeing them frankly up and down. A double nod; they'll do, the crone-judges of *la bella figura* approve, they may join the *passeggiata*. Tom

gives the old ones a dignified half-bow as they pass, gets a basilisk look
for his pains. Clare staring haughtily ahead. "Full marks", he whispers,
"for the *Principessa* bit"; they're impressed, and a bit annoyed. Outfoxed.
He gets a quick elbow in the ribs.

The long evening promenade appeals to them both for different reasons. Tom, for his part, likes to look at the young women and at the
older couples. His heart is drawn to the gaggles of lithe young girls, so
full of promise, excitement, belief; he approves them and blesses them
as they pass, he wishes them well. The young men he mostly watches for
signs of aggression, some meanness of spirit that may bear watching.
He senses the unfairness of this, but isn't about to give himself a hard
time over it. More and more now though, these last few years, he finds
himself watching the old people, approving the signs in those worn faces
of lives that have been faced squarely, lines that are testament to vicis-
situdes overcome, victories doubted but accepted, defeats acknowledged.
Endurance he has come to salute as a form of wisdom. Clare, on the
other hand, unconscious of the fact, watches mostly the young couples,
the quick, boisterous children, perpetually in motion, small, dark moons
orbiting stately twin planets. Sometimes a child, sensing her avid gaze,
will give her a long, measuring look. Gravity beyond years. Often, too,
she'll be favoured with a quick, brilliant smile. I know you, the smile says.
And also, I don't know you, the quick scamper away. She is, of course,
looking for that small, grave girl-child, the one who looks on the world
with a reserved, considering air. Not today, though, not here, and Clare,
without knowing why, is slightly sad. Neither of them notices the old, old
woman in black, shopping bag limp at her feet, who watches them from
her bench under an arch in deep shadow. She blesses herself, lips working
on each other in her sunken face as they go by. Her eyes black points of
light, her stillness near absolute.

Tom is amused by the preening young waiter who dances attendance
on Clare, practising his animal magnetism to no avail. Clare looking
pointedly away says, "I hope you're not scowling at that poor boy." "Sure
I'm invisible", Tom says, "he doesn't even see me"; the amusement earn-
ing him a surreptitious finger.

"Where are you taking us, Tom?"

"Huh?"

"Well we're obviously going *somewhere*."

"Tetchy, tetchy! Here we are anyway, *Chiesa dei Novelli Innocenti.*"

"It's a church, Tom, I see that. Not particularly impressive, so there's a story?"

Tom in lecture mode: "The year is 1212. The Pope, a right bastard if you ask me, has engineered what he's pleased to call 'The Children's Crusade'. The idea being, so he says, that the innocent children of Catholic Europe will liberate Jerusalem from the Infidel Muslim by ... well, by marching there en masse."

"What, they'll just turn up at the gates and the Infidels will immediately see the error of their ways, fold their tents in the night etc. etc.?"

"As you say, etc. etc. But let's not go into that. We have this church here to commemorate a shipwreck. Hundreds of the poor mites drowned off the north coast here in a shipwreck. In fact, there's a necropolis near here, where they're all buried. Quite a sight. You want...?"

"No", shivering, "I do not. Is the church open, do you think?"

They stand at the bottom of the nave, searching. By unspoken consent they cross to the altar of the Virgin, drop coins in the brass box with the red Maltese Cross fading on its face; they light candles, they kneel, they close their eyes and pray.

Inside his head, counterpoint to the soothing lilt of his deep-grained 'Hail Mary', Tom hears Eartha Kitt: 'Sometimes I Feel Like a Motherless Child'. Clare, with a kind of subdued wonder, hears herself speaking with confidence a prayer she'd long forgotten she knew by heart: 'Hail Queen of Heaven, the Ocean Star....'

Later, walking off an indifferent dinner, arm in arm with Tom, she will surprise him by murmuring, to herself and to the night, 'Pray for the wanderer, pray for me.'

After a while: "You a believer, Tom?"

"No. You?"

"Nope."

21

She wakes with a shock. Music. The boat is moving. Light dancing across her eyes, coming and going. Irrational fear, near-panic. Engine, the engine's on. Take a breath. Hold it. Let it go. Take a breath … I'm in the forecabin, she tells herself, it's morning, the hatch above me is open. We're moving. What?

Tom calls down through the hatch, blotting out the light for an instant, going by: "I let you sleep on, you don't mind? Have to top up on diesel, the guy goes off duty soon. Take your time."

Music. Where's the music coming from? She stumbles into the saloon, batting away shreds of her dreaming. Cohen, she's processing now. 'Ten Last Songs'. The song fills the cave of the saloon, she imagines the air is blue-grey, shot through with gold, gold in his voice, spilling up through the hatch and away: "Say goodbye to Alexandra leaving…" and she joins in, less and less bewildered as she comes to "…and say goodbye to Alexandra lost." In a kind of swoon, still looking around her, placing herself. But the CD's broken, she's telling herself. He said so.

Yeah? So? So he fixed it, get a grip. She takes a saucepan, fills it with cold water, leans in over the sink, pours the water over her head. Shock.

"Coming alongside!" he yells down, she feels the boat spin, feels her balance is back. "Make yourself decent, don't be frightening the poor old bugger!"

"Ah feck you!" she yells back,

"…and the horse I rode into town on, I know I know. You like?"

"Cohen? Excuse me? What's not to like. How…?"

"Ah sure I'm an electronics genius", he says, complacent. "Loose wire", he adds after a moment.

Dressed, up on deck. She inhales the odour of diesel. The old man handing the filler nozzle up to Tom is all sinew and bone in his faded overalls. He straightens, sizing her up, makes her a stately bow: *"Buon giorno"*, a pause, *"Signorina."* An arch look at Tom, who accepts the ancient compliment with a dignified nod. Starts filling the tank.

"Is that our theme for the day, Tom?" she asks him sweetly, bending to his ear.

"Huh?"

"Smug", she says, goosing him, with a nudge towards the old man, who is openly fascinated now.

"Let him think what he likes", Tom says, unperturbed. "Sure doesn't he think I've won the lottery. Down below now, woman and start cleaning."

"Yes, master", she says, and goes to make breakfast — sticking her tongue out at the old man as she turns to go down. Crowning his morning.

They're back on the hammerhead, breakfast finished, lingering over coffee.

"A lazy day", Tom says presently, "what would you say to a lazy day?"

"Hello, lazy day", they say in unison, and laugh.

"Seriously, we've three days to Palma, give or take, and the truth is, well I'm a bit tired. The heat...."

And everything else, he doesn't say, doesn't need to say, both of them feeling the weight of *all that talk* now. Acknowledging it with sidelong looks.

So many different kinds of silence, Clare thinks. "What might be good", she says, "would be to head down a bit", gesturing to the channel, "anchor off somewhere quiet?"

Tom says, "We're going to need some food, some bits and pieces. I was planning to get those in the evening, when it cools down? I think we'll stay here. That all right with you?" Not saying, no need to, I'm deciding here.

A small, unexpected epiphany for Clare: actually, sometimes, it's fine to let someone else make the decisions. To, what's the word, accede? Accede.

"You happy enough, Clare?"

"Call no man happy", she says, mock sepulchral, "this side of the grave. I'm happy, Tom, I'm happy enough. I saw him, you know, last time he was in Dublin."

"Jesus, what are you on about now, woman?"

"Cohen. At the Royal Hospital, were you there?"

He shakes his head, no: "I was here." Meaning on the boat.

"Well, he steps up to the mike, right, big smile, God he's a sexy man, what is he now, seventy something? Anyway, he steps up to the mike and says 'Last time I was in Dublin I was a young man of sixty with a head full of foolish dreams.' He's a hoot, I swear."

He smiles up at her, stands, stretches. Absent-minded, he reaches over and ruffles her hair, is pleased when she inclines her head towards him. "Ah Clare, Clare, head full of foolish dreams, eh?" Shaking his head, still smiling as he goes below, slow in himself, taking care with the steps. "I think I'll sleep for a bit", he says, lifting the desk lid, rummaging. "I think I'll sleep myself", she says, "got some dreaming to catch up on." Passing, she's going to ask him how he is but he raises a hand, and she pauses, passes on. He knows she'll turn to look at him, taps two pills into his hand, screws the cap back on the bottle. Holding her look now, he puts the bottle on the fiddled shelf beside the chart table. Raises an eyebrow at her. She nods, and turns away. After a moment, he kills the power on the CD player.

She pulls the door halfway over, not shutting him out, more answering to the animal self that says shelter, shelter.

He stands there, a palm flat to the roof as the boat rocks, something going by. Lately now, he can feel the drain. The sap falling back, increment by increment. Rearguard actions, he thinks, small groups of skirmishers blunting the attack, falling back stage by stage ... he dismisses the thought with a practised ease, ducking under the implications as if ducking under a telegraphed punch. God, he thinks then, how long is it since I've been in a fight, a good old-fashioned brawl?

He's lying on his back, the sheet cool on the length of his body. He doesn't remember getting undressed, getting into the bunk. Brawl, he thinks, there's an interesting word. Brawl. Must look it up. Something harmless about it, the sound of it. Out like a light.

Clare, barely gone under, wakes with a start. Beeswax, smoke from a snuffed candle. The smell's so precise and vivid she sits up, looking around her. I was dreaming, she thinks, but ... I never dreamed smells before. Do people smell things in dreams, I wonder? Never heard tell of it. Sinking back into the pillow, turning on her side, drawing her knees up, after a moment stretching the upper leg. Putting her hand under her face.

Must ask Tom, she thinks, must….

Evening. A bruised, violet glow in the air. They're on the jetty, squatting on their heels, washing fruit and vegetable before stowing them carefully in plastic crates. "Cockroaches", Tom told her when she asked: "What's with the basin of water, Tom?" "They live in the cardboard boxes", he said, "lay their eggs in the corrugations. Never bring cardboard on board a boat, Clare. And wash all the fresh produce before bringing it on."

A way he has of explaining things, not making a big deal of it, just passing on the lore, straightforward. Clare is so used to the nuanced barbs of the Law Library, the doublespeak of her clients, the briefing solicitors, the cattiness male and female of her habitual life that she's found it hard to adjust to this.

No, she thought then, industriously scrubbing a melon, Jack's like that, too. 'Jack'! Christ almighty, I'm calling him 'Jack' even when I'm talking to myself. Park that, think about it, though. What? Oh yes, There's 'close to me', and then there's the rest. Towards whom —the rest she means — I have an attitude of permanent and unrelenting suspicion. Well, now, isn't that interesting?

"Tom", she says, stowing the fruit and vegetables in nets hung from the roof either side of the companionway, "let's get some pizza and bring it back, have a few beers and tell stories, what do you say?"

He's head-down in a locker, stowing bottles of water, grunting and snuffling. Stiffens.

"Ah no, no, I don't mean like that, it's all right. I just mean, you know, yarns. Funny incidents. Little scandals and the like."

He perks up: "Salacious?"

"Only if funny."

"Huh."

"A break, like?" she offers.

"Mitching school? OK by me."

"Good, I'd like a pepperoni, extra garlic, olives, double cheese. Please. Thank you, Tom."

He's halfway along the gangway when he thinks, Christ, how does she do it? I've been, I've been *despatched*.

"That was yummy, thanks, Tom."

"Yummy? Yummy? You sound about twelve." He snorts, "Yummy!"

"Behave. Now, a story, Tom, if you please. A true one. You want a second beer? No? Sure? Go ahead so."

"OK, here's a true story. Friend of mine, trad musician, wanted a bodhrán. You, know, that flat drum…"

"…Tom I know what a bodhrán is, for God's sake."

"You do, you from the big Georgian house an' all?"

"Don't make me come over there."

"So, he's just out of jail…"

"…For what? What was he in for?"

"In for? Oh, drunk driving."

"He got jail for drunk driving? Come on, Tom, no one gets jail for drunk driving."

"With seventeen pints in him? Plus, I should mention, he'd been shagging the apple of the Judge's eye, I should mention that. Jail it was, jail he got. So he's out, but while he's in there he gets it into his head that he needs a new bodhrán, right? Only of course he's banned from driving now, too, isn't he? So, I don't know how he managed to persuade me, I suppose because I was playing a bit of trad at the time, I get to drive him down to some wild place in the west where a figure very well known in the music business has a little sideline in making bodhráns. We get there, we call up to your man, and there's bodhráns in various states of undress all over the gaff. Dozens of 'em. 'Keeping busy?' says I. 'Oh Jasus I'm flahed to the ropes', he says, 'flahed to the ropes. Can't keep up with it at all, at all.' So the pair of them are hugger muggering in the corner and the gist of it is, we're to call back tomorrow morning and he'll have a bodhrán for me bucko. We're in the pub later on, bit of a session going on, nice and mellow, and this little fiddle player comes sidling up to me. 'You were up with yer man?' says he. 'We were', says I, wondering what's coming. 'Are ye staying beyond?' says he. 'We are', says I. 'I'll give a call in to ye in the morning', says he. And with that, he's gone. We're contemplating death and the rasher the next morning, swinging this way and that, unable to make up our minds, when I see your man the fiddle player at the window. Beckoning. Out we go, a fine, fresh morning, and he's a hundred yards down the road, lookin' back at us and pretending not to know us. So, on with us and we follow him where he's disappeared down a little boreen. Walking past an overgrown gateway and we hear 'Psst! Pssst!' And him so close he could reach out and touch us. 'Folly me', he says, 'folly me, men. Now', he says, ducking under a bush on the banks of what by the sound of it is a big stream or a small river. 'Now', he says, what d'ye think of that now! 'There's what looks like a fallen tree spanning the river, the water combing though it, the branches all bleached bare, like. Only it's not a tree, it's a bloody big dam of bones. Big bones, little bones, all tangled and heaped, all through-other. Bodhráns is it?' says me man. 'Bodhráns! 'tis like the elephants' graveyard around here since yer man above started in on the bodhráns. An' I wouldn't mind, nearly all them bones is dogs. God be with the days when the bodhrán was only the skin of a goat. Christ but it kept the numbers down, didn't it! Now every feckin' eejit in the world' — he makes an exception of my pal with a big sweeping gesture, fair dues to him — 'now every fecker in the world, from, from Doolin to Dusseldorf, thinks he's a dab hand at the drummin', and where are the skins to come from, can ye tell me that, now? I'll tell ye where. Dogs. That's what them bones are there, everything from a peking-ease to a dubberman. Vans in the night, boys, vans in the night! Where is it all going to end, tell me that now, that's what I want to know; where is it all going to end?' And with that, he was gone! Melted away.

"We got the car, anyway, and drove up to collect the bodhrán. It was a thing of beauty, I have to give him that, a beautiful, clean sound off it, but all the while, sitting there in the big living room he'd converted into a, a sort of showroom I suppose, nursing a glass of poitín, I felt like I was surrounded by collies, retrievers, pit bulls and greyhounds, terriers and spaniels, wolfhounds and huskies, all kinds of Alsatians and, up there on top of the dresser, neat as the halo on a holy picture, what was left on God's earth of somebody's pet Chihuahua.

"I went back to jazz for a while after we got home; somehow I couldn't face a bodhrán for a long time after that."

"Holy Mother of Jesus, is there a word of truth in that?"

"Every word of it Gospel, I swear. Speaking of which...."

"What? Speaking of what?"

"Where do you get all these quaint expressions anyway? A city sophisticate like you? What have we had lately, let's see: We've had Holy Mother of Jesus, Holy Mother of God, Mother of Divine God, yes sirreee bob and I don't know what else?"

"Convent school, Tom dear, five years' penal servitude with culchies and nuns. It leaves its mark, let me tell you. OK, my turn:

"It's my last term at school, OK? A real hot day in April, we're out in the woods, me and two other girls."

"Oh good, I love these stories."

Sternly: "Tom, behave. There. Is. No. Sex. In. This. Story."

"There we are in the woods, Jacinta Meehan, May Curtis and me. Sunday, we've been for a long walk up in the hills and we've, what, an hour to tea time. They're dying to ask me if I have any draw, but don't dare to. Tongues hanging out of them. Tell you the truth, I could be a bit of a bitch in those days, I know that's hard to believe — don't snigger, it's unseemly in a man. Then I think, feck it, they're OK for a pair of culchies so I dip in the pocket and bring out a big fat spliff, all ready rolled and raring to go. Jacinta has a light going so fast I know she's had the lighter in her hand all along, hoping like, so we take a big, deep hit each, right, vyin' with one another to see who can hold it in the longest, when out from behind a tree steps who other than Sister Imelda. Your two wans went to bits, spluttering, waving the smoke away, beetroot red in the face, jabbering. I was, I have to say, as cool as a breeze. I remember thinking, OK. We're fucked here. Expelled, riot acts, the whole kit and caboodle. Weeping parents, shock, horror, the works — and so what? Ice cold, I tell you. Now this Imelda was hard as nails, the coolest customer you ever met, something about her when she looked at you that made ice trickle down your back. How am I doing here? You're getting the picture? I remember being amazed, while this is going on, at how matter-of-fact I was being about it. I remember calculating that, no matter what, the school wouldn't call in the Guards. Bad for business, you see. Oh I had them sussed. Might have been awkward, having the Guards called in, what with my dear old Ma being the supplier of the dope in question, but I reckoned there was no danger of that so — what's to worry about, right? I looked at Imelda, Imelda looked at me, and she saw it in my eyes. That I just wasn't bothered. She smiled at me, right? I swear, a real smile now, not something creepy or malicious or anything like that. She didn't give the other two a look. She smiled at me and then, I swear this is true, she winked at me. Wow, I thought, this shit is really weird, looking down at the number smoking away between my two fingers. She didn't say anything, just made a gesture at me: give me that. I stood up, a bit woozy by now, and kind of floated across to her, gave her the joint. She held it up under her nose, sniffed, wrinkled her nose, looked me straight in the eye and took a good long hard drag on the spliff. I didn't dare look at the other two, I couldn't take my eyes of Imelda. I couldn't believe how long she could hold the smoke in. When she let it out, it came out in two long thin jets from her nose. 'You two', she barked. 'Get over here.'

"'Now', leaning down over them, she was pretty tall, Imelda, 'if either of you breathes a word about this, ever, to anyone, as long as you live — believe me, I'll come in the middle of the night, when you think you couldn't be safer, AND I'LL TEAR YOUR THROAT OUT WITH MY BARE HANDS! Be off, now! Be off! You, Hogan, stay where you are.'

"Oh Jesus I stayed all right, I couldn't move anyway. Rooted to the spot I was. All the bravado withered away out of me.

"'Walk with me', says she. My feet must have been working OK because I remember us passing through the trees. 'Do you know what you're doing with this?' she asked me. No answer, of course, I mean what could I say to that? Even if I could get my mouth to work? Which I couldn't. 'It's not bad stuff', she says, 'but I'll tell you, it's nothing to what we used to get out on the missions.'

"I often thought since, that of all the words she'd uttered in her life, none could have given her as much satisfaction as those. I mean, put yourself in her position, right? The drama! Oh boy was she enjoying herself. Practically purring.

"On she went. 'The thing is, Miss Hogan, it's not the best thing in the world to be smoking this, so close to your Leaving Cert, is it? Do you agree with me? Of course you do. So, lay off, d'you hear me? D'you hear me, Miss? Take a break from the recreational substances.'

"Somehow I managed to convey to her that indeed I was hearing her. 'I don't imagine those ninnies will be after you for more', she said then. 'Terrified, I think is the word I want?' 'Yes, Sister', I said. That's the word all right. 'Ah', she said, 'regaining our composure. Good. Composure is more important than you could ever imagine, Miss. Remember I told you that when you find it out for yourself. I told her I would.' 'You'll go far, Miss Hogan', she says to me, 'but, if I may? A word of advice?' The Bullet. Asking me if I'd mind a word of advice? 'Please', I said, and then I heard myself say, 'I'd value some advice, actually. Any kind of advice, really.' I didn't know I was going to say that, I can tell you. She gave me that smile again, and she leaned towards me: 'Discretion', she said, 'a little discretion never goes astray. Now, you'll probably find you have a surplus on hand at this point?' She held her hand out to me. I dug out the bag of grass from my pocket, took a good pinch out of it after thinking about this for a second or two, gave her the bag with the rest of it. Vanished into her robe. Like that. 'There, gone. Take your time going back, Miss Hogan. Don't be rushing.' And as she melted away into the trees she turned and looked back at me and said: 'A lovely woman, your mother. A lovely woman.' And, there she was, gone."

Clare, flushed, drains her beer, absent-mindedly crushing the can. Far away in herself, hardly aware she's finished her story.

"She knew?"

"Huh?"

"Sorry, sorry, I mean she knew, your mother...?"

"Oh. Oh yeah, well she must have, mustn't she? I often wondered how she knew, but she was a dark horse, Imelda. You know what I figured out, long after?"

"What?"

"My Mam must have been doing a small bit of dealing on the side; not business, mind you, more habit I guess. Once a hippy ... Or maybe somewhere along the line she'd connected with Imelda, maybe she used to send her the odd present, I don't know. Anyway...", brisk now, feeling the cool of evening on her bare arms, "...did you like my story?"

"Oh I'll be telling that one, you can be sure of it. You make a pretty good fist of telling it, if you don't mind my saying so."

"Ah go on out o' that. Now, here, is there a plan?"

"There is, there is. We're leaving in, oh five minutes? That suit you?"

"Five minutes! Now? In the dark?"

"Trust me, Clare, it's one of the best feelings in the world, you'll see. The town going about its business, the moon coming up, stars coming out ... slipping your lines, catching the ghost of a breeze, sail going up, drifting away down-channel, everything getting quieter, quieter, the sea calling...."

She's on the point of slagging him for being a romantic eejit, assuming he's being arch, when she feels the silence in him, thick and slow, and looks up. He's looking south, down the long, dark defile that will take them to the sea; he has a hand on the boom, the boom creaks as it gives a little to the weight of his leaning body, groans and swings back. The water is lapping at the hull, she can see the sound register in his eyes, and she sees that Tom is far, far away, in a place where nothing can reach him, a place to which she cannot go. She's afraid to make a sound, because if he looks at her now she knows he will look at her as a perfect stranger.

After a while, judging the moment with her eyes shut, her breathing slowed, she says, very softly: "Something you want to show me, Tom, is that it?"

Ah, he thinks, not looking at her yet, how quick you can be, Clare, how quick. And yet....

A team again, quick and deft. She stops for a moment, get the sequence right now. OK, springs — the lines back from the bow, forward from the stern, that stop the boat moving forward or back. Springs first. Tom is ahead of her, already unhitching the inboard ends. She pulls the lines to her, coiling as she goes, hands them back aboard. Next, quick look up to see the wind, unhitch the bow line, run it once round the cleat, free end back on board to Tom. Now, same with the stern line. Salvation in practical things, she thinks, pleased with the thought, pleased with her own spare movements. Free end of stern line to Tom, step aboard, up to the bow. Engine on a few moments for it to warm up. "Ready?" Tom calls. "Ready." "Slip away, then." The line coming back on board, a snake's head lashing the water as she coils faster and faster. Free the line, bring it back. Tom hands her the stern line, she stows both lines in the locker, straightens and looks back. Surprising always, how quickly the land slips away from you. The town in its lit tiers, all that subdued bustle, that noise, the deep pockets of shadow, the small, intense blazes of light, and the lit windows here and there, the patches of dark between them, the lives going on in little rooms, in the streets and the piazzas and the boisterous cafés.

Leavetaking, she thinks, and she gets what Tom meant now, that sweet melancholy suffusing her bones, turning them soft, as she feels the boat dance sideways and on, sideways and on, leaving it all behind, leaving it all....

"Careful, now", Tom whispers, close beside her, the wheel making small movements under his hands, brushing her hip, "Careful, now, don't say a word or it'll vanish, don't say a word ... sssh, sssh ... Here, take the wheel, gently now, see that red, that green? Between them, straight down the channel."

He has the main up and drawing, he has the staysail up, land breeze from the west filling the great, curved shapes. The boat heels, just a little, steadies. I reckon there's enough wind for the jenny, Tom says quietly, and he's quick, practised, the furling line running free, the sail running smoothly out. The boat heels again a little, and grips. "Bang on", Tom murmurs, "right in the groove." He switches the engine off.

She can feel the whole weight of the boat in her hands, the curve of the hull though the water, the long dip of the bow, the lift of the stern a moment later; she can feel the wind on the sails, in the sails, those curves, those perfect shapes, the curve of the hull underwater precisely and perfectly in balance. The strong pull onward, the boat a live thing under her hands.

Then, "Tom…?"

He gestures upward: the running lights bright and clear at the masthead. She looks down behind, sees the sternlight washing her calves, white and soft. She smiles, shrugs a shoulder at him, a gesture of apology. He puts a hand on that shoulder, leans in against her for a moment: "Way ahead of you, girl", he says, "way ahead of you."

And he is, she thinks, happy enough to acknowledge it, he is. He is indeed.

Down past *Isola San Pietro* they run, Clare still at the wheel, seeing the fishing boats come and go, holding her course, relaxed, confident, competent. /

"Run on down past the point", Tom says after a while, "we'll run on past a bit then come about. I want to see what the wind's doing."

Nothing suggests Clare's heard him, not a twitch, not a sound, but he knows where she is, he knows it's registered, isn't bothered by her silence, her rapt absorption. Ah the sea has her now, he thinks, going below, the sea has her now and if I've given her nothing else.…

He switches on the navtex, leans on the chart table, closes his eyes for a moment, checking the signs. Not bad he decides, after a while, not bad, the day's rest has done me good. But he's man enough to face it, too; a bit weaker, all the same, he acknowledges, just a little bit, but weaker. No pain, that's the good thing, not at the minute anyway. Now, what's this? He fumbles for his reading glasses, peers at the words on the small, glowing screen. There's a small low off the coast of Libya, small but intense, he sees. Stationary. He scribbles a note on the pad. Does a quick computation in his head. OK, we have, what, oh westerlies, light and variable. Good enough, good enough. So we'll head up a little more north, then, should make good progress tonight, see what tomorrow brings. He saves the message, switches off. Something niggling. What? Ah, of course, Ruth's photograph. He switches the radar on to warm it up, crosses the galley, rummages in the locker beneath the sink; he sprays a quick dab of cleaner on some kitchen paper, carefully washes the glass of the photograph, rubs it dry with a second sheet of the paper. Kneading the wadded paper between his hands, he stands there a long moment, looking down at the photo. Ah Jesus, he breathes eventually, such eyes you have Ruth, such eyes. Feeling the pressure rising, crushing it down. Down. Making fists now, his gaze unlocked. Staring into the void.

Suddenly angry with himself. Time enough, he warns himself savagely, time enough now ... get on with it.

So long alone he's never sure if he's speaking aloud when he talks to himself.

Clare, up above, is just quick enough to look away. He stands there looking at her, something cold in him now, remote and impersonal. He stands there looking at her a long time but she never looks down once.

Her heart pounding. Her breathing, thank God he can't hear it, sharp with dread.

The wind is fresher than he'd expected. He wants to think about this, he knows he should think about this, but decides, fuck it, suits us, what does it matter anyway? Clare is, not anxious exactly, but wondering why they're still going south. Let her wonder, he thinks, then he catches the meanness of it, and is embarrassed.

"Soon now", he mutters, gruff, watching the wind.

She doesn't mind the gruffness, is pleased, and just a little relieved that he's caught her mood.

"OK", he says after a minute or two staring away behind them, "that's it, we'll tack now. Come round to, oh, 315 to 320 degrees, there or thereabouts."

"Ready about", she calls, forcing the volume into her voice.

She tacks, but she doesn't come round far enough; the genoa backs, caught the wrong side of the inner forestay and suddenly they are dead in the water, wallowing, the jenny making a horrendous noise as it flaps and beats.

Tom catches his own sudden fury, channels it into a roar: "It's OK, it's all right, could happen to anyone, stay where you are, just keep her head up as much as you can." Working furiously, he winds in the jenny, sweat pouring off him, his breath coming in short, explosive bursts. With staysail and main out to starboard now, her head comes around neatly and Tom, suddenly full of energy, hauls the genoa out on the correct side. It fills with a crack and then they are off again, bearing up the west side of the island.

Clare, shaking, is mortified and inexplicably afraid. Tom, on the other hand, is suddenly full of robust good cheer.

"Jasus, eh? Whew! That woke us up, eh? You all right, Clare?"

She gulps, nods, reluctant to meet his searching look.

"Ah go on out of that, what are you, morto? Are you, Clare, are you mortified?"

She won't meet his gaze. He sees she's seriously upset, and now he's puzzled: anyone would be embarrassed if that happened to them, he knows this, he remembers how it felt the few times he did it himself on other boats. The helpless sense of his own utter stupidity. The nausea at making a fool of himself, the … And then, he gets it.

"Clare, Clare, you afraid I'll judge you for that, is that it? You have to be perfect all the time, is that it? Perfect all the time", his sureness growing now, "or something terrible will happen. Is that it, Clare?"

She nods, looks at him for an instant, looks away again. Her face still set.

"And something else there, too, Clare isn't there?" — he's letting her follow his thought processes now, gentling her along with him, bringing her along, "and I know what it is, you see, I saw it, I know what it was. Clare? Look at me now, please."

Standing back a pace, giving her room. She looks at him. "It was the rage, Clare, yes? Yes?" (God, if I get this wrong, a part of him, off to one side, is thinking….) "Clare?"

Then, very loud, "Clare!"

Her head shot back. Fury in that look, pure ice-cold fathomless fury.

Anything he said now would have been wrong. He stood there, let it wash over him. Unmoving. Unblinking. You might have said, touching her with whatever it is that comes out of the eyes.

She says: "Yes. The rage. Just for that moment … but OK, I see it wasn't me, it's OK now. I see it wasn't, what I mean is, I was the one fucked up but you weren't angry at me, I mean…."

"Ah Jesus, you're confusing me now. Take it easy, take it easy."

A hand on her cold forearm. She doesn't flinch.

"You OK, now?"

"I am, yeah."

"How a Corkman says 'no.'"

"What the fuck are you on about?"

"How a Corkman says 'no' — 'I will, yeah.'"

And she laughs. We did it again, she thinks, and he sees the thought flash in her face, and he laughs too.

"Here", he says, "give me the wheel. Now, sit out there to the side where you can see beyond the jenny. OK? You see that, up ahead? The light?"

"You mean up there to the right? I mean, to starboard, Captain sir, oh please don't hit me, I'm only a learning sailor."

Meaning: I know I screwed up and I know it's not all that important but I'm sorry anyway and yes you frightened me for a second and I understand it was impersonal rage but it scared me. And I'll explain this in a while. And it's OK now but give me a minute. And thanks.

"The light, Tom?" she prompts.

"What? Oh, oh yeah. Down in the chart table, Admiralty Chart E1090, on top of the pile, bring it up will you?"

She raises an eyebrow.

"Trust me", he says. "The chart? Please? Trust me."

"I bet you say that to all the girls."

"I do, and they do, and they're right to, too."

"You could sing that, if you weren't tone deaf."

And she goes down, humming experimentally.

He switches on the autopilot, satisfied that the wind is steady enough. He spreads out the chart, takes a torch from its pouch by the hatch.

"Now, here, right, Capo Sandalo, you see it? That's where the light is. Now, see what's written here by the lighthouse symbol? See?"

She peers down, recites "'4W20sec 134m 24M.' So?"

"So this tells you the Capo Sandalo lighthouse flashes a white light four times every twenty seconds. And that the light is visible for...?"

"Twenty-four miles?"

"That's it."

"God that's smart. So, all the lights have different combinations of flashes and times, yeah?"

"And colours, sometimes there's a red sometimes a green. Say you have a light with a white and a red in it? That'll be set up so that, for instance, you can only see the red inside a certain arc. So, it might be that when you can see the red you know you're in the safe approach channel to a harbour. For instance. Clever, huh?"

"Smart as all get out. And, you can see this light for twenty-four miles? Must be up pretty high?"

"The tower is 134 metres tall, how about that?"

"And?"

"And what?"

"Tom, dear, we've seen other lighthouses along the way, lights anyway. You're making a point about showing me this one, right?"

"Well, it's just that I have a thing about this one, about Capo Sandalo I mean. I love the name, that's part of it, I suppose. Ca-po San-dal-o. Got a ring to it, hasn't it? But that's not it, either. Well, it's a part of it I suppose...."

"Tom, I'm going to brain you, I swear."

"Right. I'm rambling. Well, I always think there's two Mediterraneans, right? East of here is, I dunno, different? Up there, Italy, then France, away to the west Spain, and up behind them Germany, Poland, that sort of thing. I mean, east of here is small villages, Byzantine, Greek, Asiatic, Egypt, what they used to call the Levant, you know what I mean? No? Well, up there and west it's all business, cities and mega-cities, industry and plumbing fixations and...."

He's floundering, embarrassed to be making a bad fist of this.

Clare, though, surprising him, gets it. Or so he thinks at first.

"And back there is dreams, unbroken history, clear light, blue waters, things as they have been for thousands of years? Olive groves, ancient Gods, nymphs in the woods, camel trains out of the desert, rose red cities half as old as time? Get a grip, Tom, you see the kids wearing Nikes? You notice they have electricity, cars, airports, factories?"

He's being very gentle when he says "Clare, you don't understand what I'm telling you. Back there is where I'm most alive. No, that's not quite it. Back there is where I found it. Back there is where I'm happiest. No particular reason, it could have been anywhere. Some people love the piny woods, some people love Berlin, New York. Some of the guys I grew up with would be lonesome and lost ten miles from where they were born. You take where you're born as a given, you can call it home, but I think everyone has a place in the world. You find it if you're lucky. That, back there, is where I found it. Call it home, for want of a better word. Home."

Up there ahead, steady and bright, the four white flashes promised by the chart. They count to twenty. Four white flashes again. And again. And again. They close their eyes, they count the seconds ticking past. Four white flashes. Darkness. Eternal dark. Four white flashes.

22

"You go down," he'd said, "back to watches now, OK?" And, "that was a good story, I got a laugh out of that. Was there a word of truth in it?"

"You'll never know", she said, patting him on the head, "you'll never know."

He'd watched her hesitate, on the point of peering at the radar, then move on. Figuring, he has the watch, he'll be keeping an eye. A small act of trust, a small triumph for cool consideration.

Sandalo comes up abeam, and he bends to the north west, curving up and away for Palma. Before sending the chart down he'd traced their proposed route for Clare, a long, flat curve towards the French coast, to fall in on Majorca from the north. Three days or so, he knows from experience, at the speed this boat is comfortable with, in the present conditions.

He wants to look down now, confident she's already asleep, to see if she has her hand under her face. Something about that gesture that has his attention and won't let go. Something inside him that answers to it, some hidden yearning towards … ach, he couldn't say.

Sandalo on the quarter. Presently, Sandalo astern. The long, slow rhythm of the night.

The wind freshens, dips, come up again and steadies. Strange, he reflects, how a boat will prefer one tack to another, no matter how carefully you trim her. *Lon Dubh*, he found out long ago, is happier on the port tack, with the wind coming from the left. Now he remembers that, as a boy, his first bicycle, he always preferred turning left to turning right, would let the bike lean way over when turning left, would be far more hesitant, circumspect, turning right. Anything in that, he wonders? Nah, probably not. Still. Maybe the hull isn't perfectly symmetrical, he thinks.

Could be, could be … Maybe the rudder isn't exactly on the centreline? Could be, could be … He's had this same conversation with himself, how many times now? Answers himself: every single voyage I've undertaken. And why is that, Tom? Because I enjoy thinking about it. Because it does no harm. Because it means every voyage reminds me of every other voyage, one blending into the next. And I like that. Present conditions. The phrase floats up into his musing attention, is floating past when he reaches out and takes hold of it. Present conditions, present conditions. "Fool", he says then, out loud, immediately anxious he'll have woken her. Fool, he thinks quietly. Where's that wind coming from? West, a bit of south. He scans the horizon, south and west. Nothing he can put a finger on. Checks the wind speed gauge, though he doesn't really need to, can feel the increase in pressure, slight as it is, on his cheek. Only a knot or two, he thinks, and it's steady, too. Keep an eye on it, Tom. Just keep an eye on it, that's all.

Lull then, long, absent-minded lull, the bit of him needed to keep an eye on the boat looking after itself; the bigger part of him gone away into a waking trance.

He'd decided, setting out, to say nothing to her of that low over the Libyan coast, but now when Clare wakes, comes up with tea, he slips below for another look at the navtex. Hmm. He thinks, beginning to track north. Maybe I'll stay up for a bit, see what happens.

"What is it?" she asks him, not confronting him, exactly, but letting him know she has a sense that something has his attention. Letting him know she thinks he should tell her, trust her.

He hesitates, not because he's reluctant to speak but because this thing, if it is a thing, is way below the horizon of what they need to deal with. And of course, he thinks then, there you go, Tom, shouldering the responsibility. Always the assumption, eh? That other people aren't as ready to face things as you are? Mr leave it to me. Mr you don't need to worry.

"Eh, Tom? When you've finished beating yourself up there?"

"Look, I'm not sure what's going on here. There's a bit of a blow down there, away south west, off the coast of Libya, right? There's a chance it'll track north, might intersect our path, you see? Or it might go away to the west, you never know with these things, late-summer storms, small and intense, often they blow out."

"Tom, look at me. The wind is up, right? Only a small bit, but I can feel it. It's gone south a bit since I went below, hasn't it? It has. Correct me if I'm wrong here but you seem a tad nervous, do you mind me saying that? I mean nervous about telling me we might be in for a hard time, am I right? Not a rhetorical question, Tom. Am I right?"

He knows he's been found out, feels a bit sick about it. Nods.

"So, you're protecting me, is that it? Do I look like I need protecting? Have I asked you to protect me? I'm getting a small bit anxious now, Tom, and it isn't the weather. Well, the weather a bit. You're the sailor here, we know that, and I'm OK in a boat but I'm not a sailor. But, Tom, do me a favour, will you? Always tell me what's going on. Always. I thought that was the deal here, you know?"

"Yes, but, this might come to nothing, no point in…"

"…In getting me worried. Yeah. Tom, if there's a fucking hurricane going to come and swallow me up, I'd prefer to know that kind of thing? Get my head around it? That make sense to you, Tom?"

Every time she says his name it's like a thump on the side of his head.

"Ah look, look, I'm not getting at you, all right? Take it easy here, now, I swear I'm not getting at you. Are we heading for trouble? Just tell me."

"We could get a blow, yeah. You want we should turn back? Plenty of time."

"Jesus, did I say anything about turning back? We're taking this bloody boat to Ireland, aren't we, because, because … oh never mind because. For fuck's sake. Look, try this, OK? Right here, right now, all on your ownio, what would you do? What would you do, Tom?" She shivers, says half to herself, "Getting a bit cold here." Then: "We could get a blow here, you say. Fine. Right. So, what do we do? Come on, just tell me, what do we do?"

And Tom, on a parallel track all this time, miserable, head down, realises he's not worrying about how she'll cope, he's not worrying if the boat is up to it: he's worrying about whether or not he's up to it.

Witch that she is, Clare pounces: "Aha! Ye poor ould bollix, you're worried about are *you* able to cope! Gotcha! In the name of … of course you are! Sure do you think for a minute I'd have set foot on this boat if I didn't think you were? Do you not remember me telling you about the storm we had one time I was in Majorca? Do you not remember it was this time of year? Do you think I imagined we were off on a jolly around the lake? I made up my mind about you before we'd lost sight of Sicily. Sure the shape the boat is in tells me all I need to know!"

Oh but Clare isn't finished with him yet: "OK, fair enough, we've dodged this way, we've dodged that way, but you won't tell me what's wrong with you. I'm not a fucking clairvoyant, but you say it's not your heart and of course I believe you, so you're not going to die on me, are you, Tom? Fine. Right. So if it's going to take two of us to get through whatever's coming, all right, all right, don't faff at me, *if* there's something coming, OK? If it's going to take two of us, tell me what we're going to do and we'll do it the two of us. Right."

"Clare?" — tentative.

"What?!"

"Clare, where do you get the breath for all that from?"

Before she's recovered from her astonishment he says, off to one side in a stage whisper: "Oh Mother of Divine Glory, now I'm going to get the ten kilowatt glare. Stand by, stand by."

And she's laughing so much she can barely get the words out: "One of these days, so help me I'll fucking kill you. I will. I swear."

Something old and clotted inside, scar tissue, black and ancient and twisted, some old hurt that's gone bitter inside him, eases away in Tom's bones. It's an astonishing sensation. Warmth, a suffusing warmth, a soft glow in his chest, a series of sharp intense shocks walking up his spine. Clarity. His head full of light. He has to sit down for a minute, gather himself, let this wash over and through him.

Clare watches him thoughtfully, knowing to say nothing more. At ease herself now, but damned if she could tell you why. "Bloody hell", she mutters, "would you look at that? Amazing, or what?!"

"Some trip", he says to her, coming round now.

"Some trip indeed, old man. You're not wrong there. Now…"

"…If I was on my ownio. Right. Clare, best thing you can do is go down now and make up a couple of flasks, soup and coffee. Some sandwiches would be good, and in the drawer under the port settee there's a bag full of chocolate bars and whatnot."

"Sweets, you want sweets? Oh, I see. For the sugar. And while I'm doing that?"

"While you're doing that I'll be hauling in the jenny, putting a reef in the main, putting another lashing on the anchor so it doesn't fucking break loose and knock a hole in us. I'll also, in my spare time, be getting that storm sail up out of the forecabin in case it's needed. And if you've finished your little jobs, and finished stowing away anything loose down there that could fly around and kill a person, if you've finished your jobs before I've finished mine, why you can fill in the time by painting your toenails or fucking praying to whatever mad God would listen to the likes of you. OK, Miss?"

"Oh Janey" she says, diving below, "I knew this would happen, I knew it, I fucking knew it!"

He can't resist, shouts down after her: "What? You knew what would happen?"

She calls up from the dark below: "I knew Sister Imelda would come back to haunt me!"

23

The deck work done, Tom goes down for the stormsail. The kettle's beginning to whistle, Clare is packing sandwiches into a plastic container, heel of her hand sealing the lid. Good, he thinks, moving past silently, clear thinking. Good woman. He's on his way back through the saloon, looking left and right for anything not stowed away. Clare, at the chart table, holds out his bottle of pills to him, expressionless. He takes them, shouldering past without looking at her, shoves them deep in a pocket.

Up in the cockpit he spreads the small sail out as best he can; with a torch he examines it minutely, checking the seams for signs of fraying, testing the attachment points, the reinforced stitching at the three corners. Satisfied, he rolls it up carefully, stows it on top of the fenders in the starboard locker. Clare hands him up a fleece, he grunts thanks, pulls it on over his head, thinking what next, what next? Grab bag. "Clare? Under the starboard settee? There's a yellow barrel, bring it up to me, would you? Ta." In the barrel: flares, handheld GPS, handheld radio, compass, first aid kit. To this he adds, going down to collect them, some bottles of water, biscuits and chocolate, his passport, ship's papers. On deck again he takes a quick look around, notes flying spray, the wind's come up another notch. "Clare", he says to her, "get your passport, would you? And your wallet." She hands them up, looking thoughtfully at what he's doing. Torch, he thinks, put in a torch. OK. He bangs the lid down, leans in through the hatch and shoves the grab bag into a kind of metal basket secured to the side of the steps. "Oh neat-o", Clare says, "I wondered what that was for." Her silence invites him to say something. "Had that made up one time, thought it might be handy, like." She smiles at him indulgently. Fuck it, he thinks, will it never go away, this need for praise from women? But of course he is pleased.

Everything's moving too fast, he thinks then, standing, stiffly, to look around him, above him.

Under reduced sail, the boat's motion has changed, become — not sluggish, exactly. More wary? He thinks, something like that. I could have left up the full main, he thinks, ah well, better to reef too early than too late.

"Come on up, Clare, bring us a coffee if it's handy; take a break."

"I'm leaving the wet-weather gear here, at the bottom of the steps", she says. "Will I dig out a pair of trousers for you? Might get a bit cold for shorts."

"Good idea, but maybe not yet. Leave 'em there with the rest. Come on up."

A craving for company coming over him, for talk.

She plumps in beside him, handing him a mug, chinking hers against his. She looks up as the main flaps once, twice. Raises an eyebrow at him. What are you thinking about? The look asks.

"One time, I'd got roped into a race, don't know how, don't like racing, too much shouting. Anyway, four other guys, I only knew one of them, we'd played a session or two together. We didn't get along very well, too many personality types, know what I mean? Off Baltimore, this was. A kind of general air of crankiness, tetchiness all day. So, making back for Kinsale, night coming on, it got really dirty, all of a sudden. Big, dirty squall. Next thing you know we're being blown up, down and sideways, all over the place, too much sail up, too close to shore. And here's the thing: not a word said, suddenly you'd think we'd been practising for this. All together, working away, doing all the right things, minding each other, covering each other, like a machine — you know the phrase 'a well-oiled machine'? Like that. You'd swear we were best of mates, been sailing together for years. No bother on us at all. And here's another thing: when the squall blew through, you know, then we got all embarrassed, hardly a word said after that, a grunt here, a mutter there. We could hardly look at each other. Separate ways, the minute we landed in Kinsale. Not a word said. Never saw any of them again after that."

The boat hesitates for a moment; a slight shudder, it plunges on.

"Tom, are we overdoing it, do you think?"

"What do you mean? All this…"

"…No, no, not the preparations, that's only common sense, sure. No, I mean are we making too much of all this? Us?"

Water slaps against the side of the hull, loud. Once. They listen, it doesn't happen again.

She tries again: "Don't tell me you haven't thought about it. I turn up in Siracusa, cheeky strap, *forward* my Mam would have said? I inveigle my way on to your boat and the next thing you know we're sailing for Ireland. Come on, Tom!"

"If I'd a thought of it like that you wouldn't be here."

"Come again?"

"In the Café di Duomo? When you said you weren't going to sleep with me? If it was all a bit of flirting I'd have bought you dinner and taken you back to your hotel. Grand night, lovely night, blah blah — and I'd have sailed away the next morning without giving you another thought. Believe me."

"Would you really? Seriously?"

"But it wasn't like that, was it? We started something, and the only way we'll find out what it is, is by finishing it, right? Like, you're tipping away on the piano, say, little riffs, not thinking of anything much and you hear something — a phrase, a run of notes? And a bit of you, far away at first, starts going hmm, and you keep going, following it, yes this, no, not that, like following a thread, right? And the closer you get to it the more you start to wake up and, if you're lucky, if it comes to something, suddenly you're wide awake, it feels like more than awake and you have it, you have it now, just a matter of finding, finding the final shape. That's it. The full shape of it."

"So, that's what we're doing, you reckon? Following the thread? All will be revealed, is that it?"

"Well, yeah, I suppose?"

"OK, so." Like that.

"I mean, don't you think?"

"You say so."

The boat heeling suddenly, buffeted once, twice. The slap of water again, heavier now, and another, and another. He eased out the main-sheet.

"Clare? Talk to me, what's wrong?"

She's ice-cold, her words like small, carved stones, carved out of the darkening air: "She used to say things like that. Sandra. All very cosmic: the fates, karma, the warp and woof of life, going with the flow, the journey's what matters not the destination, you have to listen for your inner voice, man, it's all written down, it's in the stars, it's destiny, man, destiny…. Fucking shite! What was so fucking cosmic about marrying Rory so's she could live in comfort, have her bloody horses, her bit of dope, her fucking memories, her might have beens? Tell me? Law? You want to know why I did law? Because law is about consequence, about facts, you did it, you didn't, you're guilty, you're not. Choices, Tom! Fucking responsibilities! Making decisions, seeing things as they are, as they fucking actually are!"

He won't engage with this. He just won't deal with this now. She can fucking work it out for herself. The wind *is* up, definite now. A line from Dylan comes into his head, 'not dark yet, but it's getting there.' Yeah, yeah, yeah. She wants practical? She wants actions and consequences?

"You want actions and consequences, Clare? You think this is a good time to have this conversation? Right here? Right now? Well, listen to me carefully now, listen to me now, Clare."

He feels it immediately, her full, live presence in the actual moment. Her direct, unwavering stare at him.

"Right. It's going to get cold now, very soon. Layers, you need layers. Put your waterproof trousers on now, best thing is tights underneath, then track bottoms if you have any? No? OK, soft trousers then. Don't put your jacket on until it actually starts to rain. We're going to have very heavy rain, I can smell it coming."

He's down below, talking up through the hatch, putting on trousers, waterproofs, transferring his knife to an outside pocket. "Here, here's a knife. Keep it where you can reach it. Get rid of the sneakers, sandals are better, sneakers hold water, they'll make your feet cold eventually. You with me, Clare? Lifejacket, harness, here!"

Up again, scanning all round him. The stars receding under flying shreds of cloud, the moon — gone. "Go on below, now, do as I'm telling you. Have a quick gander at the radar, would you? Tell me what you see."

South west, fuck it anyway, there's a long fetch in that, that's a lot of open water. Hope this is quick now. Lights! "Clare!"

"Nothing!" she shouts up, "nothing!"

"What?"

More measured now: "On the radar. There's nothing on the radar."

"I'm glad to hear it, the masthead light has gone out. Check the switch, will you?"

She toggles the switch a few times, he sees her do it. Double checking. Looks up again, nothing.

"Forget it, loose wire or something." At least the running light is on.
Craning back to make sure. Double checking.

"Clare, under your feet there? Bring up the big flashlight. If we get
too close to anything, you shine it on the sails, you understand?"

The wind stronger now, climbing a gradient, steady, inexorable.
Nearly a half gale already, he thinks, lovely, fucking lovely. Washboards,
what's wrong with me tonight? Washboards.

Clare is back up, hands him his lifejackets, harness. He buckles up,
goes around her, slides the hatch cover towards him, locks it shut. Now
just a small, vertical opening down into the green-lit cave below.

"OK". Rummaging in the port-side locker, "You see these?
Washboards they're called. They slide down into the channels there in
the hatchway, you see? This one first, good, we won't need the other one
unless we're taking heavy water on board. Jesus, I nearly forgot...."

"The radio", she says calmly, "I switched it on. Channel sixteen, yes?"

She's clipped to the U-ring on the cockpit floor. The boat heels
far over, she takes the strain on her harness, holding it in one hand.
Automatically. Looking directly at him now. Poised.

He sees it, sees she's going to be fine. He smiles at her, crosses to
her side, grabbing her round the waist, pulling her down onto the bench
beside him. "Jesus", he says, happily, "You're some woman..."

"...For one woman, I know. God but you can be very fierce sometimes. Are we all right again now?"

"All right! We're about to get our fucking heads kicked in and she
asks me are we all right!"

After a while she says, serious now: "Are we, Tom, going to get our
heads kicked in?"

"I think I'll take in that second reef now", he says; then, turning to
look at her: "Probably. Maybe."

Something uncomfortable ... he shifts his hip, pulls a fleece hat out
of his jacket pocket, looks at it stupidly, grunts, pulls it on. Looks around,
ahead, astern.

"OK", he says, "this is fine for now."

The boat has dug in at a definite angle of heel, is scudding along on
a wash of black water coursing by her side. Sometimes the foam off a

wave blows into their faces, caught in a back eddy, but mostly it flies away to leeward in great sheets, fanning back from the plunging bow. Like a hunter, Clare thinks drowsily, coming on from a canter to a gallop. Big heavy horse, slow to get going, unstoppable then, needing her head. A splash has her instantly awake.

"You OK there for a while?" he asks. She says she is.

"Grand, so. Don't worry about the autopilot, by the way, well up to the job. Shove up under the spray hood, there, you'll be out of the wind."

She shuffles along, and Tom stretches along the seat, head against her hip, pulling the hat down over his face.

"Think I'll have a bit of a quick nap, so. Call me...."

And he's asleep.

She sits staring straight ahead of her for a minute or two, gaze unfocussed, thinking nothing at all, and then she stirs, looks down at him. Unbelievable, she thinks, who would believe it? And she lifts his head gently, inches towards him so she can lay his head comfortably on her thigh. She puts a hand on the side of his face. She leaves it there.

24

He's curled up into a half crouch, Clare following him, inching along the seat at intervals as he moves in his sleep, still cradling his head. Now she's out from the shelter of the spray hood, has been for a long time, and her face is wet from salt blown in from the larger and larger waves that are buffeting the port bow. Increasingly often, gouts of cold water are sheeting back from the foredeck, over the coach roof to burst into a fine spray off the hood.

Clare doesn't mind. Nor does she mind the low moan of the wind, the occasional shriek, the sullen thunder in the reefed-down mainsail.

She has her head back, watching the stars that have come out again into a clear sky, when the boat falters a moment. The wind drops, uncertain, resumes. The sky is a kind of milky dark, she's just decided, having given it some thought, like ink diluted with milk, maybe. She bends to look to the south west, and sees a broad, dark band across the horizon. Uneasy without knowing why, she gives Tom a shake, meaning to be gentle, but overcome by a sudden start of anxiety.

He comes to, comes upright in a single fluid movement, animal in its grace and directness. He glances at her face, follows her eyes and comes wide awake. "Washboards", he says, a hand in the small of her back, pushing, "get the rain jackets, a flask, quick now. Quick." Another glance to check that the autopilot's functioning and he's moving forward along the side deck, downwind, scrabbling and crabbing to the bows. Get it down, man, get it down, now. Now. A rattle behind him. Shit, harness dragging between his feet. Quick, clip it over the jackstay, tug, tug again. On. The short swell is almost two meters now, the foredeck lunging and yawing from side to side. He scrabbles at the halyard, kneeling at the mast, and then scrambles forward, starts hauling the staysail down in clumsy, urgent handfuls. His fingers popping the piston hanks, unclipping the sail from the forestay as each hank comes within reach. Faster, he tells himself, not daring to look at the coming squall, then daring, then wishing he hadn't. Somehow in all this, hardly knowing he was doing it, he has the fore hatch open, and now he's stuffing the stiff sail down the narrow opening, punching it, hammering it with his free hand, fast as he can, gallons of whatever going down with it can't be helped, can't be helped....

And a waterfall smashes through him. Jesus, Jesus it's cold, he's thinking, knocked to his feet by the wall of black water, gasping for breath as the wind batters him to his feet, lifting and hammering him at. the same time. He's banged about on his knees now, arms flailing, his neck pinned on the wire forestay and he's scrambling, desperate to get the hatch closed, before the bow goes down too far under this press of wind, these falling black tons of water. The boat far over now, the roaring press of the wind pinning her down, walls of black water falling broadside on her gleaming flank. All he can do, feeling suddenly faint, very faint, falling very far away, very far ... is hook his elbow around the inner forestay, almost hanging down the deep-slanted deck, and let wind pour over him, water pour over him ... weak, feeling weak — and two things happen at once: that thing inside him, deep down in the cells, in the once-and-only animal body of him roars, he hears it come up through him, unstoppable, deafening — and a brilliant light blinds him, stabbing him through the eyes, piercing deep into his skull. /

He closes his eyes, then, and his left arm comes up like the arm of a powerful, practised swimmer, he feels this happening in slow motion, his arm curves up, and as his fingertips touch the stay he opens his hand and reaches just that bit farther and snaps his hand shut around the wire in a powerful, unbreakable grip.

He pulls himself to his knees, he feels the boat under him, a living thing, powerful and sullen but pulling on undaunted. He feels the water boiling around his feet, feels the pull of it, this way and that, and knows he can beat it. Slowly, a brute himself now, he pushes and pulls himself to his feet. The deck is plunging and rising now — but what of it? He rides it, he's snarling. He looks back, head up and back, he looks back to see Clare scything through the dark distance between them with the powerful torch, swaying, one hand on the boom, her mouth opening and closing, opening and closing. He can't hear her, and she can't hear him when he roars back at her, downhill, then uphill, then downhill again, wrestling himself vigorously back, until he's almost there and she hears him calling over and over, "Are you clipped on? For fucks' sake are you clipped on?" And then there are tears streaming down her face and she nods, blinding him for a second, and tears on his face and he ducks his head and comes up smiling.

"Give me a minute, give me a minute, whew that was rough, give me a minute" — he's on his haunches on the cockpit floor, wedging himself into the corner, coughing and spluttering. "Give me a minute, the storm sail, the storm sail..." and the spasm that hits him almost snaps his neck as his head shoots up. Grey light, bright fog, a terrifying draining inside, bones going to cold water, something bilious and hot, a lump in his chest. Not pain so much as a vicious, implacable subtraction. No, he thinks, no, not now, not here — and it passes, oh thank you Jesus' Mother, thank you, lie down for a minute, thank you, thank you.

Clare scrabbling in his pocket with one hand, with the other shifting from handhold to handhold, fighting for balance, wind whipping about her, the boat almost broaching, lying far over and hanging there an eternity, two, coming back but nearly out of control now, on the brink....

She forces the tablets between his teeth, he swallows, more reflex than act of will, and he's trying to get to his feet again, on his knees now, Clare trying to press him down, muscling her away, trying to prise the locker open. Failing. Head down at last, head hanging down. A moment, a long moment.

He pulls himself to his feet. Slowly, lurching a bit but slowly and steadily he gains his feet. He gestures mutely to the locker, and Clare says, "I know, I know, the storm sail, I'll get it, sit down, I'll get it, I'll get it."

And Tom ... accedes. Very simple. No other way. He won't get away with it a second time. All right. OK. Clare. Up there. Has to be.

She has the sail out, is running it round and round in her hands. He mutters, pointing: "The halyard, here?" She nods. "Tack, here?" "Tack?" "See that loop?" "Yes." "Shackle at bottom of the inner stay." "OK." "Sheets, here. The clew, the clew, right? I've left the staysail sheets knotted together round the stay. OK? Pass each one through the clew, here, you know how to make a bowline? You do. Leave about a foot of tail. Clare? Be careful; you terrified?" "Yep." "Good, that's what makes people careful."

"Tom, what are you doing?"

He's behind the wheel, leaning over to switch off the autopilot.

The wind a banshee howl now, but she hears him, and he hears her. Battered and staggering and cold and wet. He says, "I'm going to bring her head into the wind. We'll be banging into waves now, Clare, you hear me? The head will be going down and up like a train, OK? There will be a lot of water up there, listen to me now, when the deck's coming up against you, you go forward. Stay still when it's falling away from you, OK? Hands and knees, Clare, hands and knees. You ready? Of course you are, you're a fucking marvel, Clare, I am stone mad about you but I haven't the strength to drag you out of the water so stay in the boat, will you! Stay in the boat!"

Feet braced wide behind him and to either side, his whole chest flat to the wheel, Tom wrestles the boat into the wind. He thinks his heart is going to burst, feels the whole weight of the boat against him, but lovely boat she is, fucking lovely boat, oh you beauty you, you beauty, round she comes, sluggish at first, knocked this way and that, bucking and sliding, but round she comes, and suddenly she is light under the wheel, the reefed main is flapping like thunder but the motion is easier now and Clare's off, amazingly fast. He watches her go, his hands minding the boat. She's at the mast already, so agile, wow, the sail in a roll under her arm and she's using both hands to hold on. Now she's at the forestay, unclipping the halyard. Good, Clare, good. Watch the water! Christ, disappeared there. Hanking it on, good, good, Christ she's fast. The tack now, snap shackle, tugging, checking, oh good, Clare, watch ... grand, and the clew, the sheets now. Yes! And now back at the mast foot, so fast, so fast, hand over hand, the small orange triangle flying, up, up, snapping like gunshots; mast winch, the last few turns, Jesus born to it, born to it — haul in the sheet, Tom, that's it man, that's it. Still head to wind, make it fast in the tailer for a moment, call her back, back now, Clare, come on, come on ... and she tumbles into the cockpit, suddenly lanky and bony and folded this way and that, but no need to tell her, straight to the winch, tail in her hand, two turns still on, braced.

Tom spins the wheel, brute force and fast. Her head comes around again, bearing away, the deep-reefed main filling, the orange triangle up there filling ... harden it in. Clare, more, more, that's it, that's it. The engine on all this while, bubbling away in neutral —when did I? Never mind, he shoves it into gear. //

And suddenly, grace. Respite. The rain still sheeting down, sluicing them through and through, the wind a long, keen moan still, small dip and fall in it, but the boat puts her shoulder into the water and stays there, carving a groove for herself, slicing deep and powerful into the heaped, dark waters, tossing out spray and plunging her head rhythmically, but plunging on, plunging on into the night.

Clare, her chest heaving now, all tension sprung out of her, taking deep breaths, the deepest she's ever hauled down into her lungs, has time to say, pointing feebly, "Christ, Tom, your jacket, you'll catch your death!" And hearing her own words, freezing in superstitious horror, did I just say that? Oh my God did I just say that? — and Tom in a heap against her, shaking with cold now, drenched to the bone, relieved by the autopilot, can only say, struggling with breath: "You know, you know, you know, Clare, you have, a certain way, with words."

After a while she says, "Tom? You don't mind me asking now, but — are boats meant to be out in the likes of this? Fuck me, are people meant to be out in the likes of this?"

Tom, too far gone by now to be bothered playing with her, says: "You mean you'd like to steer for a while?"

And by the sudden flush in her blood, Clare realises that's exactly what she'd meant. Though some praise for her heroism would be nice, too.

"You're a hero", Tom tells her, giving her goosebumps, "You're a grade one hero, you are." Then: "The wheel's yours, try not to hit any rocks."

He unbolts the hatch, slides it back slightly, lifts the top washboard, wriggles in and down, backwards. As he's reaching to slide the hatch forward again, his blood runs cold: water, he hears water gurgling below. He cuts off the surge of adrenalin with an act of will — from when I was shoving the staysail below, that's all, no point in telling Clare. Too tired, he sees that, just too tired, not concern, not shielding her. Too bloody tired. He reaches for the bilge pump switch, presses, hears it cycle on. Fine. Fine.

He's stripped, vigorously towelled, half dressed again. He's at the chart table, soothed by the green light from the radar, the bright orange panel of the radio. He's only mildly annoyed he'd forgotten to punch out the alarm perimeter to eight miles. He does it now, is pleased to see — nothing. "The only idiots out here…" he says, and hears that he's talking out loud to himself again. He slumps on his arms, head to one side, staring steadily at the picture of Ruth. Ah Ruth, he says, silently this time, Ruth, Ruth, did you hear me calling you up there? I thought I was a goner when I was wrestling that bloody sail. I thought I was a goner when I collapsed — yes, yes man, that's what it was, you collapsed, face it. In the cockpit. Ah dear God I miss you every minute of every day. Are you waiting, I wonder? Like you promised? See you over there, remember? That's what you used to say. Every night without fail, just as you were going over: I'll see you over there, give us a shout if you need me.

Enough! He bangs the table, thinks guiltily of Clare, Christ she'll think I've keeled over!

"Where are the flasks, woman? I need coffee, can't find a bloody thing down here, wherever you've put everything. Woman! Coffee!"

"Tom?" Sweetly.

"Yes, dear?"

"Find it your fucking self, I'm kinda busy!"

He drops the flask and two metal mugs though the slot, wriggles through after them, face scrunched up with the effort. He picks up his jacket, puts it on. His life jacket, his harness, he clips on. He hands her a mug without speaking, pours. Pours for himself. Flops down beside and behind her.

She takes a scalding mouthful. She says, 'Typhoons."

"Typhoons?" he repeats, feeling like an imbecile, "what about typhoons? This isn't a typhoon; it's a gale you eejit. In fact", looking around him now, properly, "I do believe it's on its way down. Not by much, but down."

"Could've fooled me", she mutters, then, louder: "I said typhoons and I mean typhoons. Hong Kong."

"What in the name of…?"

"Jesus, Tom, pay attention, will you?"

"Clare, I know there's a point in there somewhere?"

"Oh you are a fool, aren't you? Where was this lovely boat built? Answer: Hong Kong. Who told me that? Answer: You did. Look at her, Tom, look at her pulling away! Oh they knew what they were building all right, building for typhoons, God bless them or Buddha or Confucius or whoever, whatever they believe in, bless them. You want a go at this? No? Good."

Serene as be damned, he thinks, in honest wonder. To the manner born.

And then he thinks, once upon a time that would've been me.

He's watching the masthead dancing figures of eight against stars that are getting brighter and brighter when he notices. "Clare", he says, nudging her with his coffee mug, "Clare, look up."

"Masthead light's come on", she says, matter of factly. "Must be a loose wire" — and gives her attention to steering again.

After a minute she says: "You better fix that. When you have time."

25

They tough it out until dawn comes up, sudden and hard and bright. Tom peers at the compass through salt-encrusted lids: still more or less on course. Amazing. They've been taking it in turns to doze, without speaking of it. Clare shifts where she's tumbled at his feet, curled around the pedestal of the wheel. "Turn off the shagging light, would you, Tom? It's hurting my eyes." He pulls the hood over her eyes and she subsides, grunting. He unfolds himself, stiff and bruised, sluggish and muzzy-headed. He climbs to the afterdeck. An arm around the backstay, he pisses copiously over the stern. "Disgusting", she murmurs. "Men." He could have sworn she was asleep again. He looks down and sees she is. Clutching the backstay now, he turns to survey last night's damage. None. He can't believe this; he rubs his eyes, he looks again. Nothing. Stanchions, check. Stays, check. Mast, spreaders, radar dome, antennae: check. Unbelievable. The orange storm sail is bleached along its foot, salt already drying in the rising heat. Anchor! He cranes to look. Still where he lashed it, when, only yesterday evening? Unbelievable. He shakes his head: get over it Tom, would you? This time you got a pass.

She's awake, grumbling and batting at whatever she's tangled in. "Grr..." she says, clawing her hood back, sitting up, squinting at him, looking away again with a snap, the sun hurting her eyes. "Tom, I hope that's you up there, I can't see a thing." He jumps down. "Did you just jump? Jesus, Mary and Joseph, you're full of beans." She can see him now. "No", she says judiciously, "you're not."

He musters enough energy to disengage the auto, bring the boat head to the steady wind, backing the storm sail, stalling her when she loses way, lashing the helm on opposite lock until she is hove-to, riding the high swell peacefully, bobbing her head as if in approval.

"Sleep, Clare", he says. "Come on, come with me." She crawls on her hands and knees, stops, head down. He slides back the hatch, removes the washboards, carries them down with him, stashes them under the steps for the moment. The floor's bone dry. Thank God for deep bilges, he thinks, and he drags the mattresses from the settees, lays them on the floor. Opens out two sleeping bags, lays one on the mattresses. Gets cushions, a pile of them. She's regarding him blearily from the hatch. "Don't think I'm up to it, Tom", she says. "Never fancied you anyway", he manages a weak grin. "Get yourself down here." Unsteady, her foot slipping once, she backs down the steps. She unzips her jacket, raises her arms, eyes closed. Soothing her, murmuring half words, he undresses her, helps her lie down. She curls in a ball. He covers her with the second sleeping bag. She bats the mattress behind her, feebly. "You too, Tom, snug up to me would you?"

Then, oblivion.

Loud. Something loud. An elbow jabbing his back. He opens his eyes. Gloom, rocking gently. "Telephone, Tom, answer the phone would you? Radio, I mean, I think it's the radio." He hears it, sits up with a start.

"*Lon Dubh, Lon Dubh, Lon Dubh*, this is yacht on your starboard bow, yacht on your starboard bow. Over."

He just sits there, stupefied.

The message repeats. He crawls to the nav table, grabs for the fist mike.

"This is *Lon Dubh*, over."

"Ah *Lon Dubh*, this is *Spirit of Glandore*, Channel twenty-four, repeat two, four. Over."

Glandore? I'm dreaming, Tom tells himself, though perfectly aware he isn't. He scrambles up through the hatch.

A trim white schooner is standing off his bow, making very slow way as she moves towards him. 200 yards, he registers automatically, west to east. *Lon Dubh*, pronounced it properly. Fuck it, tricolour on her stern. He looks down at Clare, sitting up now, alert, as he taps in the digits on the fist mike.

"*Spirit of Glandore, Lon Dubh*. Over."

"Ah good afternoon, *Lon Dubh*. I observe you lying hove to with a storm sail flying. Just checking to see if you need any assistance. Over."

Tom is utterly charmed by the friendly formality of it. And baffled, too; an Irish boat, what are the odds?

"Ah, negative, thank you. Catching our breath. Over."

"Yes, caught out in that last night, were you? Where from? Over."

"Siracusa, Sardinia yesterday evening. Bound for Howth. Over."

"Howth, eh? Almeria ourselves, for Lesvos; rode over the top of it. Hairy, wasn't it? You must have caught the brunt. Any damage? Over."

"Also negative, I'm happy to say. Over."

To Clare, tugging at his ankle, Ssh! Ssh!

"Well, *Lon Dubh*, we'll be pushing on. Fair winds. Over."

"Tom, Tom Harrington. I'll look forward to buying you a pint one of the days. Good luck to you. Over."

Four of them there in the cockpit now, waving as she glides by. Tom waves back.

"Gerry, Gerry Murphy. Make mine a Murphy's, up the rebels! Best of luck, now. *Spirit of Glandore*, out."

Irish? I don't fucking believe it. Cork boys. What are the odds? What are the odds? — Clare elbowing up past him, waving like mad. A cheer from the other boat, pulling away strongly as her jenny comes rolling smoothly out.

"Well you've done wonders for my reputation anyway", Tom tells her, big grin on his face, leering at her.

Clare, stark naked but for a scanty pair of panties, looks down at him imperiously. "Quite deliberate, I assure you. Your reputation needs all the help it can get. Old man. Sure they all probably know you. Is that right, by the way? No damage?"

"No damage", he tells her, "isn't that something? And I got you into bed! What do you think of that?"

"You tucked me up like a baby, Tom, you big softy. Coffee? With a dash of whiskey?"

"Sounds good to me; I'd put something on, though, boiling the kettle."

"Tom?" — feline, silky.

"Yes, dear?"

"You do realise you're wearing even less than me?"

"Ah, but I'm not making the coffee!" He ducks the flying cushion with ease.

All's well in their little world as the afternoon tips, begins the long slide into evening.

Always a definite moment, Tom thinks, even as a boy I used to notice that. Summer, you'd head out after breakfast into one of those endless days, the whole afternoon before you and then, maybe up a tree or chasing a ball. Or later, older, in town, hanging around outside Eason's hoping some particular girl might just happen by, might even look at you for a second; you'd feel the blunt tip of it in your chest, a slight dull prod — and everything changed; you'd wake in the morning like a pup going 'where's the ball? where's the ball?' and you'd mill into the day, all charged up with the sense of possibilities and then, oomph!, you'd see the end of the day up ahead, never mind that you wouldn't see your bed before midnight, you'd see the end up ahead and that changed everything.

Where did I read that, I wonder? Lovely phrase that: 'an agreeable melancholy'. I spent my life meaning to write things down so's I'd remember where I read them. Scalp feels hot, getting thin up there, Tom; maybe a touch of sunburn, eh?

She plops a hat on his head, the brim flopping around his face. "Getting a bit red there, Tom. You'd want to watch that, your age."

Done it again, he thinks; what can you do but laugh? Some woman.

"Drawing well now", she says, "pulling away good-oh. Heading for home, eh, Tom? Think she's heading for home, think that's what has her flying?"

"Ah, but home is back there, you know?" Looking back over his shoulder. Sandalo. Siracusa. Ikaria, the Aegean….

"Not what the Glandore Cowboys would say, Tom. Flying the flag and heading west?"

"Well", he concedes, "it's one way of looking at it."

Lon Dubh is driving on. Blue water again, throwing out bright fans of spray, in a good groove, her suit of white sails standing full and taut in the wind and light. Must be making eight, nine knots, he thinks, on a beam reach, her favourite.

"You think a boat has a soul, Tom?"

"Three of us pulled through last night, Clare. Can you feel what she's feeling? Can you feel it?"

Tom seated behind the wheel, Clare perched up behind him to one side. She puts a cool hand on his neck, brim of his hat scuffing her forearm. Here we go, he thinks, bracing himself, here we go.

"Tell me about her, Tom. Tell me about Ruth. That's Ruth, yeah? In the photograph?"

"God damn it", he says, getting up in a burst, heading for the hatch, "what's wrong with me? The forecabin cushions, they got soaked last night when I shoved the staysail down, didn't even think about that when we were getting it back up again. Give me a hand, will you?"

After a moment she follows him down. "Not too bad", he says, grunting, dragging a long cushion back through the saloon. She passes him wordlessly, without looking at him, contrite and shy. They lash the cushions, one above the other, to the windward mast shrouds, high up as they can get them. Tom sits in the cave of shade they make, back to the mast, patting the dry deck beside him. Folding her legs gracefully under her, Clare sits, facing him at first, then wriggling around when he pats the deck again until they're sitting shoulder to shoulder.

"Like a tepee", she says. "Mam had a tepee, did I tell you that? Great big panels of heavy, white canvas, she had a sailmaker down in Cork make them for her. Five big poles, I remember, we'd lace the panels together, we'd have it up all summer. Made Rory uneasy, I think he was afraid of what the neighbours might think. Asked Mam if she wouldn't mind putting it up in a little field we had near the house, in a grove of ash and birch, you know? I loved that little field, full of wild garlic."

Prattling a little bit, giving him a choice here, and Tom knows it. Says nothing.

"She used to sleep out in it, you know. Warm summer nights I'd hear the kitchen door open, I'd look down and she'd be crossing the yard with a couple of blankets under her arm. Janey, it's coming back to me. She had a camp bed there after a while, old wood and canvas army thing. This Doctor, O'Brien, we were having a picnic in there one time, Mam and me, and O'Brien would be out with his dogs, we'd often see him. This day he's standing there where the flap is folded over, right, the light behind him so's he's in shadow but sure we knew him well. A nice man he was. Always had a bit of a twinkle for Sandra, he had. He sat down and had tea with us, no bother. Very relaxed kind of man. I remember him saying he'd always liked sleeping under canvas when he was a young man. He'd been in the British Army ... I bet that's where the camp bed came from! Do you think, Tom?"

"Ah, Clare, he says, Clare, Clare, it's OK, it's all right."

Soothing her, soothing her. Settling himself.

"So. Ruth. We met in Paris. Les Deux Magots, you know it? No? Always loved Paris, easiest place in the world to disappear in. I'm sitting inside, reading *Libé*, inhaling a *maïs*, minding my coffee and my own business. Invisible, right? Coming into summer, fresh kind of day. I look up, this small, wiry woman is … threading her way through the tables outside, staring in at me, all the way to the door, right back over her shoulder. Long, brown hair in a kind of loose ponytail. Neat shoulders. And I go, 'Oh!' Like a very small turn over inside my head, you know? As in 'Oh, there you are.' I stand up, I turn around to the door, she walks up to me, a bit shy but bold, too, you know the way; she puts out her hand, cool and formal, says 'Ruth.' Of course I say, 'Tom', what else would I say, and she sits down and I sit down and we just … we just sit there looking at each other.

"Just, looking at each other. No bother at all on us, take all the time in the world, sure where are we going anyway?

"This old waiter, he's a bit used to me, I've been in town all week doing some session work, right, doesn't matter, this old, old waiter, skinny as be damned but tough as old boots, big droopy white moustache, he's by the door staring at us. He looks at me and then, I swear, this big, unholy grin comes over his face, I smile back at him, shrug; she turns, sees him, I can't see her face. He draws himself up, right, and gives her the most formal bow, you should have seen it. Pure dignity. And she nods, and she turns around and looks at me and she has this smile on her face … God you should have seen Ruth's smile, I can't….

"There you are, I remember thinking: ah, there you are. No big deal, don't get me wrong here, not thunder and lightning, suffocating heart, not like that. Just, quiet and certain as you like: there you are. That's how we met. Ruth."

"You used to smoke? Tom…?"

"Yeah. OK. All right. In the wine store, saloon table, in at the back"

She comes back with a large bottle of water in one hand, unwrapping the cellophane from the cigarette packet with her teeth, gas lighter sticking up from the back pocket of her shorts. She lights two, inhales down to her toes, plucks out one and hands it to him. "A bit stale", she says — "good, though." "I used to smoke for Ireland, one time", he says.

"Anyway, Ruth is a radio journalist, arts and politics, very French sort of gig. The day before I leave, two, three days later, she says, dressing, examining a tooth in the mirror: 'I have things to do, Tom, I will see you in Dublin. Soon. I promise.' I said, 'OK, grand.' So off she went.

"Three days later she phones, says 'I'm at the airport. I'll see you soon.' I just stood at the back window of the flat, looking down into the garden. There's a ring at the doorbell … She stands there looking at me, I stand there looking at her. That's it, then, we're both thinking. Here we are then. The traffic going by in the square.

"'I went back', she tells me later; we're standing there looking down into the garden. 'I went back to the café. I brought him flowers. Roses.'

"I knew of course she meant the old waiter. 'What'd he do?' I asked her? 'He was very formal. He said he wished us every happiness. He said he met his wife in the very same way. He said we were very lucky.'"

"God", Clare sighs, "the French, eh?"

"I didn't say Ruth was French."

"I meant the waiter. Eh, she wasn't? French?"

"Cork, born and bred. Father and mother factory workers, scholarship to UCC, Honours French, off to Paris with her. Turned out, we knew half Ireland between us, we even had friends who'd been trying to introduce us to each other for years. We found out all that later.

"So, anyway. I was getting divorced, she was in a dead-end life with some fella, nice fella but it had kind of worn down over the years, and … there you are."

Fluent as he is, she catches the false note. He feels it from her, makes a face.

"OK, OK. I was getting divorced, yeah. Been married four years, disaster. Never should have…. Look, my fault, her fault, nobody's fault. She…. Look, I made a deal with myself: I took all the blame, never said a word about her after, never. I kept to that, I'm keeping to that. People think what they like, OK? Leave it at that."

"Jesus, Tom! I only…"

"…I'm sorry, I'm sorry, I don't mean to sound angry … forget it, right? Let's forget this, Clare, it doesn't matter, all right?"

"Look…"

"…Sssh, Sssh, sit down, don't get up, sit down. Give me another one of those."

She lights two, not looking at him. Afraid to. Afraid of what she might say. They listen to the boat for a while, regaining themselves. Settling.

"People make mistakes, Clare, right? So, anyway. What she'd done, Ruth? She went in to her boss and said: 'I have to move to Ireland now.' She told me. Her boss just looked at her, very nice woman by all accounts, Ruth always said. She looked at her for a while and she said, 'OK, we can have a correspondent in Dublin, why not? I'll fix it.' And she did."

The staysail snaps, shuts for a second, fills again. It's starting to get dark. Tom gets to his feet, levering himself up with a hand on the mast winch. He's staring off behind, Clare is staring up at him, when he says: "Fifteen years, we had fifteen years."

Dreading the moment, but knowing she has to ask, Clare puts her head between her knees, takes a breath, asks: "What happened?"

God love you, he thinks, it's not easy, is it, life? Be careful of what you ask for. "Last Christmas", he says, putting a hand on the top of her head, still looking back at the foaming, roiling wake, the night dark weaving into it now. "She died last Christmas."

26

The boat plunging on, the water darkening, the dusk starting to drift in. Tom bends suddenly, takes an electrical fitting in his hands, pushes the two ends closer together. Ha! Raised eyebrow from Clare. "Masthead light connection, must have got knocked loose", he explains.

Silence again, a different kind of silence you'd say, the whole horror and weight of last night lying heavy on them. And what he'd just said. "Ruth", he'd called, "Ruth, Ruth, I'll see you over there." Had she heard, Clare? Had she heard him howling? Yes, yes he thinks, she heard. And, so what, eh? Life and life only.

"I know", she said, unfolding smoothly, beginning to gather in the still-damp cushions. "I know, let's make a curry. Unless, unless you want to, you know, take a nap? You're OK, aren't you?"

"Curry would be good", he says; "from scratch, eh? We're in no hurry, are we?"

Sensing how close they are to discussing his collapse.

Neat deflection, she thinks, neat bit of footwork there, Tom. You're some man.

The moment expands. Then, sensing each other's hesitation, both at the same time, each says "we're some team, huh?" "We are", he says. "We are", she agrees.

They're peeling and chopping at the saloon table. Tom says: "Sweep a garden, any size." "Be here now", she responds. "One of Mam's favourite sayings." Deepening her voice: "Be here now, man."

After a while she says: "You'd have loved her, Tom, Swear to God. She was … something else. There's another one. God!" "Another what?" "Another one of her sayings; she'd a way of shaking her head when she'd say it: 'Something else, man.' Jesus!

"What? What?" He thinks she's cut herself.

"No, no, I'm all right. I just remembered something, that's all. That time she decked the guy, in Arizona? I remember it now, isn't that strange.... We'd arrived back at the ranch, remember I told you not a word said all the way back, twenty-five miles it was? Yeah? She slammed the door on the pickup, me by the other hand, and she looked back down the road, the dust settling, and that's what she said. She just kind of shook her head and said: 'something else, man. Something else.'"

They eat in the cockpit.

"Tell you one thing", she says, her mouth crammed full. "Tell you one thing…"

"…The sea air really gives you an appetite, I know, I know."

"OK, OK, don't be smart now. Hear that a lot, do you?"

"Uh-huh."

"You have many people on this boat, Tom?"

"Always in small numbers, Clare, only in small numbers. People I know. Never a stranger. Never a whats-her-name."

God but you're quick for an oul' fella, she thinks. Caught out.

"Don't you be trying to catch me out, now", he says. "You'd want to be quicker than that."

What can I say? she mimes, bowl in one hand, fork in the other. "Anyway, this is delicious."

Meaning, OK you get that one, but see if I care.

It's full dark and they're still sitting there in companionable silence.

"Clare", he says, "last night?"

She stiffens, on guard at once, no telling where this where this might be going. He makes his voice soothing.

"In my experience, in my experience, right? Listen to me now. After a blow like that, you know, it's best to let it go until you're ashore? You know why? I'll tell you why. You might think, OK, we came through it, it was awful but we came through; nice sailing today, tomorrow's going to be good, best time to process all that fear and confusion is now, right? I don't think so. Want to know why? Because you'll edit it out. You'll learn nothing from it. It goes in, though, every second of it goes into the dark in your mind and in your body and if you don't process it, sometime, the next time you're out and you get in a bit of a blow it'll come barrelling back and you'll be terrified, properly paralysed and terrified, OK? You have to think about it, let it come up, but you do it in a safe place, you do these things in a safe place."

"OK", she says after a moment, "OK, I get you. I understand."

He looks at her to see if she does, and he sees that she does and he lets out his breath in a long sigh.

"Twigged that I don't like being lectured, have you?"

Look of surprise on his face. Gotcha, she thinks. Even-Stevens.

Fascinating, Tom is thinking, watching her out of the corner of his eye. Here we go again, you can actually *see* her shaping a question, turning it this way and that way first.

"Tom, did Ruth like sailing?"

Not, he notes, 'Did Ruth like this boat?' Not 'Did you and Ruth spend a lot of time on this boat?'

Ruminative and wary: "Did Ruth like sailing? Did Ruth like sailing? There's no easy answer. We spent a lot of time on this boat, but not necessarily sailing. She loved the Ionian; we'd potter about, one island to the next, maybe we'd tie up in a town for a couple of days, maybe we'd find a small cove and anchor there for a while. And the Aegean — Ikaria, Samos, one time up as far as Chios, Lesvos. I remember that; Meltemi when we were thinking of leaving. She got the ferry, I brought the boat down. Aghios Kirikos. No bother, we'd it worked out. She used to say, 'I'm a Cancer, crab, I like to be close to the water, not on it or in it.' She wasn't afraid I'd drown her or anything like that, you understand?"

Christ! Ice on his neck. The weight of a word. For a sickening moment he feels the immense, sucking void under the boat, the vast dark space beneath; the boat an impossibly frail and *unlikely* thing sailing over millions of tonnes of … negative weight. Negative weight, negative weight? What the....

"One time", hurrying on, "one time I was talking about maybe bringing the boat home for a while. To Ireland, right? We were in the kitchen, mid winter; I can see it in front of me, we were in the kitchen and she said to me, straight out: 'You can sail it without me, pal. If you think I'm going to dress up like the Michelin man to get cold and wet and frightened....' Ah she could be very funny sometimes. A lot of the time. Nearly all of the time."

"Do I remind you of her, Tom?"

"No." Quick and brutal. "No, Clare, you do not." On his feet suddenly, gathering in the dishes, moving away. "No, you don't. I'll get these,

I need some sleep now, Clare, will you be OK for a while?" Not waiting for an answer. Not caring for any answer other than yes.

She manages: "Yes. You go down, of course, of course." In what she hopes is a normal voice.

Unheeding, unhearing, Tom goes on down. Bang on the radar, alarm zone, what? Four miles. Hot water. He washes the dishes, stacks them to drain. Clare hears him banging, thinks: angry.

Tom just wants it done. Strip. Tie off lee cloth, just in case. Climb in. Sleep. Sleep now.

He falls headlong into the dark, dark void.

Up there in the starlight, the moon coming up across the black waters, Clare's at the wheel. Struck in the face. No ground under her. Inconsolable weeping. If she moves, she'll die. She knows it.

Maelstrom.

Oh Donal, Donal, I'll tell him your name tomorrow, I will, I'm sorry, I don't know what I was thinking of, keeping you safe from him, keeping you safe from them all. Oh Donal mind me, I can't do it all, I can't, I can't, I need minding, I need you; not safe, just private, oh God, I mean private, all to myself, you and me, Donal, tell no one, tell them nothing! Nothing! Why tell them something they can't understand! Let them guess if they've wit to, guess if they can but never tell, unlucky, oh black bad luck if you name it. Mam! Poor Rory, poor poor Rory, the loneliest man … Poor Mam, poor Sandra, poor all of us —dear God what a world….

And on, and on, and on. On into the night, her hands minding the wheel, her hands tending the mainsheet, sweeping the hair from the back of her neck, a reflex, over and over tho' she knows her hair's short now, remembers the day in Kinsale she had it shorn. On into the night and down and in for the bottled griefs, the small black boxes, numbered and stored, and the nameless fears in the dark upper rooms, the things that come in and out under the eaves, the slights, the words left unsaid.

And Donal. Ah God love him, my lovely, lovely man. God love you Donal as I do, as I do love thee, your snuffling just before you wake. The way you peel apples. The way you do go away from me in the dark, thinking away so loud I can hear the thoughts tumbling in your head. You don't know that I'm keeping vigil, sometimes I'm hardly breathing for fear you'll cop on. The prayers I do say for you! And then, you think I'm asleep and you lean up over me, watching me, watching over me, the tenderness pouring out of you. Ah Jesus the fights, never mind the fights, sure who cares about fights? What a cunt I can be. And the soles of my feet burning, burning when you make me come. And the way you die for an instant when I make you come for me, come for me Donal, oh come for me, hearing myself saying it.

Can you feel me, I wonder, the pain and the dark and the boat rushing on? Oh what was I thinking of, what was I thinking...? Oh wait for me, love, wait for me, I know you will, I know you'll wait for me, right now you're lying awake in our lovely cloud bed, the white sheets, the soft down pillows you laughed at when I bought them, the white cover you bought me in Edinburgh, knowing it would please me, the beautiful white embroidery, no, lace-work, that's it, white lace-work; Donal, Donal, the things you do find in the world for me.

The things you find in me.

And on into the night, the grief subsiding, the clarity after tears, that place you find when grief has died down, burnt out, been doused in salvation of tears.

Long after midnight, she's wide awake. Playing with the sails, humming short snatches of songs that she didn't know she knew. Wondering if there'll be time to wash her clothes in Palma. Fucking sea-gypsy, that's me. How'd you like that, Mam? Ah sure clean dirt, clean dirt.

The instant she hears him stir she locks off the wheel. She marches to the hatch, leans down and in, hands on her hips.

"Donal", she roars down, "Donal, his fucking name is Donal, right? You hear me? And he's selling his fucking house the instant I land in Dublin and he's moving in with me for the rest of his fucking life and I don't want to hear a word from you about it — and another thing, don't you ever, ever cut me off like that again. Ever! You hear me, you fucker!"

A long, long silence.

'Do you hear me? Do you hear me talking to you, Tom Harrington?"

A shorter silence, then: "Clare?"

"Jesus, he speaks! He lives! What!"

"You're, eh, you're talking to me? Oh. I thought, you know, maybe you were, eh cracking up? Talking to yourself? Talking to some old judge in your head, like?"

She shakes her head in disbelief, rocking on the soles of her feet, staring off into the night. Thunderstruck. A master, she thinks. I swear to God a genuine twenty-two-carat dyed-in-the-wool fucking genius of a Zen master! How does he do it? How. Does. He. Do. It?"

"Oh, and Clare, you wouldn't happen to have made some coffee?"

"Make mine black" is the best she can manage. She storms back to the wheel, damned if she's going to let him hear her laugh out loud.

He brings her coffee, kneeling at her feet, the wheel bumping his shoulder. Head bowed, offering the cup above his head, both hands. She feels a sudden stab of sorrow, some dark regret, a ghost in the air around them both — blown off immediately in a gust that keened for a moment in the shrouds, then died away.

Her own soft voice surprises her: "Ah get up, Tom, get up. A pair of us in it. Get up, sure aren't we a team?"

When he stands and looks at her, and she sees his eyes close to in the light from the compass and the moon, she leans in and kisses him on the cheek and pulls his head in besides hers and whispers: "I'm sorry, Tom, I'm sorry for Ruth, I'm sorry for your troubles."

And then, to herself, faintly, "sorry for all of us, the living and the dead."

"What's that, Tom?" Pointing. "On the port bow, a little below, there, see?"

A faint blaze of white. A green.

"Motor yacht, probably. Crossing our bows, she's a good bit off, nothing to worry about. Not that you're worried, I know, I know. Well spotted."

"How close would you say it is?"

"Oh, I dunno, 'bout two to three miles maybe?"

"So?"

"So?"

"So, Tom, the radar's switched on, right? So why isn't the alarm sounding?"

He comes back up: "Volume was turned all the way down."

She shrugs, "We haven't hit anything, have we? Been run over?"

"I'm very sorry", he says, "my fault entirely. Jesus, wonder how long it's been like that? There could have been anything...." Grey in the face. "I should have twigged, this morning, that Irish boat ... nothing. No sound until the radio. Jesus, Clare, I'm sorry about this."

To Clare, it's a thing of nothing. A mistake, that's all. Nobody died, move on. And then she understands that Tom feels he's losing his grip. Cannot think what to do about this. What to say.

She gathers herself by force of will, says: "I'm going down, I feel pretty whacked all of a sudden." She's about to ask 'Are you OK up here?' then thinks better of it.

Down at the chart table, she's filling in the log. Every four hours, one or the other of them has been doing this. She flicks back a page, is amused to see Tom's brief note on last night under 'Observations' : "Near gale, gale, two reefs, storm sail. All well." Mister laconic, she grins, flicking the pages backwards. Terse to the point of boring, she thinks, you'd never think … what's this? On the inside back cover, a half-sheet of typing paper, sellotaped lightly top and bottom. Words from a poem, or a song, looks like.

She turns the page into the light:

Some morning, some clear night,
you will come to the Pillars of Hercules.
Sail through if you wish. You are free to turn back.
Go forward on deck, lay your hand on the mast,
hear the wind in its dipping branch.
Now you are free of home and journeying,
rocked on the cusp of tides.
Ithaca is before you, Ithaca is behind you.
Man is born homeless, and shaped for the sea.
You must do what is best.

She reads it through twice, shrugs. It means whatever it means, I guess. She snaps the log shut. She calls up, crossing the saloon: "Hey, Tom, pills? No? OK. Good night." And to herself, shedding her top and shorts, climbing into the warm sag they've been making between them in the mattress, "good night sweet prince…" but cannot, worry it as she will, remember the rest.

Tom watches until he's sure that yacht has cleared their track. He stands at the hatch, out of sight should she glance up, and listens intently until he's sure Clare's asleep. He slips down quietly, makes sure the alarm zone's out to eight miles even though he's only just reset it, be sure, be sure, and turns up the volume. As he goes to tiptoe out and up again, she opens one eye. He freezes. I was sure she was asleep, he thinks. The eye closes. She is.

He brings up cushions, a small fleece blanket from the unused bunk. Be a laugh, he thinks, if we have to change tack, we'll keep heading for the wrong bunk. OK, not so funny. Ah so what? Grump, grump, grump. He makes himself up a nest in back of, to the high side of, the wheel. Keep a lookout, he thinks, just in case. Wedge myself in there against the slant, there. Good. Still on the port tack, amazing. Can't think how long it's been. Seems like forever. Good course now, glance at the compass, pulling away north of the island, just so, just right. Nice. Making good time, too.

Ah Ruth, he thinks finally, relenting. Dodging the issue as usual, that's what you'd say. Knowing full well it's just my way of getting the head around something that needs to be done, needs to be dealt with, needs to be … Yes, well … I couldn't bear it, you see? No, she doesn't remind me of you. Nothing reminds me of you. Not like that, no explaining to people, thank God I've the sense not even to try. Could've explained it to *you*, of course, but then that's the point, isn't it. Remember the first time we heard Sinéad singing 'Nothing Compares'? Remember, Ruth? How you turned to me and said 'Isn't it weird, she gets it, but Prince doesn't. She gets it.'

We weren't even a year, then. People used to say, in the bands, after I came back from London, before I met you, that I was a bully. That I always wanted my own way. They were right, of course, in a way, but they couldn't see beyond the gig, most of 'em, and I was so far inside the music by then, they'd just make me angry. I wanted it to be right. And it got to be a habit, being right. You told me I was addicted to being right, always having to be right, Tom. Always having to win the argument. And I'd get so frustrated, you couldn't see … and then one day I caught myself listening to you make, oh I dunno, some opposite case anyway, could have been about anything, and I was listening, you know, asking myself is she right, or am I right? How do I put this, I was outside the question, and, it was only a question. You never had any idea what you did for me, had you? And isn't that what you were always saying to me, too?

Remember I used to call it 'soaking up the rays'? We'd be lying there in bed, just lying there, backwards and forwards between the two of us, not even talking most of the time. Remember? Soaking up the rays. Oh dear Jesus my heart is broken with loneliness for you. Did you see me collapse last night, did you? Were you worried for me? I'm sorry for worrying you. Jesus, Ruth, was there ever any two people talked as much as we did? Non-stop. Sometimes I'd wake up there beside you and I'd be exhausted, I swear I was half-convinced we'd been talking to each other in our sleep all night! Nothing that wouldn't interest us. Nothing. Where did we ever pick up all that ... stuff! You have to laugh, one minute it's astrophysics, next it's me with my Ph.D in pruning, you with your fully-worked-out solution to unemployment, on and on and on. Ah but we had great laughs, though. You'd wonder sometimes, did we know we were happy? Remember how everyone, everyone, who came into the house used to say God there's great peace and light in this house! And ten minutes before that we'd have been in despair at the dust, the clutter, the books, the paintings the instruments and all the ... stuff! Saying we need a bigger house, we need a bigger house, over and over like a mantra. Knowing that if we lived in a mansion we'd still need more space ... what were we like?

Tom, coming up for air. Looking around, sniffing the wind. He folds the blanket neatly, puts a cushion on top of it, goes for 'a walk around the deck.' His own phrase for a minute inspection of anything that can wear, chafe, work loose, do damage, fall overboard, crack your skull or sink the ship.

Coming up for air. Into what element?

Nothing? Good. Nothing? Good. Nothing? Good. Meaning, everything looks OK.

I wonder, though ... looking up the mast. That staysail halyard, when did I change it last? Could be chafe there at the block. Should I climb the mast tomorrow and have a look, I wonder?

Linear time stuff, that's what you used to call it. Linear time is real, Tom, don't be such an old hippy about it. God but you could be very fierce about some things. Took me a while, and then I just ... got it, I suppose. Paint is peeling on the door? Scrape it off, undercoat, paint it. Everyday maintenance. The door won't paint itself just because you can say the word 'samsara', Tom. Take care of things. Do the ordinary. But, see the forms under the forms, OK? See what's through and under and over and behind things. Come on, Tom, you do it all the time, you just don't fucking pay attention.

Oh you could be a wagon, no two ways, but I loved every molecule of you, the smell of your skin, every dress you wore, the things you would say that only you would say, or how when you said completely ordinary things, if the light was in you they'd just reverberate through me. How when you were away I'd often pick up a shoe, say, one of your favourite shoes, and just hold it in my hand and feel you walking. For God's sake, you'd say, some agnostic you were, for God's sake, Tom, you know the way you're always trying to explain to me that you can feel a sound out ahead in a song you're producing? Something not there yet, but you can get the song to there? That's it. Nothing more peculiar than that. You do it all the time. Just, do it more!

Bossy. But, you were right. I felt so stupid when I got it, that it was there all along and I just didn't get it. You used to have to smuggle your clothes out to Oxfam, remember? I'd be in bits. You can't throw that out, I'd be, you wore that in Athens that time … or, not that jumper, you had that on when we went to … couldn't bear to … couldn't bear to.…

Can't bear this any more. These long, intense conversations. /

For Christ's sake, Tom, conversations! Why can't you just let go, man? She's gone. She was here, she was everything. She's gone. Not the first time in the history of the world. You have to move on. Deluding yourself, understandable for a while but, seriously.…

Then why do I feel her all around me? How is it I go on doing the everyday, no one complains, nobody's worried about me, I do the jobs, people are happy, I shop, chat, have a drink with people, I walk around and nobody's calling the men in white coats, for fuck's sake! But, she's here all the time. Natural as you like. I know she's in the ground, for Christ's sake, didn't I fill the grave myself, help fill the grave myself? And she's here, in me, with me, all the time. Who the fuck else am I talking to?

And.…

And.…

I'm weary, he thinks, sitting down suddenly on the foredeck, legs hanging over the side. I am so, so weary. And besides … oh let's not go into that just now. You have a choice, still.

I have a choice, he repeats to himself. No choice at all, really, is it? No.

Then have some style, man, have some style.

Sea legs a bit wonky, he says to himself, scuttling back. No surprise there. I think I'll steer for a bit. Pick a star and hang it there for a while, halfway along the lower spreader is always good. You always liked doing that. Using a star to pull yourself up the line. That's a nice phrase, isn't it: Shaping your course? Just so. Shaping my course.

Lulled, lulled, the long trance of helming at night, creak of the gear, slight shifts in the sound the wash makes, running back along the hull. Breaking at intervals for a sip of water, a long, slow look around. Fishing boats register, first one then after a long interval another. One heading north, one heading south and east, both crossing behind him, their lights barely visible, outside the zone so nothing to break the silence.

'Do I remind you of her?' her question. Ah no, and yes. A bit. So quick, so sure and unsure. Leggy and bony and sharp, where she was … petite and a warrior. A spin or two ahead of you in the cycles, my dear, a spin or two ahead of us all was Ruth. The great cycles of being and becoming. He thinks about tenderness, slowly, not so much thinking perhaps as rehearsing his memories — pictures, the feel of a touch, the yearning inside. And he thinks that perhaps the tenderness he feels for Clare is the tenderness of a scarred and battle-shrewd veteran for a young huntress, clean-limbed, grey-eyed Artemis, isn't that the phrase, where they do float up from? I wish her well, he thinks, a moment of clarity. She wants me to, and I do. A blessing, a way of looking at it I suppose, she wishes a blessing. A benediction.

First rose flush in the sails, how it always creeps up on you when you've made your accommodation with the night. *Fiat Lux*, the phrase wells up and stands in his mind. Let there be light.

Must have tranced off again, he thinks, I heard nothing, watching her come up, still trailing wisps of sleep, silent and grave. She hands him his mug of tea, bends her head, sips, looking about her. Everything familiar and, at the same time, strange. He stands to one side, she steps in, puts one hand lightly on the wheel.

A day for silence, the kind of day it will be. Each senses it, in themselves and in each other. Something between a respite and a truce. The stars receding, the night's work done. The moon staying on for a bit, a pale firm ghost of herself.

He squeezes her shoulder with his free hand, she bends in a little towards him, a soft, unspeaking nudge, and he goes down.

27

The sun through the porthole beside him has made a warm spot on his hip. He wakes without opening his eyes, feeling the warmth there, savouring it, but when he goes to stretch, when he opens his eyes, he feels his bones clamped in a vice, his breathing laboured. Christ, he thinks, that's bad. No doubt about it, knowing it will ease before long, no doubt about it. Getting worse all the time. Not by much, but getting there. Hums to himself, sadly, 'not dark yet, but it's getting there'. His other favourite line on the album: 'trying to get to Heaven before they close the door'.

He gets himself onto his back. Pills in a minute, he thinks. Sweating, though he doesn't feel terribly warm. Ah well, must try to be calm, eh? Take it as it comes.

These last years, Dylan's narrow, haunted face. Those eyes of dark suspicion, the gunfighter's pencil moustache. Jesus in heaven, how does a man stay sane in this world and write so many fucking beautiful songs? Don't follow leaders, how right you were. Have I done good? I made some good music in my day, didn't I? Smiling now, he feels the smile as a kind of easing, softening his face, knows that softening, eventually, will work its way down through the cramped muscles, the dark mass in his chest, down to, he wriggles them experimentally, his toes. Ah but Jesus in heaven, man, there were some good moments, weren't there? Don't go there, though, pulling himself up, gently now, not now, not the time or place. The old guy, Sheriff, what was his name, on the banks of the river in *Pat Garret*, Slim Pickens, was it? Gut shot, looking one last time at the only world he knows, will ever know. 'Knockin' on heaven's door'. Jesus, how simple, and what it says. Four chords and it says it all. What was I dreaming about? Yes. Van, 'Snow in San Anselmo', best song he ever wrote. Heard him sing it live in London, where? Ah, Finsbury Park,

The Rainbow was it? I think so. That summer, was it before or after I came home, saw her there, hit her, before or after? Can't remember now. Van in a pink jacket, white trousers, spasming across the stage, closest he ever came to dancing. Yes! Pasadena String Orchestra, that cellist, my God, every head in the place switching Van, cellist, Van … such an extraordinarily beautiful woman. Bewitched, the whole place bewitched. Wonder why he never re-recorded it? Story there. Ah, better; feeling the long bones begin to soften. Pills in a sec, easy does it. The sax solo at the end, so beautiful, such an elegant production, too, the strings, the choir, but not a bit cluttered, lovely big vaulting spaces in the sound. So … full. That solo, dying away at the end, just so, just right. Not Richie Buckley, who was it? Jack Schroer, Jesus where did that surface from! Ah Richie, genius; can look at that axe from across the room and make it sing to him. Enough, enough! Ready now, easy does it.

Carefully across the floor. Pills. A swallow of water. A look at the barometer. Small joke: Steady! Steady! Log, she must have come down and made an entry, no, two. Ah, letting me sleep again. Fair dues, I needed it, and if she's able and willing … Very quiet up there — a quickening, senses firing up: no, all's well, he feels it in the boat's long lope, the contented creaking and settling of timbers and gear, the dip and swoosh of it all. In good hands, he thinks, another lovely phrase: in good hands. Ah Clare, he thinks, Clare whoever you are … and tears start in his eyes; *he picks her up in his hand and holds her cupped there against his chest, small, vulnerable creature, soothing and humming softly, soothing.…*

Full waking suddenly. The shock of it. Four-square on his own deck, by God. Alive and be damned to it all. Bollocks! Bollocks!

The hatch gone dark: "Are you swearing at me or God, or have you just discovered something interesting about yourself?"

Composed and, demure is it? Cool as you like, anyway. He flushes with happiness: "Forgive me, my dear, you must forgive an uncouth old man his seamanlike way of expressing himself."

Thank God, she thinks, keeping the relief out of her voice, thank God; he didn't look well there all night, sweating and … dexterous old bastard with the words, too.

"Ah c'mere", she says, coming down; "it's a lovely day up there, hop up there now and get the sun on you, I'm starving. You hungry? Sleep well?"

"Grand", he says, "grand", beaming up at her. "Ex-cellent" she says. Liar, she thinks, but admiringly. Fair dues to you. You're some man.

He's below again, washing up, when he feels the boat hesitate, wallow, pick up again, but tentative, unsure.

"OK, Clare, windshift coming, let's get to work. Knock her off auto, there. I'll get the preventer."

"The what?"

"Ah. See this here, this sheet from the boom, here, follow it forward there to where, see, it turns through that midships block there and comes back to this winch?"

"I saw that but I didn't know what it was for."

"Always ask, Clare, always ask, never any harm in asking." Not a rebuke, simple advice, taken as such. "Last thing we want is a gybe, right? Wind shifts behind us, boom slams over, somebody in the way gets skulled or worse, maybe gooseneck breaks, there, where the boom joins the mast, follow?"

"I do, I do."

"So this preventer, well that's what it is, right? Prevents that happening. Now, wind's been, what?"

A second or two before she realises he's waiting for an answer.

"Huh? Oh, sorry, south west."

"Yep, consistent, more or less consistent, but it's fluky right now, isn't it? And it's going to shift right round there to the north. Trust me. So — see, it's banging off west, now, see the sails beginning to slat? Keep her head there in the wind now, best you can."

Swiftly, smoothly, he rolls in the genoa, centres the staysail, the main.

"Now what?"

"Now we wait. We're losing way here, switch on the engine a minute, Clare, would you? We don't strictly need to do that, you understand, but we're making such good time, don't want to lose the momentum."

She looks at him blankly. She's in no hurry. /

"Ah, you're right of course, we could just sit here and wait, of course we could. Just, I find it satisfying, you know? Maintaining an average speed, keeping the boat going?"

Clare nods, but what she's thinking is: Donal, I'd love to get back to him now, but ... I should see this through. I could, what's the thing they say, I could jump ship in Palma, but God love him I've more or less promised Tom I'd take the boat home with him. Donal will understand, I see a long phone call coming up; Donal will understand, and besides, sailing up into Ireland, all the way up from the Med....

"Clare? Clare? Hello? Earth calling Clare?"

She starts, blushes, recovers. Smoothly on to the offensive: "Earth? You think you live on planet earth, do you? More like, more like ... Planet Water!" Charmed with the idea: "I like that, Planet Water, what do you think, Tom?"

Tom stroking his beard: "I dunno, I dunno, sounds kind of ... hippyish?"

"Ah feck you...."

"And the horse, I know, I know. Right, here we are, feel the wind on your cheek now? Feel the strain coming on the wheel? Now, what're we going to do here?"

She considers, says: "It's going north, right, probably your oul' whatsit, Meltemi, right? Soooo, sure we do nothing at all, we keep on this course, yeah?"

"More or less, you've got it. But, it's not like turning a page, is it? Wind's not going to go from bang on the nose to north like the flick of a page? So, bear off a bit to the south, nice and gentle, keep the wind on the beam, ninety degrees more or less, right? Then as the wind goes on around, you follow it around."

"Right, I see that, gotcha."

"Except", Tom adds, watching her slowly feed the wheel through her hands, "except that we want to go a bit north of west, fall in on Majorca from the north, isn't that right? So when the wind settles, what you do, you point us up to, oh, about 310 to 320 degrees. OK? Got all that? Oh and when she's nice and settled, then you can roll out the jenny again, OK?"

"Yessir. Three bags full, Sir. And while I'm doing all that?"

He climbs up past her on to the afterdeck, cushion under his arm.

"While you're doing all that, this old man is going to get some heat into his old bones. Top up the tan."

"God", she says, struck by the thought, "I'd love a swim."

He props himself up: "We can do that, you know, heave to, trail a safety line over the stern. I wouldn't do it, though, not myself personally."

"You wouldn't? Why?"

"Sharks", he says.

Shocked: "You're not serious?"

"Nope", he says, complacently. "First lie I've told you."

It is, yeah, she thinks, and falls to wondering if maybe she has some Cork blood in her after all. Mam, she thinks, it wouldn't surprise me, it wouldn't surprise me.

And so the long day passes.

They come and go, they make snacks for themselves and for each other, they drowse in the sun. Clare goes down for a while, makes up the bunk on the opposite side. Fresh sheets, she thinks, and then after a minute she takes the old pillowcase off, folds it neatly and tucks it in under the fresh pillow. It takes a bit of wriggling to get comfortable. She misses the familiar sag their bodies have made in the other bunk.

She showers when she wakes, and he showers after her. Fresh clothes, each decides. Big lunch, they decide, wordlessly. Long, lazy, near-silent, companionable lunch.

Repair work by increments. Building the peace. Replenishment.

Clare on the side deck, soaking up the sun. Tom thinking, they always look uncomfortable, thongs, You feel they'd cut into you, wouldn't they? Clare without raising her head saying: "I can hear you thinking, old man; they're not, as a matter of fact. Uncomfortable." Her snort when she hears — nothing. Ha, gotcha!, she thinks happily, subsiding, snuffling contentedly.

Later, Tom on the foredeck stretched out face down, head propped on his folded arms, arms flat on a salt-raspy cushion. Like flying, he thinks, then: no, not *like* flying, flying. Would eternity be like this, Ruth, do you think? Catching himself, hearing himself, stiffening — and relaxing. Ah sure only natural, he tells himself, after all that time only natural not to be used to it yet. Habit's a queer thing, though.

Almost, but not entirely, convincing himself. Almost, but not entirely, home free.

The long day passes, as these days do on long voyages, on the open sea. Wind, sun and water; water, wind and sun. Everything blue, everything white, the glinting of water, the tactile pockets of shade; everything tilting and rolling, borne up and borne on, metal and wood and canvas and water and air, a small and sufficient buoyant world, packed full of itself, and all the time in the world to be at home within it.

When dusk began to come on, Tom went down to bake bread. When the full dusk was landed around them, she followed him down into the dark saloon. She switched on the radar, her eye flicking a moment to check the batteries are charged; she made an entry in the log; she took a pencil, dividers, she checked their position again and made a small X on the chart, a small circle around it; she followed the long line of Xs back down the curve to Carloforte, the steeper dip down to Gozo, the climb up to Isola Capo Passero, she peers at the chart to make out the name, and then Ortigia, Siracusa.

"Seems a long way back, doesn't it?" — Tom has turned to watch her.

"Sure does", she says, and hesitates, unwilling to say more.

They sit at the saloon table, peeling and chopping. Onion, garlic, cucumber, pepper, tomatoes, kalamata olives. A big hunk of cold Feta cheese, sweating slightly. It crumbles under the knife, finding its own faultlines. Tom crushes lemon juice into a bowl, she adds the olive oil, thick and gloopy, green in the light of the lamp. She beats the dressing in a bowl on her lap, the bowl on a tea towel draped across and between her thighs. Tom leaning over and drizzling salt, pepper, into the mix. The bread, wrapped in a cloth, is cooling on deck. She brings it down, inhaling the smell of it, head bent over a sudden breaking-though of childhood.

Tom has cleared the table. He spreads a white cloth over the shining surface, an intricate trim of lace along its edges. Ruth's, she thinks, Ruth bought that cloth — and then, seeing his face, his hand smoothing and smoothing the fabric, she thinks: no, he bought it for her. She sits on the low side, smoothing her short, red skirt. She thinks for a moment, rises, goes through to the forecabin, returns. A white cotton blouse, long sleeves, round neck. Buttoned all the way up. Her silver bracelet. Tom, opening a bottle of wine, looks at her for a long time, then nods soberly. Unwilling to see him naked, she fiddles with cutlery, glasses, straightens the tablecloth. He's put on his grey shirt now, his black linen trousers.

All this, not a word said. All this, the air around them charging up. It's warm down here, from the oven, but they feel cold. She feels it on her neck, she feels it spread across her breasts. She waits, forcing resolve she does not feel. He feels the prickle in the hairs on his scalp, feels — it's time. We're here.

He pours the wine, intent on the red stream purling into the polished glasses. The wink of bubbles. Eyes locked now, the weight pressing down on them, they chink; the light catching the flash reflection, the sound echoing in the stilled cabin.

28

"Cancer, Clare", he says, putting his glass down, his head down. "Cancer. I have cancer."

The lit oil-lamp above the table sways, steadies. The boat rocks a moment late, then steadies, holding her course. Time swells around them, pushing backward and forward. Tom's hands flat on the table, palms down, pushing down to brace him up. Then Clare's hands on his, light and firm.

The three questions, Tom thinks: what kind, how long have you ... how long do you ... He can almost always tell now, with his friends, who will ask which question.

Clare's silence saying: You choose, Tom. It's your story. I'm here.

He lifts his hands, he sets her hands free, thanking her with the touch. He begins to serve them both. "I wasn't expecting it, to be honest", he says. "A bit of a shock, really. Well, I guess I was still in shock after, well, Ruth, you know, and I was low on energy, very low on energy, and I went to the Doc, check-up sort of thing, and a week later I pick up the phone and he's saying, 'you have to come in to see me, Tom, I have something to tell you and it isn't good. Some time today, tomorrow, in your own time.' Used to be a bass player in college, the only bass player I've ever met who had women running after him. You couldn't ask for a nicer fella to tell you.... He told it like a man, you know? Straight and simple. Explained what I had — I won't go into it, you don't mind, pretty much everything; explained the options. What it felt like was — you know the expression 'hit by a truck'? If all your concentration was on the moment of impact, and you could freeze that instant until you'd had time to examine it? Like that. Past, present and future — all of it in the one instant and pretty much unbearable, actually. I was ... way beyond numb. He's not a very big guy, Tony, but blocky, like. He came around the desk after a while, I'm just sitting there staring into, staring into … and he put his arms in under my armpits and he lifted me and he put his arms around me and one hand on the back of my neck and bent my head down. And he kept his hand there until I started to cry, and until I'd finished."

All this time as if holding the most ordinary conversation in the world, sipping wine, going through the motions of eating. Except Clare has broken three, four chunks of bread into tiny pieces. Except every now and then Tom's fork rattles uncontrollably on the plate. Neither flinching from eye contact, neither hesitating to break it.

"Do I sound too fluent, Clare? It was much more broken up than that, you know what I mean. Time broken up into I don't know what, not like I sat down, we talked, I got up and left, all in a line kind of thing. Of course it was." He pours more wine. "A jumble of impressions, that's what people say, isn't it? Only afterwards, of course, I had to sort it all out, naturally. You know what I felt, walking out the door? I felt sorry for poor Tony, not because of how often he has to do this kind of thing, tell people, that's all part of the gig, isn't it? What I felt sorry for was, he knew I was going home to an empty house, and he wanted to say, come home and have dinner with Kate and myself, but he knew he couldn't do that. It wouldn't be right."

Silence. He's looking away aft, at the moon hung in the dark oblong of the hatchway. Like a Japanese lantern, he thinks. Precisely like a Japanese lantern. She gives him the time, then she asks: "What did you do, Tom?"

"That was, what? The first week of March. The fourth of March. A Tuesday."

"Tom, what did you do, Tom?"

He looks up at her and he thinks: God, the things you do understand. And she reaches out and presses his hand, and her eyes say: go on.

"I walked out to the kerb, not really seeing anything, and I put my hand up and there was a taxi coming and he brought me home. Putting the key in the lock I felt a kind of excitement, you know? Bursting with news, holding it all back until I could tell her. And I closed the door behind me and the house was so full of her that had been empty for months I was full sure she was upstairs somewhere or out in the back garden or … and then I collapsed at the end of the stairs, in a heap I was, in a heap. I couldn't catch my breath, like someone had thrown a huge bucket of cold water at me and my, I couldn't catch my breath. The only light in the house coming in from the streetlamp outside the gate. I don't know how long I … it was dark anyway when I got home. I went up to the back bedroom. I pulled the curtains shut. I took all the paintings off the wall, I went up and down the house collecting every picture of her I could find, I didn't know we had so many, pictures of her on her own or pictures of the two of us, I hung them on nails there in the back bedroom, hammered in more nails when I hadn't enough. I went and got books she loved, brought them up. I opened the cupboards, her wardrobe, the drawers full of her things that I hadn't been able to bring myself to open and I picked out special things, things she'd loved herself, things that brought back a particular memory. Things that, that still had her smell on them. When I'd find something like that I'd hold it up to my face, you know yourself. The way you do. And shoes! God she loved shoes. I put out shoes, too. Then I felt suddenly ravenous; without particularly thinking about it, you see. I ate out of the fridge, whatever was there. I made a bowl of muesli and I ate that too. I made tea, put all the things on a tray, biscuits, shortbread, and brought that up. She loved candles; there were stashes of candles all over the gaff so I got candles and candleholders, candlesticks, and I set them up all round … Clare, are you sure you want me to? OK, I set them up all round the room, clothes like kites hung everywhere, even from the lightshade, in heaps around the room, the books and all that, I switched off the light and it was like — magic. I sat down against one wall and I shoved the door closed with my foot and it clicked, a nice, soft, definite sound. All that soft light from the candles, such a glow off them all together, all of the flames standing up, not a wisp of a draught anywhere.

"I sort of noticed then that I still had my coat on, I still had my shoes on. I took them off, and I didn't know what to do with them, the shoes hanging from two fingers, the coat over my arm. I remember standing there and I couldn't think what to do with them. Then I went out again, and the candles all danced a second or two, and I went into my workroom and I took off all my clothes, every stitch and, I wasn't even having to think about this, I put on all soft things, you know, I put on things she'd bought me or that we'd bought together and I put on a thick pair of woolly socks that she bought me and I went back in and closed the door again and sat down again.

"I sat up all night, I think, or most of it. I must have gone through our whole life together that night but I remember it the way you remember big nights of complicated dreams, I can pick out bits and pieces, colours, events, things said, that kind of thing, but it keeps getting away from me any time I try. I was frozen when I woke up. The heating had gone off in the night like it always does on the timer and I was in a heap in the corner, my face in her clothes, bits and pieces of her clothes on top of me, all around me, and pictures in the corner I could see when I opened my eyes whatever way I looked in the angle of the room in the corner. Like a burrow it was, I remember thinking that, and bits of jewellery and God knows what. I don't know how I didn't burn the house down. All the candles had gone out."

His head in his hands. His breathing jagged and uneven. His will telling Clare to keep back now, keep back there a minute, understand me please, don't let me down now. And Clare, understanding, holds herself very still, hands in her lap looking right at him so that when he raises his head he can see he has her full attention. The best understanding she can give him.

"Six months to a year. That's what he said, the specialist Tony sent me to; six months to a year. Impersonal. Cold. Fair enough, you'd go mad I suppose…. Then he started rattling off all these treatments, assuming of course that I … o' course I know there are good ones, I've met a few, but Jesus, Clare, did you ever have anything to do with specialists? Don't, that's all I'll say, don't. I wanted to tear the fucker's throat out, sit on his fucking chest while he's bubbling blood and air, look in his eyes and ask him, 'What do you think about death now, pal? What's it like to come down off your fucking mountain and rejoin the human race for your last few fucking minutes on earth?' I mean, Clare, rage! Real fucking rage, you know!

"And not about me at all, you see, seeing it even while I'm taking the ten deep breaths, it was about Ruth and that fucking, fucking…. And then it all went away. Like that. Gone. Just icy cold impersonal, standing up and shutting him up with my hand held in front of his face and saying 'Thank you for your time, Mister. Eh, I'll deal with this now. You must have a busy morning ahead of you. Good day to you.' His mouth just opening and closing, outraged he was; he looked, well, lost? And no satisfaction for me in that, either; I was past that, well past that. And me walking out the door. Like that."

Slaps the table. Rises.

Hands still in her lap, Clare looking up at him.

Of course her head is spinning with questions, fragments of useless plans, helplessness, the urge to hold and console, the desperate search for the words, any words, that would be … adequate. She considers this turmoil with a part of herself that she's had flashes of before now, intuition she calls it, or instinct, when she calls it anything at all, pays it anything other than fleeting attention. She considers herself considering this turmoil, better, she *notices* herself processing what Tom is telling her, and what's going through her mind. I know this, she tells herself, clear and sure. I know this — but she has no words to say what it is she knows. And that's all right, too, this also she knows.

Surprised and not surprised by a kind of … unexpected faculty? Is that it?

And Tom sees all this happening, feels all this happening, in her, in the bond between them, and is glad he's told her; he feels her connect with herself, and he feels their connection. No big deal, he thinks. No need to talk about this.

As if *this* has been out there all along, this whole and adequate moment so full of its own weight and light and charge — and either they'd make it to here, to this now, or they wouldn't. And they have.

Everything squared away. The peace of the night, the onrush in dark waters, the tall sails pressed over, leaning south.

Side by side on the coachroof, looking north and west, the moon riding companionably up there; "A lantern", Clare said, not knowing why. Tom laughed, grateful for the warmth in that laugh. "A Chinese lantern", she added.

"Painkillers is it, Tom", she'd asked, helping him clear away their supper dishes. "Morphine, I suppose?" "Yes", he'd said, "something like that." "So, no chemo, no radiotherapy, no nothing?" "No." Not terse or curt, a simple 'no'.

Looking north and west.

"So", she says, "bringing the boat home, eh, Tom? Bringing it all back home?"

"Yes", he says, "home. Bringing it all back home. Heading home."

She considers. She says, "I'll help you."

He says, "You have. Helped me. You do."

"No", she says, "I mean I understand what you're saying, and I'm moved, I am, thank you. I'm very glad that I came on this trip with you, Tom, I am. And, I know it's a help, me being here is a help. What I mean is, I'd been thinking about bailing out at Palma? And now, no. I'll bring it home with you, Tom. I'll bring it all the way home with you." A pause. "If you want me to? If you'll have me along?"

"Ah look", he says, "you might want to think about that, you know? Might be rough."

"Ah Tom, Tom, you're some man you are. Some man for one man."

He's on the point of ruffling her hair, upwelling of affection, gratitude, when she looks at him and he looks at her and soundlessly, separately, heads bowed, they both begin to cry.

They weep for a long time. Sorrow.

For the living and the dead, Clare is thinking.

For the living and the dead, for all of us here, Tom is thinking. And for myself, why not? For myself, too. Just now, right now, for me.

And the boat speeds on under cold stars, bearing them up and on, on through the rushing dark, serene and indifferent to whatever being human means, serene and indifferent as the riding moon.

You'd say the boat is sailing itself, so smoothly they move between watch and watch in the long hours, so tactfully they do what needs to be done. The small things that matter: housekeeping, seakeeping, watching and tending.

The boat, and each other.

Clare, gone down to sleep if she can, at the least to be alone for a while.

Tom, more acutely than ever now, thinking about managing the dosage, about walking the line between pain and no pain. The seduction, the sweet seduction of that.

Clare, between brief dips into fitful sleep, going over and over in her head the things she might have said, should have said, could have said, may find herself having to say tomorrow. And the next day, and the next. Arriving at Dublin in her head, brought up short: too far, she thinks, too far ahead to think about that. Donal, I'll call him from Palma; he'll know what to do. No, he'll know how to talk to me about what needs to be done.

Tom is listening to a voice in his head, going: Lovely, oh lovely, Tom, that's just lovely. He smiles. Hello, Ma.

The low onrush of her familiar voice: Fair dues now, you have your own way of doing things, I never got in your way about that, although, God knows, I didn't understand what you were going on about half the time, but, I mean to say, what are you like! I mean really! I'm not saying a word, now, against that girl. She's a lady, Tom, a lady — written all over her. You can tell she got good rearing, even in the bogs of Tipperary. What had anyone from Tipperary ever to do with the sea, would you tell me? No matter, although your Aunt Mary, remember, went out with that sailor fella one time, remember him with the Teddy Boy cut of him, and he was from Clonmel. Tipperary, now, where would you be going! But ah, Tom love, that was a hard burden to put on anyone. And she hardly knowing you, all alone on a boat in the middle of the ocean, God love her, to be hearing the likes of that!

As vivid before him as ever she was. Ah, Ma, he smiles, sure don't be going on, now, isn't she well able? Isn't she, Dad? Ah.... And his mother, sceptical in her own inimitable way, and loving, loving, saying: She was sent from God, Tom, she was sent from God. You should be down on your two knees.... The Da there beside her, nodding away in agreement....

Then: ah sure they're neither of them there, what am I thinking of? Light down there to the south, single white light, loom from below the horizon, no sound from the alarm so I'm guessing something big a long way off. Keep an eye on that. Just in case. Pulling lovely, still, we've been blessed with the winds. Well, apart from ... and sure that didn't do us any harm. Course is still good anyway. Deya tomorrow evening early, should be picking up the island at first light, shouldn't we? Check in a minute. I don't feel too bad now, not too bad at all. Warm night, too.

Then: the long procession he's gotten used to over the months since March. The long farewell, he says to himself, thinking of Michael Hartnett's lovely, chilling line: the long subtraction has begun. Friends, mates from the business, not everyone; the ones he could trust to accept it for what it was, is, not make a fuss, let him be, accept his take on it all. Keep their mouths shut, too. For a while, before he went off to prepare the boat, after it came to him that the thing to do was go down for the boat, calling people up, calling round to see people. Judging the moment, telling them. Getting better as time went on at helping them deal with it, at letting them see he's dealing with it. How strange is that, he'd sometimes wonder, and then think, not so strange, really. The ones who went out of their way to avoid him, after. Few. The ones who'd ring up, call round, not overdoing it, either. Taking their cue from him, the tempo, the rhythm of it. What was left of his life, the way he was living it? Not one of them arguing with him. His gratitude for that.

The ones who'd come to him out of the dark, conversations with them; like this, now. And the former lovers, them too, and not his ex-wife. The roads not taken.

That morning, he'd woken up cold and cramped in the back bedroom, tortured by fear as he would be for days yet, though he didn't know it would be only for days, not then; unable to leave the house, to wash himself, change his clothes, answer the telephone. Open the curtains, every pair in the house closed. People thought, he supposed, that he'd gone away. Until a voice inside him said: No. Not like this, Tom. Don't be demeaning everything you've been and done. Don't be disrespecting what you've been given. You're not the first, no, nor will you be the last. And the voice, himself, whoever, whatever, saying: It comes to us all, Tom, sooner or late. Everyone has to face it. And seeing his father's face from years back, bent over the coffin. Absolute grief, overwhelming. And seeing now, then, seeing the man straighten, oh Jesus so slowly but straighten and put his hand one more time to her cold, cold cheek and put his other hand out to Tom then, and turning, the pair of them, walking out through the opening crowd, the crowd gone very silent, dear God so silent, and walking out shoulder to shoulder with, feeling the thump of it in his chest, a man.

The dignity of him. Mortally bereft, and stepping out. Taking each hand in his as it was offered.

29

Clare has to fight her way out of sleep, hot and muggy, head in a fuzz and sweat. Damn, forgot to undress; fleece half wrestled off, over her face. A warm bed in a cold room, Rory's prescription for a good night's sleep. And how right you were, she thinks. Not the worst, poor man, not the worst. Her mother in her dreams: that fork in the road one time down in Kilkenny, slate country, the surprisingly poor and scraggy fields in the richest of counties. Slate outcrops everywhere, narrow lanes, burrowing and twisting themselves, tracks of some creature unable to find safe ground. In the dream. They'd gone to look at an Irish Draught mare that Sandra had heard about, in the way she had of hearing about such things. The black Toyota pick-up, the horsebox jolting behind. They'd come to a Y-fork, nothing about the choices to suggest which was the better option; green tufts of grass in the middle of each road, the hedges closing in. June, the air heavy and damp and hot with pollen, loud with all kinds of flying things, biters. *Arizona, the pick-up*, Clare unable to tell now, waking, if this is a memory in the here and now or a flashback from the dream. In the dream, Sandra, barefoot, bewildered and, yes, poor; long, scraggy dress, torn at the hem, trailing. Unable to find her way, sad that she had to leave her daughter here in this place. Telling her this with her eyes, a wry grin on her saying sorry, Clare, sorry, looking over her, past her, her eyes faraway, saying 'something else, Clare, something else....'

"You about ready to get the head down, Tom", she calls, advancing unsteadily towards the hatch, balancing two mugs. "I made cocoa."

"Cocoa, cocoa? Jesus, where did you find that?"

"In my bag, Tom. I brought it in case I'd trouble sleeping. Sandra used to make it for me when I'd be going through bouts of insomnia, when she was being all smothery and maternal. When she wasn't saying,

'Why don't you just work at something until you're so tired you can't keep your eyes open?"'

Cripes, she thinks, listen to me ramble; why couldn't he just have said 'thanks', or 'no thanks?'

"Thanks", he says, 'just the thing. Just sitting here thinking, you know, happy enough to sit on for a while unless you'd rather....."

She's listening very carefully to the tone of what he says. Fearing, what? Desolation? Weakness? No, she thinks, the forensic self having a word, not because I fear not being able for it, because I'm afraid of what it'll mean to him if he crumbles now.

What he was thinking before she came up, as she was beginning to stir in the dark below:

Ruth before me
Ruth behind me
Ruth above me
Ruth below me
Ruth beside me
Ruth inside me.

The morning he decided to be grateful even for his own death, abject and wretched though his fear was, his craven animal whiny snotty self-pitying fear; to *try* to be grateful, then, to try, he made up this mantra, sipping a cup of tea in the kitchen, looking in wonder at everything she'd touched, thinking never again, never again, never again, making himself think this at first, then, learning as days went by, permitting himself to think this, as he had not done since the day she died. Could not and would not do.

Wrote it all down on a fresh page of the phone message pad, the previous pages torn out and scrunched in a ball, shoved deep in the bin, too painful to see her hand there, her spirit reaching down through the pen into the faint channels the writing made on the shiny pages.

On the bus one morning he'd laughed at himself: you and your mantra, it's a prayer, Tom. Invocation, deal with it.

As in, a door o.pening for a brief instant into childhood: Hail Holy Queen Mother of Mercy hail our life our sweetness and our hope.... On the upper deck of the 32A. Not an atom left in him of that believing child.

"Tom, your cocoa's gone cold. Give it to me here, I'll go down and heat it up. Just give it to me, OK? It's no bother; it's fine. Aren't I on watch?"

He hands the mug over, scarcely registering her, her words. Minimally present to the here and now.

Whenever he feels the acid bile of panic near, has to swallow hard, bring his breath under control, he recites this mantra. Sometimes he seeks it out as a way of ordering whatever he's doing, bringing himself to the place of order, calm thought, effective action. Sometimes the mantra has his full attention, thought propagating thought as he considers the words, as the words bloom out and out; sometimes, when he's feeling more than usually tired, say, or the pain is bad, the words are hardly words at all, it's the breath rhythm that works its magic, the way that he breathes, saying the words.

Something else to keep an eye on, Tom. This tendency to drift away; want to watch that, old son.

When she comes back up, she asks, "You sailed the boat in worse weather than the other night, Tom?"

"Hmm? Oh yeah, this boat and other boats. This boat? Only on my own. Wouldn't stay out with anyone else. Wouldn't go out if the forecast was bad, would run for cover if I saw bad stuff coming."

Jesus, Tom, she thinks, have you any idea what that sounds like: only on my own?

"Were you scared, times you were out on your own?"

"Scared? Of course I was scared. I'd run a mile from sailing with any-one who says they're not scared at some point in rough weather. Either a liar, means you can't trust them, or a maniac, which I personally trust even less. Sure I was scared, but, you know, you have to sail the boat, that's all. Sail the boat, sail the weather, make good choices."

"That's it, huh? 'Make good choices'? Just like that?"

"Well, yeah. You shouldn't be out there if you can't handle the boat; the weather is just kind of an upping of the ante."

"And on other boats?"

"Oh sure, there've been some hairy moments. Mast in the water, water getting in down below, guys too sick to be any use, guys going helpless, useless would be better, with fear. Once, an engine fire off Finisterre. Put that out and the steering started sticking, lovely. Clare, people are scared all the time in this world, you know that. Some people are scared, petrified even, by things you don't give a second thought to. The other night, that's what you're getting at, isn't it? That was a gale, Clare; gales happen, we nearly got caught out, we caught a pass because we kept our heads, we did the right things."

Then, softly: "I saw your look, Clare, don't be forgetting I'm an old witch now. Don't be afraid to ask me anything. Am I scared of dying? Of course I am. Am I afraid to talk about it? No. What I say depends on who's asking, of course. Here's a good one nobody's asked me yet: are you afraid that there's nothing after this, Tom, just an eternal void, and you'll be awake forever alone in the void remembering everything and everyone you touched, tasted, felt, everything you saw, heard about, read about, thought, and all you have for eternity is the sum of what your attention brings with you when the lights go out forever? You feel up to asking me that one, Clare?"

A challenge, not hostile, a question that asks: how far along the road are you, Clare, what are you up for at this point in your life? Reality check.

She shakes her head. "Jesus Tom, that's really terrifying. I'm not able for that. Are you afraid of that?"

"Oh yes I am; anytime I give space to that thought I feel fear like you would not believe possible. Believe me, you don't want to give that thought too much of your attention."

"Tom? I'm sorry, I was going to ask you about, about Ruth? What you said down there...."

"Ah Ruth, yeah."

Relief, a hand opening the dam gates for him; right question, right place, right time. Right person? He looks at her hard, her open face, feels the under-pulse of the journey, sees for a flashing instant that look in her eyes, Ortigia ... Ah nothing's for sure, he tells himself, nothing is certain, ah look, let it go, let it go, man....

"Well, look, OK. Like this. We didn't know she was sick, not as such. Did I tell you the Radio France gig only lasted a few years, no? Well she taught in the prisons for a while, some stories there, my God, and then, the, the last few years she was working with immigrant children; you know, literacy work, that sort of thing. Only, she started feeling less and less able for it. 'No energy', she used to say, 'I've no energy, Tom.' We thought it was the change, you know? She'd be on the web trying to ...

I suppose trying to diagnose herself. Not the kind of thing she'd talk to her friends about, and she didn't trust doctors. So, one day, coming back from a bit of work in London, I had an idea. We had this friend in Japan, a lovely, lovely man. A Professor, mad about Irish poetry and Irish music. You know, trad. Really knows his stuff; ah feck it I'm straying here, anyway, I rang him and said, he lived in Kyoto, I was thinking of bringing herself over to the Buddhist temples, that sort of thing. 'Oh', says he, 'perfect! Perfect, Tom san! I was wanting to come to Ireland again, why do we not simply swop our house, you and me, and you stay here?' Jesus, I nearly cried at the look on her face when I told her. Ah fuck it, I did, I cried, she was so happy. So that's what we did. We were two months in Kyoto, every day we'd go to one of the temples, sit around in the gardens, not exactly meditating, OK, not exactly just hanging out either. Kinda hard to describe. 'Soaking up the vibe', she used call it, half laughing and completely serious. It got so some of the monks started recognising us, but they gave us loads of space, you know? No questions. They might beckon us in for a bowl of tea now and then, they loved Ruth, I swear, they used to just beam at her. Whatever they saw. And for a while, she blossomed. I used to slag her that it was because everyone was the same height as her and she'd spent her life looking up at people. 'You were just finding life a pain in the neck', I'd say to her. And, she was better there, you know? For a long while, weeks on end.

"Only there came a time I got impatient, sarcastic like, you know, a bit cynical. Everything started to seem like, a scam? She sat me down, very quiet in herself by this, and she said: 'Tom', she said, 'listen to what I'm going to tell you. You have to see what's through and under and over and behind things. You have to pay *real* attention. Stop trying to be so smart you can't be fooled. Why are you always worrying about people putting one over on you?' And, I got it. I was all right again. I could see why the monks'd be beaming at her.

"Then one day, out of the blue, we were walking around the edge of a moss garden and she turned to me and said, 'Tom, let's go home. It's time to go home.' Well, OK, I thought, and I phoned our friend, Mutsuo, and he said, 'No bother, I'm thinking of heading up to Rann na Feirste for a while anyway'; the accent of him perfect, I swear, Rann na Feirste, and I thought, feck it, we're not short of a few bob, and I bought us two first-class tickets home. 'Jasus ye mad bastard', she said when I told her, but what with the bigger baggage allowance and the amount of paper, ink, silk and I don't know what else that she'd been buying, me egging her on of course, when I wasn't buying stuff for her, anyway she agreed that it made sense of a kind — though she knew full well it would have been cheaper of course just to pay the extra baggage charge and fly normal — anyway I, I kinda suspected … or maybe I just thought that after? No. I had an instinct.

"So, we're back in Dublin, what, two weeks, and I discover she's gone to the doctor. 'Tom', she says to me over breakfast, 'he wants me to go into the hospital for tests.' 'What kind of tests?' I asked her. You know how your blood goes cold when anyone mentions tests like that? 'Just tests', she said, and she wasn't a bit scared or anything, her that hated doctors, and hospitals even more. Just, thoughtful. I brought a book with me when we went in, but after we'd done all the paperwork she turned around to me and said, 'Tom, Tom', she said, 'why don't you go out for a walk, why don't you? Come back in a while when they have me all sorted, processed, whatever they fecking call it? Anyway, love, it's a lovely day out there, come back in a few hours.' And I kissed her, gave her a bit of a cuddle; I was, you know, doubtful, but Ruth had this amazing smile, she could light up a room she could, and she just smiled at me and said, 'Away off with you and let me have a bit of peace.' And I looked back when I was going out the door, she was talking away to this oul' wan, and she felt the look on the back of her neck, must have, and she turned around and gave me this long, slow smile. Ten times a day I'd fall in love with that woman, even when I felt like strangling her for the lighting bitch she could be when the humour was on her, ten times a day but never, never, Clare, as true as God is my judge, I never felt more in love with her than at that very exact moment. And I could read it in her eyes, plain and shining, that she felt the same.

"And I went out. And I had a coffee. And I wandered into town and ambled a bit, over towards Merrion Square and walked around in the gardens there, we loved the gardens there, and I went into the National Gallery for lunch and when I was thinking that's enough now, I better head back, I was waiting to cross at the lights on Clare Street and I got a call on the mobile. They'd like to talk to me. No, Ruth wasn't available to come to the phone just now. So I switched off the phone, calm as you like, then I stood in the road in front of a taxi and when he started swearing at me, I said cold, and he knew better than to say another word: emergency. And to the passenger I said, fifty euro, get out of the taxi for the love of God. A right sourfaced old bastard he looked, too, banker, solicitor, something like that, you know the way you can tell instantly, the lips pursed — and he jumped out and said, 'For God's sake man, I don't want your money, take the car, go on.' And he put his hand on my arm and just looked at me. So gentle. Jesus! 'Go on', he said. Unbelievable. And the taxi crashed through a red light and tore off into the traffic.

"And the driver said 'Hang on in there, pal, the missus is it?'

"'She's in a coma', the nurse said. 'To be honest, we don't know what happened.' In a coma. 'We can't let you in yet', the staff nurse said. 'Get a gun', I said, 'and a man with a very steady hand to use it, but in I'm going' — and in I went. It wasn't Ruth at all. It was very like her, but it wasn't Ruth. Like wax, her face was, I put my hand on her lovely face and she was cold, she was very cold. Tubes everywhere, machines beeping and binging, a tube up her nose, two drips in the one arm, I couldn't understand why two in the one arm, I kept worrying about that, how distracted I was. They kept coming in and looking at me but they were afraid of me, I could see it, they knew I would kill if I had to, I had that look on me, I knew full well I had. I grabbed this young intern: 'You', I said, I looked at his nametag, his coat bunched up in my fist: 'Herlihy', I said, he didn't like that I'd copped his name, 'get me a good man in here who knows what's going on or I'll find you and kill you. I will.' He believed me. 'Now!'

'Mr Harrington, Mr Harrington, this isn't helping, please, can we just step outside for a minute.' My age, smooth, oh so fucking smooth. 'The wrong man', I told him, straight up: 'you have the wrong man here, Mr whoever the fuck you are; I want to know what happened here, I want to know what you propose to do, I want to know exactly, but exactly what happened and what is going to happen to make it right.'

"Do.I.Make.Myself.Perfectly.Clear?

"Vocablulary, vocabulary and accent, you have to hit these bastards right away with the class thing, make them wonder just who you might be, what kind of trouble they might be heading for. Terrible, but true. And you say it loud and slow, so that he knows everyone can hear you.

"To be honest, I don't blame him for being terrified.

"You wouldn't believe, they got the Guards.

"They got the police to remove me.

"'Tommy Earley, the barrister, you probably know him? A good man, isn't he? I had him in there in half an hour and what he didn't tell them, what he didn't threaten them with. I was let back in. 'The Team' were doing all they could. 'The Team' were carrying out tests, oh comprehensive tests. 'The Team' would keep me fully informed. 'Who's in charge?' I kept asking them, doctors, nurses, anyone I could get to stop for a minute and talk to me. 'Who's in charge?' Oh 'The Team' this, 'The Team' that, evasions and fluttery talk and no answer, no answer. Then or ever, no answer could I get. All night I stayed there, and all the next day. They gave me a chair to sleep in. The tea ladies brought me food and you could see the nurses didn't like it but they said nothing and after a while they began to soften. A bit. Every now and then the, the specialist, Harney his name was, fat, sleek, pompous bastard, but scared of me now and right to be, right to be, I didn't know how much anger I had bottled up inside me, the years it must have been there, me not knowing ... he'd sort of sidle in but I'd confront him. 'I want to know', I'd say, and off we'd go again: 'The Team', 'The Team'....

"Oh she went hard, Clare, she went very hard. The second night. I knew it was coming, you know. Little things. The nurses beginning to give me small, guarded looks when they thought no one, I suppose the Ward Sister, could see them. They'd bring me cups of tea. They'd come in and plump up her pillows, adjust the tubes when they didn't need adjusting, that kind of thing. Oh, I knew, and they knew. Only nurses in and out now. Not even an intern.

"'Is she in pain?' I'd ask them, 'is she in pain?' Over and over. 'No', they said, brusque at first, what would I know, but softer and softer as the night went on, and then the Staff came in and she said, 'You should go on talking to her, Tom.' She called me Tom, and I nearly lost it then. She put a hand on my arm, just like the fella in the taxi, and I thought how do they do it? Night after night, week after week, how do they do it? And she went out. And she closed the door behind her. First time it had ever been closed.

"'I'd started talking to her, to Ruth, the first time they left me alone with her and I never stopped, I never stopped. Even when I was nodding off to sleep I'd be getting up and going in and chatting to her, I'd be holding one hand, and then the other. Anything that came into my head. Things we'd said, things we'd talked about, stories about places we'd been, things we'd seen. Anything that came into my head. Never a minute when I wasn't touching her; every now and then, very carefully, I'd lift her up off the bed and put my arms around her. Cold and hot at the same time. Face like grey wax and livid blotches of heat under her arms, under her small, lovely breasts. Oh I prayed and promised to everything, everyone, every God ever thought of, I said Hail Marys, I said sutras, God only knows what I said but all under my breath in case she could hear me and I'd panic her. Me, praying for her! Bad enough to be in a hospital! That would have rattled her, let me tell you, me praying.

"She went hard, and I don't know was it whatever was wrong with her or that she didn't want to go but she went hard. Rattling and wheezing in her chest. She'd rise up off the bed with the effort of breathing and there'd be a kind of gurgling and the first few times it happened I swear, I swear I thought she was going to open her eyes. I did. But she never opened her eyes. I had her hand in my hand and I had my other hand on her brow and no matter how sweaty she got, she'd get sweaty for a few minutes and then cool down again, I never took both hands off her. I'd mop her brow with my sleeve, a cloth, anything. I knew she was going over, I was doing my best to help her and I'd get terrible spasms of guilt, could hardly breathe myself, would she think I was wanting her to go over, would she get it into her head I wanted rid of her? Oh Jesus those were the worst moments, but then somewhere between midnight and five in the morning when she died, somewhere in there I *knew* she was going over. I just *knew*.

"So I had to help her, you see. So's she'd know this was real and then she'd be OK. The staff came and gave her a shot, just before the end. They know, too, do you see, the nurses. The death veterans. They can time it to the Nth. So the Staff opened this little plastic case, says 'Do you want to step out, Tom, for a minute?' and I give her credit, I looked at her and said, 'No, you go ahead', and she took out the syringe and put the tip of the needle through the seal and drew up whatever the dose is, for the pain, you see, there must have been pain then, and she looked at me again and I nodded and she drew up a little more. And she looked away from me then, and very tender she was, she found a vein and pressed down on the plunger, and dabbed the spot with cotton wool, and she still wasn't looking at me and she went out and she closed the door.

"And I looked at my Ruth, and I saw it come over her. Heart's ease. An end to struggle. The body come as far as it could on the long journey, the spirit easing away. Like, a flush of nothing. Ease. And that last time, that last breath, I was sure she'd open her eyes and smile the big, dazzling smile at me one last time as she went over but, no, no smile. I had my lips on her lips, and I was saying over and over: 'Wait for me, love? I'm here, love, I'm here. Wait for me, love. It's all right, everything is all right, you can let go, you can let go. I'm here, love. I'm always here, I'll always be here.' The same words, over and over, my breath, her breath, until there wasn't any breath at all and my own lovely Ruth … my own lovely Ruth … the colour back in her face again, like she'd look in our big bed of a morning after a good sleep, coming round; the nuzzling movements she'd make, her hands folded over and batting at me, oh I loved her hands; her body searching for mine in the bed, the small grunt as she'd nest in beside me, the sun coming in the window and any minute her eyes would open and she'd see me, and then she'd smile, that big, slow smile … and I'd melt … I'd just …melt.…"

Asleep. He just, fell asleep. Clare watching in wonder. Just, fell asleep. She felt a sudden stab of fear. She started forward, put her ear to his mouth. Felt the soft, slow puff of his breath. Relief. Relief.

Wind, the main slatting, uneasy, boom trying to shift, settling again. Going, she looks around, what, going, make a decision, Clare, west. It'll go west. Tom? Wrap him up in a minute. First, what, we have to tack of course. The whatsit, preventer? No, took that off.

Tommy Earley, ask him about Tommy Earley. Oh God, oh Jesus, poor, poor Tom. Check, OK, sleeping away.

Here it comes now, windshift. Put your back into it girl, is he waking? No. Right, centre main. Engine? No, noise, won't need it. OK, ready to bring staysail round, attagirl Clare, doing well here girl, hey, getting good at this, fuck! Sheet jammed, no it isn't, OK, before it starts flapping, here it comes, here it comes, now. Wheel over, ninety degrees now Clare, get her set first, then ease her back, that's it. Good girl yourself, there! Sheet, staysail sheet, knee to hold the wheel where it is, need to be a monkey, God, there. There. God but it shifts fast, must ask Tom, what if it had gone east, have to gybe, maybe not so easy? Charmed, we've been charmed here, never, what's the word, headed. Hardly ever.

"Nice, nicely done." What!

Tom, hand gentle on her hip, a pat. His hand falling away.

"You OK, Tom? Want to go down for a bit?" Meaning, you must be drained after that, are you in bits?

He shakes his head no, slow motion, dreamy and drowsy. Did well there, Clare. In good hands. In good hands. And, gone again.

Should I try to wake him, get him to the bunk? Ah don't be stupid, leave him be. Fleece blanket, that blue yoke, cushions, so on. Right. Swings down below, supple, catlike. Gathers things up again. Tucks him in, plumping cushions, checking his breath, small fussings, cool and crisp. "There." Hears herself, *there*.

Then, shaking, shaking, having to sit down. Shock, finally. The wash of it all coming over her, overwhelmed. No. Not overwhelmed; the black weight of his sorrow, such nightmare, all of that falling over her with the weight of, the weight of ... but not overwhelmed. No. Keeping composure but *feeling it*, feeling it all. For ... she can't tell for how long. As long as it takes, let it be, let it come. As long as it takes. And way down inside, a voice she can almost, almost hear, saying: good, Clare, be easy, that's it, good, good....

And ... well. The world goes on. The world goes on, she says, coming to; the world goes on and where, I wonder, is Majorca?

Tom? Sleeping, so peaceful, he can't be comfortable, can he, but peaceful, look at him there, look at him there, all right for now, he's all right for now. Check in a minute again.

Right, let's see. OK, this sets the rings out, let's try twenty-four miles. There! Ah would you look! I'm brilliant, I am. Bang on the button. The beam sweeping around and around — like a hospital monitor! Janey, there's a thought! Cat scan, something like that. Leaning in to the green screen, the ghostly glow. Tracing the outline, from nine o'clock to twelve, of the oncoming island. Would I be able to see it from the bow? If it was daylight, I mean? No, just on the edge of the range, but, what, about twenty-two to twenty-three miles, too far down over the curve I suppose. Look at that, though! Windshift. Just right, imagine. Magic. Carry us right over the top, handbrake turn, there, hang a left, down we go. Magic.

Down here, sitting back to take a look around, everything's fine. Everything, just so. Oh, the bunk, of course, change the bunk again. Laundry in Palma, mustn't forget. Tom!

Grand. Still sleeping. She listens to his breath, senses he's coming to. Sits back and waits.

"You awake now, Tom? Good man, good man. Here, have this glass of water. Careful now, there. OK my man, time to get you into your bunk."

Tom, very faintly amused, exaggerating his feebleness; letting her feel he's aware, druggy, near spent, is happy to be taken care of.

She tucks him up, she takes his face in her hands. "Jesus, Tom, that was a tough deal, eh? How did you get through it? How can you bear it? How did you do that?" Not needing an answer, not wanting an answer, she can't tell. She lays his head on the pillow. He closes his eyes.

She's climbing back up when he says: "Clare?" She freezes, doesn't turn.

"Clare, I didn't know, didn't know I was going to ... but I'm glad I did. I had to tell it, couldn't tell anyone, you know? All bottled up, God it came out in a rush, though. I'm sorry if that was hard. But, thanks. Thank you."

Tears starting, she won't allow them. She's going to go on up, but she backs down the stairs, she walks across, squats on her heels. She looks at him levelly, and she says: "Tom, Tom, we made a deal, remember? A compact. A long time ago, Tom, a long time ago. So, we trust it. Yeah? Isn't that it, Tom? The deal? Trust?"

He smiles up at her. He says, "Yes, dear. You're right of course. You be all right up there?" "I will", she says, "I will." Then: "Janey! I forgot to report. Majorca ahead and to port, we'll be clearing north of it while you're asleep. OK? That OK?" He squeezes her hand: "That's fine, Clare, fine. You sail the boat." He goes to sleep.

30

"Tom, you mind if I ask you a question?" Her small teeth nibbling the last of the melon off the rind.

""You always do that?"

"What, ask questions?"

"Not what I meant, I mean gnaw things, the way you do. You do it with bones, too. Nibble, nibble, nibble."

"That annoy you?"

"No, not at all, just curious."

"Used to annoy the hell out of Sandra, for some reason. Funny enough, Rory never minded. You'd think Sandra, her and her cookouts, she loved the American word, cookouts … no, what I was going to ask you was…"

"…Oh Mother of God, this isn't going to be a cosmic question now, Clare, is it? Because I'm not…"

"…Up for it, I know, I know. See, Tom, if you'd only let me…"

"…Get on with it, I know, I know. So, what's the question?"

"Do you know, you can be one very annoying man, do you know that?"

"Is that the question?"

"Jesus Christ! Will you … Oh. Oh very funny, Tom, very funny. OK, all right, you got me. Very funny."

"Go on, do the Princess sulk, will you? Ah go on."

"The what? The what?"

Uh-oh. Step away from the car, Sir. Hands where I can see 'em. Tom's survival instinct cutting in. So, "All right, I'll stop, I've stopped, see? So, what's the question?"

"Why are we here?"

"Ah Jesus, you promised!"

"Here, Tom, here on the north bloody coast of Majorca. Which, as you can see if you follow my pointing finger, is over there. You see it, Tom?"

"'Deed an I do, your Honour, and why wouldn't I, and it there crawlin' along beside us this past four hours for all the world to see, you'd think it had nothin' better to be doin' only crawlin', crawlin', like...."

"Tom Harrington, I swear, I'll swing for you, so help me."

How do we do this, each of them is thinking, how do we do this?

The shadow coming over Tom's face, then; coming, and as quickly going. Clare's quick frown of concern. Who we are, Tom says to himself, it's who we are. And Clare thinks, how am I able for this? But she knows she is, she knows.

"Tom, why didn't we just cut in from the south? Shorter, for one thing."

"Ah! A surprise."

"What? A surprise how? What surprise?"

He makes her wait, then says: "You'll just have to wait and see, won't you?" And ducks. Just in time.

Clare stalks past him, follows the cushion down below. This, she announces, is a bona fide huff. A sulk, if you will. You hear me, Tom?

"No."

Shaking her head, chuckling, she falls sound asleep.

Hours later, he tacks the boat; smoothly and quietly. The westerly's a bit stronger than it had been, and as *Lon Dubh* heels over he hears a muffled crash from below. Oh fuck, he thinks, I'm in for it now.

"Tom", she says sweetly, "you tacked."

"I did", he says.

"And the starboard side came up, Tom?"

"I suppose it did."

"And I fell out, Tom."

"Are you, eh, bruised? Hurt?"

Wait for it, he thinks, wait....

"Nah. I'm fine. Don't worry about it. I'm starving, you? Be up in a tick."

Gone. What do you make of that? Some woman. I thought I was dead there.

Late afternoon. Backs to the guardrail, sun on their backs, feet braced against the coachroof.

"Tom, last night, Ruth dying … I have to say this, Tom."

"Go on, it's OK, I'm OK with it, what is it?"

"It sounds like serious negligence, Tom."

"Tommy Earley's on it. A slow business, you know that. Won't bring her back, I know that, but you can't let something like that go. You know what, Clare? Makes no difference to me now. She's gone — and soon I'll be gone, too."

Flat. Declarative. Plain as that. What can you say to that, Clare asks herself. Nothing. Nothing at all.

"Come on", he says, "we're here."

A notch in the cliffs to port.

"OK, wind's not going to help. Best if we get the sails in."

Engine on. She winds in the jenny, coils and stows the sheets. He drops the staysail, unshackles the halyard (halyard, he tells himself, meant to check that, remember to do that first chance), unhanks the sail, bags it. Lashes the bag to the starboard guardrail. Right. He drops the main, flaking the folds neatly on the boom. Clare hands him the sail ties, one at a time. He goes back, says: "Up into the bow with you."

God she looks good up there, he thinks, engaging gear, pointing the bows towards the cove opening before them. Imagine some young fellow in there seeing us come in. She'd take the eye out of him, she would. Tenderness and, is it pride he's feeling here? Wonderingly: it is, it is indeed. How strange. Or, indeed, some oul' fella. The man himself, for instance. Visitation! Manifestation!

About here should do, he thinks, looking back into the wind thoughtfully, coasting off a bit to one side. Here. No need to tell her what to do, he admires; she's freeing the anchor, stepping off to one side, clear of where the chain will run. "Stand by!" he calls, and lets it go, letting her stern swing towards the land. Enough, he brakes the windlass, gives it a bit of astern to dig the hook in. "OK!" he calls, "lash it off there. That should do." Engine off. Settling, bows into the wind.

Low cliffs, she sees, some kind of building there to the right, turning to look landwards. Ridge there, God look at that. Long, flat-topped mountain beyond that, high, really high. Big presence there, she thinks. Calls, "Tom?"

"Deya", he says, "up there behind the ridge. Place called Deya."

That's a strange look, he thinks. That's a very strange look.

"Deya", she says, and he's lost her, she's away in herself. What's this, he asks himself, what's this now?

"Sandra", she says finally, sitting down on the deck, crosslegged, staring away inland. Away from him. He sits down behind her, giving her space, close enough that she won't have to strain if she wants to talk to him. "She always wanted to come here. She'd read it over and over, like her bible. You know?" He nods. Graves, *The White Goddess*. "She'd have it down on the table in the dining room, she'd have it up by her bed, it was like the book was following her around like, like a dog or a cat. Didn't like cats, Mam, not as much as dogs anyway. In Arizona, you'd think I wouldn't remember but I do, in the glove compartment of the pick-up. On the porch. Everywhere she went. I remember she used to trance off in the tepee, reading the same passages over and over, skipping bits, turning back to read bits."

She paused.

He said: "Lot of people like that, back in the day. Women more than men, I suppose, but a lot of men, too...."

"So, eventually I read it. There's a lot in it, I can see that. Some of it gibberish, I used to think, some of it would, I don't know how to put it, wake you up a bit? You'd find yourself almost, almost ... so, anyway. There I am, eighteen, all geared up for the law, Miss Rational Mind, and one day she's going on and on about women's mysteries yadda yadda yadda, and I don't know what we'd been fighting about that day, anyway, I blew up on her. The whole nine yards. 'Man does, woman is.' 'Is that right?' I said. 'So, what exactly does that mean? Women can't do things? Women shouldn't *do* things? Mother,' I said, you can imagine how infuriating I was, 'Mother', I said, 'there is no fucking divine essence of the fucking feminine, do you get me? That' — Jesus, I can't believe I was such a prig — 'that', I said, 'is what we call out here in the real world a very fucking handy patriarchal construction. Do you get me, Ma?' Ah, Tom! 'Out here in the real world?' I was, eighteen? 'The real world'? Ah, here....

"'You stick a woman up on a pedestal, Ma, you stick a woman up on a pedestal and you worship her as the fountain of all knowledge and wisdom and do you know what you have, Ma? Do you know what you have? A fucking statue, Ma. A statue.'

"I'd have done better to slap her across the face. I didn't know what I was doing, I swear I didn't know. But, I struck home. Too deep, too far in.

"You think she struck back at me, Tom? Lashed out? — And she was a good street fighter, Tom, no holds barred when the temper was up? No. She just got up from the kitchen table, she just looked at me and walked past me. Out into the hall. Up the stairs. Up into her room. Closed the door. I was in floods, I didn't know why, not then, not for a long time after, but I knew I had done something terribly, terribly wrong. Something that couldn't be taken back."

She fell silent. She sat there, looking away up at the mountain. She turned to look at him.

"Tom, Tom what's wrong? You're as white as a ghost. Tom?"

He got to his feet, not a word, waving a hand at her as he went back; stay where you are, the gesture said, stay where you are for a while.

He dug the inflatable dinghy out of its locker; he set up the electric pump and filled the tubes. When she went to get up to lend a hand, he waved her away. He got the dinghy over the side, led it amidships, tied it off. Never once looked at her. He won't manage the outboard on his own, Clare thought; I'd better … but he brought the oars, more like paddles really, out of the locker and lowered them carefully into the dinghy. He sat down on deck, bare feet just about touching the dinghy dancing beneath him — to catch his breath, I'm sure of it, Clare thought, anxious now with concern; but he sat there, staring away to the west, unmoving. Clare watching him sometimes, sometimes looking away inland to where olives swayed in the red earth between the low bluff and the ridge, to where washes of light caught the tall face of the mountain behind.

31

"Clare?" Soft, whatever storm was in him is gone through. "Here, pet. Coffee?"

Grateful. So grateful — and then resenting being ... made to feel grateful, how dare ... and catching herself at that.

"Thanks."

Stand up, Clare. Look him in the eye. He sighs.

"It's complicated, come back and sit down with me."

Cushions piled against the aft face of the coachroof. Separate nests, close enough for talk.

"It's complicated, see. Bear with me. First thing, Ruth used to talk about maybe visiting here, but somehow she ... we never got around to it. The poems, you see, she loved the poems. Intrigued to see where so many were written. Curious man, Graves. Head wrecked in the War, you probably know this. Retreated here from a marriage went wrong, under the thumb of ... some say so anyway, how can we tell these things, really? Never went home. Or, found home here, whichever you please. Edwardian officer class gentleman, what would he have to do with us, you might think. But heads, hippies, whatever you call us, whatever we were back then, there was some ... connection. We got some connection from Graves. Doesn't matter what you call it. I'll come back to this in a minute.

"Ruth loved the poetry, as I say. Used to say you could live in the poems, they made perfect *places*, she used to say. I didn't understand her for a while, and then one day I did. You can go *in*, you see? You see what I'm saying? I mean, really, go *in*. Be there. In the, the *there* of the poem. And the *when*, the whatever time is in the poem. Well, most of 'em. Not all. So, I always had it in mind to bring her here, but somehow we didn't get around to it. So, back there, when you were ... well, last night, Ruth ... being here, it all got a bit much."

She's so relieved she wants to burst in on him and say … but he stops her.

"Wait, you're OK, there's more, there's more. That's not what came over me, not just that. What you did to your mother? Do you understand what you did there? Do you understand it now? You don't scorn what's sacred to people, Clare. Not up to you to do that. You don't agree with them, you think they believe in nonsense? Fine. Either keep it to yourself or you only discuss it when they agree to discuss it. You're not the final authority, on anything. Understand? I'm not being hard on you now, just saying. OK?

"See, I did something like you did once. Oh she had the bible, too, all the women I knew, we knew, did. But that's not it. You see — I'm talking about the woman I slapped? You remember? It's not what I said, I mean it's not something I said to her, you understand? I broke her luck. Her fate. I lost my belief in her, well that's how she put it. Here she was, not easy, you have to understand how hard it was then, trying to be independent, trying to establish her right to be herself. To make her own choices. Right? That's one thing. But, whether it was in the air or God knows what the reason was, a lot of young women then were trying to find, I don't know, I don't know how to put this — a mandate? That make sense to you? *Permission* from — something in the world, something in the culture, in history, politics, myth, who knows the fuck what?! Sorry, I get so frustrated with myself. And there were, like, sacred texts, right? Some books were treated as sacred texts. *The Golden Notebook*. Castaneda. *The Politics of Experience* — boy that one fucked up a lot of people — ah shit, your Ma probably had the whole library by the sound of her, you know what I'm talking about, right?

"So: Cass, her name was Cass, she had it in her mind that there was what she always called, 'Capital letters', 'The Path.' Right? And, we were on a path, her and me. New Man, New Woman. The capital letters, you see? Remember I told you, the night I fell into her eyes, how we felt that we were, I dunno, carried off *elsewhere*? That's where we'd go, you see, if we stuck to 'The Path.' Well, the way she looked at it, when I came home that time in London, and found her there and I slapped her and she forgave me, I forgave her, all that didn't matter, you see, not the slap. As such. Not the jealousy, as such. Not her fucking that weedy little weasel. Didn't matter. Somehow, between us, somehow we'd broken whatever held us on 'The

Path.' I should have trusted her, you see? I still don't know how I'm supposed to have done that. What, I was supposed to have known not to come home until she'd finished demonstrating her independence by fucking weasel boy? I wasn't cosmically in tune enough or what? Ah I'm being too hard, too hard. So, that was that. A favourite saying of the time, 'No blame.' The *I Ching*. Seems like, when you fall off 'The Path', there's no going back.

"I was, what, twenty-three? She was a year older. You have to factor that in here. What did we know? And, what did we think we were doing? You can mock all you want at what you call hippy shit, Clare, but in our own awkward way we were trying to find a better way of living the life, you know? That's all we were doing, trying to find a better way of living the life. Making all the mistakes in the world, but trying, God but we were trying our best.

"So, on and off down the years I'd think about her, Cass. She blew away into the world and I never heard from her again, never heard of her again. I wish her well, wherever she is. I hope life's been good to her. We meant each other no harm, we tried to be good to each other, you know? Life moves on, we find what's for us, we have to be grateful for what was kindness in our lives, yeah?

"Like, with Ruth? I figured that, good or bad, wherever she'd been, whoever she'd been with, all that went into making her who she was when she met me, when I met her. Wouldn't you have to be grateful for that? For any kindness that might have helped shape the person you love?

"And here we are in Deya. It's a beautiful place, you know? Sailed in here once, made me sorrier when I'd think about it after that I never got round to bringing Ruth here. I mean, sorrier than if I hadn't been here, if you follow me. She'd have loved it."

He stands, yawns, stretches. Big animal, sun in his bones, near the end of the day. Content.

"Big lot of stories coming out, eh, Clare? I hope to God I'm not boring you? Old fart with his life story, hah? I just wanted you to know it was nothing got to do with you, back there earlier?

"Ah sure I suppose it's because I'm dying, hah? Getting the oul' life story straight before the end. That's that out of the way, anyway.

"What do you say we take a run ashore, eh? Plenty of light left yet, big moon tonight if we stay up in the village and have some dinner, no bother getting back. What do you say? Clare?"

Looking back and down at her stricken face. The hair standing on the back of his neck. Her stricken face. Her black, electric hair. Her blue electric eyes. Her face so pale. Oh fuck, he thinks, what the fuck have I done now? What's this about? Some terrible ghost in her stone face.

Exhausted! That's it, what's wrong with me! Up all night, no more than a few catnaps! The poor child, and having to listen to me vomit up all that fucking grief, and stuck on a boat with a fella who's just told her he's fucking dying, what are you like, Tom? Where's your fucking head!

"Go down, Clare", he says, gentle, sitting on his heels so she doesn't have to look up at him, "go on down and have a bit of a sleep. We can go ashore later. It's OK, you poor thing, you must be exhausted. I'm sorry for exhausting you. Come on, then, I'll help you down."

She pulls away roughly, coming to her feet so fast he snaps back so's her head doesn't bang into his. Overbalances, rights himself. Staring up at her. Wild, my God she looks — wild.

"Stay there, Tom. Stay where you are. Don't move. I'll be back. Just, stay there."

No time to think now, don't stop to think, Clare, just do it. Here we go. Go with the flow. How right you were, Mam, go with the flow is right, fuck you and the flow, ah sorry, sorry, I don't know what I'm saying.

"Sit down, Tom." She's back on deck now. "Sit down there now." Commanding. "You'll think whatever you think, Tom. You'll do what's right, you'll do the right thing, Tom I'm sure of it."

Breathing heavily, staring straight down into his eyes, straight down through him. Pinning him there. Tom, bewildered.

"You'll think whatever you think, Tom. Up to you. Up to you. Here."

In her hands all this time, Tom knowing it's there, unwilling to take his eyes off hers, knowing it's there. He takes it in his hands, not looking yet. Feels the heft of it. Cardboard, large folder, bound with some kind of tape. Legal documents, he thinks wildly, but ... Still looking at her.

Whatever she's looking for in his eyes, she finds it. She turns, she goes back down.

Cardboard it is, a folder right enough. Bulky. Yes, ribbons, faded and worn, tied in a bow. Tug the short end, loosens, bow comes undone. Staring down through the hatch after her, can't see her, where has she ... forecabin. Door closed. So.

He scoots along the seat until he's in the corner of the cockpit, the sun over his shoulder. Paper, big wad of paper, old and dry. Near-brittle. Smell of ... must, is it? Mustiness? And now he looks, riffling the pages.

Newspaper cuttings, all newspaper cuttings. The top one dated, let's see, but before he can check the date he sees, unfolding the dry sheet, the photograph of himself. Not just him, of him and the band. FATE. Would you look at us, he thinks, startled, but what? He grips the pile of cuttings in his left hand, with his right he riffles the pages, so many pages, all newspaper cuttings sure enough. Here and there as the pages fan past his startled eyes he sees photographs: himself in fast forward, hair longer and shorter, longer and shorter, beard coming and going. Slow down, he tells himself. Slow down. Page by page, the years building up, the pile so bulky. Gigs, interviews, reviews, news items. Sometimes no more than his name, buried deep in an article, underlined neatly; photographs — Rory Gallagher's funeral, the second Carnsore Festival, with Sinéad on Grafton Street, shielding their faces from the fucker with the camera, he remembers it clearly, some rag trying to stir it up. Himself and Christy both wearing headphones, in a studio it looks like, hamming it up for the camera. On and on, so many faces, not reading the words yet, he's mostly looking at photos, some he's forgotten, some are still friends. For a mad second or two he thinks it's a Special Branch file, but sure Jasus why would they bother, all these years, but she's a lawyer, isn't she? Who knows what the fuck ... nah, keep going. OK, try to make sense of this. The first is, he looks again now, from, let's see, right enough, 1981. The last, four years ago. The big benefit in the park. What does the caption say? Oh I remember this, Ruth nearly fell over laughing: 'Still cool at fifty.' 'Still cool', she hooted, him squinting through readers at a gardening catalogue, buttering her toast for her. 'Still cool!'

Jesus Christ, Clare, he thinks, what are you ... what the ... He's confused, stunned; a little, yes, a little frightened. He looks up, looks around him, wondering: How did we get here? We. Clare. He doesn't know what to think, his mind such a welter of confusion that something inside goes: Stop. Just, stop. Slow down here. Just, stop. Still riffling the pages, transfixed now and then, people, places, events he remembers, things he has long forgotten pressing forward, one thing elbowing another, so eager for attention; so much of his life ... and the small voice going: Stop. Just stop. Stop. Until eventually, almost mutinously, he agrees with himself that he hears himself and … everything stops.

He closes his eyes, he listens. The hull creaking as it lifts and falls in the gentle swell. That short, grinding noise the chain makes over the bow roller as she swings to her anchor. A creak from the mast, another. A bird calls away to his left, another answers. Far up the valley, a bus grinding slowly downhill, growl of the dropping gears, a slight grating screech from the brakes. He quietens. His breathing, he hears his breathing, he concentrates on his breathing and he feels it slow, he feels it slow down and deepen, feels it slow until everything is calm, everything is quiet, everything is calm. He stops. He opens his eyes.

Dark down below, the cabin a cave of dark. Clare down there. Let her take her time? Call her out? Call down to her? Go down yourself, he decides, go down yourself and be calm now, be calm as you can.

Seeing what was in her eyes as she handed him this … this fucking dossier! A fucking dossier! Tom, Tom, the voice again, his own voice, his own. Tom, be calm. Tom! Peremptory: Don't be acting the fucking maggot! Oh. Right. Right, so.

Not commanding, not angry, got that wrong, Tom, frightened. So frightened. Of what, though? What's she frightened of? Of him? Why would she be frightened of him? Sure aren't I … you can be frightening, Tom, you can. You know you can. And sure, Tom, what does it matter? Nobody's died here, Tom. This very strange girl who you think you've got to know has a file of cuttings about you. So? Big deal in Dodge City, eh? Only a mystery, right? Aren't you curious? Relax now. Steady. Steady.

Looking at his hands, embarrassed by them. Unclenching them, one at a time, shifting the … file from one hand to the other.

He goes down. He lays the folder on the saloon table, is going to tie it up again, doesn't. He takes a breath, he knocks on the forecabin door. He says, low but clear: "Clare, I've left your papers on the table in here. I'm going back up to watch the sun going down, I think I'll have a beer. You're welcome to… in your own time, Clare. In your own time."

No answer. He has no idea what's going on here. He feels very peaceful. He's OK with whatever it is. He's a bit surprised by himself, but not very. He stands there a moment longer, begins to be worried she might feel threatened by this. Him looming outside the door. He goes back up and out.

He's on the afterdeck when she comes up, hands in his pockets, staring away up there where he knows the Pyrenees come down to the sea at Collioure; on across France, across Biscay, all the way up past Land's End, into the Irish sea. Home.

"Tom, Tom you forgot to get yourself that beer. Tom, here. I didn't hear you opening the fridge, you see. So I thought, like, you'd maybe forgotten it. Would you, would you like a beer, Tom?"

What he hears in her voice, he thinks will break his heart. Steady now, Tom, steady. And then he turns round; Clare, it's only Clare after all; if you'd never, if she'd never, still be Clare. He sits down, he pats the seat beside him. He takes the beer from her, already popped he notices in a distracted kind of way, oh still Clare; they knock their cans together, they look at each other. She sighs, she turns away, but she sits in close beside him. Don't make him lonely, she's thinking. Or worried for you.

"Cass, Tom, you knew her as Cass. To me she's Sandra. My Mam, you see. Her file. You probably think I'm some kind of stalker; no, that down there is her file. No, that's the lawyer in me, not her *file*, Tom. That's too heavy altogether. Just her scrapbook."

Waiting. Letting it sink in. She's thought this through: Tell him straight, blunt, let him absorb it, give him the time. If you tell him at all. Over and over she's thought about this. Had almost decided to let it go, and then, of all places, he lands them into Deya. Well, damn it, you can call it coincidence if you like but … I should be shaking, the drama! And, isn't that odd, no drama. Why so? He's very quiet.

Tom says: "Cass."

He doesn't say anything for a while. He says: "And you're her daughter." Staring at her, the last of the light. She turns her face full-on to him. "I am. You mightn't think it, but I look very like her. You don't see her in me? No? I'll show you a photo of her in a minute, if you want; from towards the end … from a few years ago. You'll see. Can't escape it, Tom, every child looks like their parents. You don't see a resemblance, Tom?"

"Cass."

"She was still beautiful, Tom. Still beautiful. She had her hair cut short, lines on her face, Tom; living, you know? Time. Still beautiful. She'd talk about you to me, I don't think she talked about you to anyone else. And only from time to time. You have to understand, it wasn't some mad obsession, don't go thinking that about her."

And appearing for the defence … he thinks, sardonic — and is instantly ashamed of himself. What's wrong with you, man?

"When we came back to Ireland, excuse me, when she came back to Ireland with me, that's when she started it. She told me she just saw this piece in the paper and thought, oh there you are. I remember her saying that: more like, 'Oh. There you are.' Something funny about how she said it, telling me, but sure I always thought she was odd anyway. That first piece, about your first band. I saw her looking at it one morning out in the yard. It became a kind of game with us when I was about nine or ten. We'd look in the papers for things about you. On and off. When the humour would take us. This might go on for a week, then we'd get distracted, she'd be trying to school a yearling, I'd be climbing trees with the O'Leary twins, whatever; just, you know, getting on with life. Then maybe one or the other of us would spot something and we'd go at it again for a week or two."

"But…"

"…Sssh, Tom, let me tell it will you? Please? So. Just a game, Mummy knows someone who's in the papers often. No one we knew was ever in the papers, Tom. Except for weddings and funerals, and that wasn't the same thing at all.

"Then I noticed we were meant to keep the game a secret from Rory. From everyone. I was, what, thirteen? Oh bloody hell, I thought, the Ma has a secret pash on this fella, Jasus! How embarrassing! I was learning to swear, you see. Maybe a bit precocious, too, to be honest. Don't laugh at me, Tom, please, not now."

"Come on", he said, "it's getting cold up here. We'll go down and light the lamp, make some tea, coffee, something warming, OK? Come on."

Taking her by the hand. Half-expecting to be rebuffed.

32

He lit the lamp. He put the kettle on. He made tea. Clare following his every movement with her eyes. He's turning from the sink, a slight swell coming in under the boat, buzz of an outboard, coming in, he judges, when ... something ... something he's missed, something ... Oh. Oh Holy Mother of God, surely ... and he hears it, he thinks he hears it, the giveaway note, the faintest hint of ... what? Yearning? Pleading? — 'you don't see any resemblance, Tom?'

Chill on the neck. Chill in the air. She's clapping her hands, slowly, softly. Applauding? Being what now, sarcastic?

"Slow, Tom, you're a bit slow but you get there. You get there."

"You", he says, "Clare, I swear, you make the hairs stand up on the back of my neck. You're...."

"Something else?"

"Not a very good time to be sarcastic, Clare. Not what I was going to say at all."

She recoils. Stares at him.

"Clare? Clare? I'm sorry, I'm so sorry, I just misunderstood, I got it wrong, OK, I'm a bit confused here. Please, Clare?"

She shakes her head. "Tom, I don't know if this makes things worse or better for you but you're still getting it wrong. Calm down a minute, I'm not made of glass, all right? We're not very good at this, are we? I wasn't being sarcastic, you don't need to be so, so abject? Is that the word? Abject. I shouldn't have said you're a bit slow. Trigger words, Donal calls them. Words that set people off, even when they're trying to be calm. Or tone of voice ... would you listen to me?! Sit down, Tom. Let's take another run at this, OK? Sit down won't you? Please? You were going to say something? No?"

Tom just can't get words out. He shakes his head, helpless. Too many shifts of mood, time pushing forward and backward, too much of … everything.

"OK, here's where we go back to, OK? You're standing there at the sink and, what? I'll say it for you, will I? You're thinking, she thinks I'm her father. Am I right, Tom? You have to help me here, Tom. I know, gawp once at me for yes, twice for no. Can you do that, Tom? Gawp?"

He can't help it, he can't help laughing. Nerves, maybe. Another part of him, appalled, asking: Christ, how did she take charge all of a sudden?

"Good, Tom, that's a very good reaction, we're making progress here" — and she sucker punches him. ✓

"You're not. You're not my father, so what's all the fucking fuss about, eh? You know what's confusing about you, Tom? One minute you get it, the next minute you don't. You in or out, Tom?"

Pushing him here. Sparks of irritation coming off her now.

"You get all these things right, I swear to fuck it's uncanny sometimes, and then you get stupid. Up there, right? For example? Some part of you got it, way back there, when I was talking about Sandra, Cass, fuck it, my Mam, all right? And you *knew* it was the same person, you *knew* it, but you wouldn't let it in. You *knew* she thought you broke her luck. You *knew* from the minute you saw me there was something up. Think back, Tom, this whole trip, right? How many times did I just float it past you, and you *saw* it, but you wouldn't let it in. You knew, Tom. You just wouldn't let yourself let it in. And on the other hand, I don't know how many times since we left Ortigia you absolutely floored me. I mean, you talk about me making your hair stand on end? *Your* hair? If mine was still long I'd be looking like fucking Medusa plugged into the fucking mains!"

"Clare?"

"What?!"

"Language, dear, language."

"Very funny. She was as bad."

"About language?"

"You're joking, right? She had a mouth on her like a dealer robbed at a horse fair."

"A what? Where do you get…"

"…Fuck it, she was as bad as you are at not knowing what she already knew! What am I saying here that you don't understand? Just — shut up and never mind, all right? We're trying to sort out why you're so smart and at the same time so stupid."

"Clare? Talk to me, OK? Seriously. Talk to me. Enough now, enough of the word games, the cleveralities."

"You think I don't know I do this? The lightning repartee? The little verbal dances, parry, thrust, tense changes, mood changes? You think I don't know I do this? Tom, I've been doing this all my life, this is how I keep myself safe, Tom, you see? You do, of course you do. It's not safe if people know that you see things, that you *get* things, right? They end up hating you and not having any idea why. Fearing you, Tom, and not knowing that they do. That poor fucking idiot I lived with, after college? See what it did to him? See why I stayed away from people after that? So let's be serious, Tom, all right? What do you want to talk about, Tom, eh? What do you want from me?"

"How about I want to sort out smart from stupid? How would that be, for a start? How about I ask you questions and you give me answers? How about that, Clare?"

She folds her arms. "Fire away", she says — and under her breath, "for all the good that'll do you."

"So, Ortigia. Start with that."

"I knew you'd fetch in there, sooner or later. Dublin's a small town, Tom. I wanted to get in touch with you, after she died, Mam, but I was in no big hurry. Yes, I did think you might be my father. I don't have a big father thing, Tom, let's be straight. You mightn't believe me, most people wouldn't, but Mam was Mam, boyfriends came and went, Rory was, just Rory, her business, not mine. I didn't need a father, I didn't want a father. But, you had an effect on her life. Right to the end. You were a presence. I wanted to find out what you were like."

"You could have done that in Dublin?"

"The wagging tongues, Tom. Nobody's business but my own. I hate people knowing anything about me. I hate it. And, I needed to be away for a while, think about Donal. I'm going to give it a go, by the way. Just a chance remark, that's the funny thing. Your name came up, in the library. Somebody said, 'I hear he's gone down to bring that boat of his home.' That's all. But you see, the scrapbook, Tom. Mentioned how you have a boat blah blah blah. Mentioned Lefkas. I called a lawyer there, marine lawyer, you might even know him, does boat registrations, that sort of thing. No? Anyway, rang him, spun him a yarn, got your whole bloody itinerary. All's I can say, it must be a mighty town for gossip.

"The web, Tom. Amazingly useful thing. You come down out of the Ionian, you're heading for Ireland, how many places are there you can call into for supplies, water, fuel? Not that many, right? So, I knew when you'd left Lefkas, figured out where you might call in, every day I'd ring the harbour office, marine police, whatever, asking after you. Different places. So, I struck lucky, right? Flew down to Catania, on to Siracusa etc. etc. Next question."

"You were planning to con your way onto the boat? For the trip?"

"Are you mad or stupid? Why would I want to do that? No, just … ah never mind, maybe I didn't know what I was going to do, OK? Maybe I just wanted you to know about Mam, how she.… And then, you looked at me. I felt it. What happened after that.…"

"And all this time, this trip, when were you planning to tell me?"

"Maybe never, I wasn't *planning*, oh Jesus, Tom, think about this, would you? Please? Look, I'm not being cruel, OK, I swear I'm not trying to be hurtful, but would you do something for me? Would you think back, Tom, I swear I hope this isn't painful, would you think back a minute to something you told me Ruth was always saying to you? It hit me like a train. I've a good memory, Tom, listen. She said: 'You have to see what's through and under and over and behind things. You have to pay *real* attention. Stop trying to be so smart you can't be fooled.' Isn't that what she said?"

Tom shaken, says "Yes, that's what she said."

'And it's all right, me quoting her? You're not offended?"

"No, I'm not offended."

"So, Tom, we can talk forever about all this stuff, but why? Why would we? Getting on the boat, right? The way we started off, I stopped caring about whether you were my father or not. No, that's not right, I was caring more about other things, different things. *And so were you*, only right now you can't remember. And sure I knew before we got to Malta you weren't my father anyway."

"You what? How…?"

"Tom, I'm a nosy bitch. You know this. Your blood group, Tom. You've one of those medallion things in the drawer there with your blood group on it. You know, Tom, you're meant to wear those things on a chain round your neck or something, not much use to you there in the drawer."

Suddenly, she's fed up to the back teeth of this. She sits straight up, her hands in front of her, fist nested inside palm.

"Tom, listen to me, haven't you had enough of this kind of — how much time do we have, Tom, how much time do we have? Look at me, Tom, don't say anything now. Enough, enough. Just, look at me. Look at my eyes, Tom. Trust me. Look in my eyes, Tom."

Thinking, dear Mother of God I hope I'm doing this right now, I hope I'm doing the right thing.

Thinking, why don't people do this, that's what Mam used to say, it's the strangest trip of all, she'd say, and it's free. And, nobody does it.

Just, with someone you really trust, and that's the only thing, you have to trust them, just — sit there and look into their eyes. For as long as it takes.

You find yourself looking first at one eye, then at the other. Looking *at*, coming back to him now. First it's looking at, so hard to focus on both eyes at once, takes time, it's distracting; her skittering around inside there, behind one eye, behind the other, having to slow down herself, no easier for one than for the other; you bring both eyes into your gaze, and then — you're in.

Tom sees: A stage, a woman dancing by herself. No, a woman dancing with herself, dipping and swaying, airy and grave; the stage all in darkness, she moves in a pool of light. Ruth and, somehow, not Ruth but that's OK. Dancing him out … something he almost knows. In a full, satisfying silence. To a music she hears but he doesn't need to hear. He registers this, that he doesn't need to hear the music. She stops, just so. Looking away from him, to one side. Such grace, her walk so matter-of-fact. On the edge of the pool of light, a table. On the table, a box. She puts her hand on the box. Oh Ruth, my love, your hand … she tips the lid open as she steps away. One movement, the other, the lid fully up as her foot lands on the floor. Tom looks in the box. A stage, a woman dancing by herself. No, a woman dancing with herself, dipping and swaying, airy and grave; the stage all in darkness, she moves in a pool of light.…

Clare sees: A road climbing up and away from her, steeply, bending to the right. Hawthorn and honeysuckle, the deep hedges on either side, the ridge ahead bright, the fork in the road just before the ridge. A frieze of ash, birch, rowan along the dipping ridge. Sandra in the apex of the fork, her bright face towards her, that long, brown, embroidered dress, that turquoise and silver necklace. Her elbows tucked tight to her ribs, her palms upraised. Her long hair flowing, buoyant, floating in the no-breeze. When she sees that Clare sees her, she smiles. Oh God, that enigmatic smile … she turns away, she walks away taking both roads at once. Not two Sandras, Clare understands this, checks with herself that she understands this. Not two Sandras. One Sandra, *Cass*, two roads, each climbing up and away, steeply, bending to the right. Hawthorn and honeysuckle.…

Breathing so deeply, the heart rate slowed down so far, it takes time to come back. They take their time, they have all the time in the world. Tom has to lie down now, worn out; the pain at the edges, beginning to creep in. Clare is exhausted, drained. Weary and slow, they drag themselves to their separate beds, boat on an even keel, neither bunk favoured over the other. Nothing to think about, nothing to watch out for. Sleep, sleep.…

Pain's back, he thinks, waking. Hours later, the body clock knows. Well fuck that for a game of soldiers. Get up, fumble in pocket for pills. Clare? Not here. On deck, so. The body knows. The moon's brilliant silver through the hatchway, spilling down the companionway. Companion, he thinks. Good word. Lucid now. Slow, lucid. Good.

Waiting for him, two cigarettes between her fingers, unlit. She grins at him, bold child, fires up the lighter, inhales both, hands him one.

"So, Tom, we good again?"

"We're good. I'm hungry. You?"

She doesn't answer his question, looks away back out to sea for a moment, then says: "She never mentioned you hitting her, OK? In fact, now that I think of it, she never really talked about how you were together, about how you parted? It was all 'Oh, yeah Tom, I remember a gig he played in…' and 'One time, we were going along Portobello Road and…' or maybe 'He used to have a beard, you know…' or — you know the sort of thing. You might have just shared a house or something, you know?"

"Oh."

"Ah Tom, don't be stupid, OK? Of course it meant something to her, don't be stupid now. She just didn't want to let me in on it, you see? I *knew* you'd been important to her, all right? I knew, and I'm pretty certain she could see that I knew, she just needed to keep that locked up safe inside her, wherever she put it when you drifted apart, see? Like when she walked out of the Arizona life and into life with Rory, and she just parked who she'd been? But that Sandra never really went away. Maybe she was waiting for me to be old enough to ask the right questions?"

"And then she died." Tom is shocked at his own unexpected words, the bluntness.

Clare leans back into him, he makes a circle around her shoulders with his arms, and she says, "Yes, Tom, then she died."

And after a while she says, "yes, Tom, I am. Hungry, I mean."

They beach the dinghy on shingle, pull it up beyond a thin scurfy line of dried kelp. They look around. Ramshackle building at the water's edge to their right. On the concrete veranda, an old man in his vest, hands clasped on top of a walking stick. He salutes them with a jut of his chin. Tom gives him a brief wave, leaves the oars in the dinghy. The path to the villages is steep enough. As they come to the ridge, passing among olives, there's a step up where the path bends left. Tom remembers this. He reaches to the thick olive branch above his shoulder, his hand finding the patch worn smooth by generations swinging up, steadying themselves down. He guides Clare's hand to the place as she follows.

"He used to swim every day, in the afternoon", Tom says. She knows he means Graves.

"Imagine how many times his hand has rested there."

She smiles at him fondly.

"I found a branch here, on the ground, took it home with me. Peeled it, shaped it, a stick for Ruth, out walking the dog. Beautiful wood, olive, the grain like human skin."

Her hand in the small of his back, the push saying yeah, yeah, keep going old man. Tom smiling at this. Dogs barking, lights in the small, old houses. They come off the track onto a dirt road, then onto the main road. Left, then, up through the village, and when you're almost past, a steep hill to the left again. Buenas tardes, buenas tardes, left and right, the old women on the doorsteps, on chairs, observing without judging, without caring much one way or the other. Tom and Clare, nothing to do with them. The church at the top of the hill, behind walls, railings on top of the walls. Big, venerable cypresses, the church a faded pink, squat bell tower. Between the gate and the church door, flat on the ground, the grave slab. 'Robert Graves, Poeta.' The lettering amateurish, perfect.

There's nothing here. A small Mallorquin churchyard, a dead English expatriate. Night in a small village, far from home. Two more in an endless, inexplicable stream of visitors. Some man who was famous once, Inglés, who knows what people do? Or, Ai! Don Roberto, still they come!

And: here I am, Ruth, still on the curve, still learning and up for it, but I'm dying, Ruth, you know that. Here I am, full moon over Deya, my God that big black mountain, would you look at the ball of the moon rolling along that ridge, here I am, Ruth, and here you are, and oh God, Ruth, I'm scared, you know, what if I'm wrong?

And Clare: Well, Mam, what did you make of that, back there? And here I am, eh? Deya. Who'd have believed it, maybe you would, maybe you would. More your daughter than maybe you thought I'd be, eh? So, not him after all, Mam, eh? You're right, Mam, this life? Something else, Mam, something else. Ah, but Sandra, Sandra, weren't you very lonesome all the same? And where do I go from here?

"Like we're towing the moon", she says, voice hushed, her hand trailing in the silver-black water.

"Feels like it", Tom grunts. "A wonder it didn't occur to you to do the rowing."

"Don't you know, Tom Harrington", haughtily, "that class of thing is beneath the dignity of a Goddess? Where were you brought up at all? Ah! Men these days...."

33

"God", she says, back of her hand to her brow. "Another bloody day in Paradise, honestly wouldn't you get sick of it?!"

"You're in good form this morning."

"Shut up, you."

They motored out with the dawn, the big red ball of fire on the black wall behind them. "I want to get a good offing before turning down for Palma", Tom had said, "wind's still in the west, but it's got a bit stronger, and there'll be all kinds of people coming up and down this coast anyway. We'll stay out a bit, OK?"

Now they have all sail set, running south on a beam reach, sweet and true.

"Pass me the coffee, would you?" she says.

"I tidied away the nest, too", he says.

"Well aren't you great?" she says. "Now the milk."

The wind pouring down on them from the west, strong and steady, *Lon Dubh* carving a valley of creamy white water out of the deep blue, flying south. What we must look like, from the cliff over there, she thinks, oh beautiful, beautiful.

"Tom, do you think are we carrying too much sail?"

Reading my mind, or reading the wind, the boat, he wonders?

"Ah no", he says, "we're just about on the edge; see, I let out the main a bit, let out the stays'l, the jenny and, presto!"

"I thought maybe we were pushing it a bit, you know? You love this life, Tom, don't you? I can see you out here on your own, you know, I can see what it must be like. The rush, Tom, it must be a rush, eh? On your own, like this?"

Tom, hearing the question under the question, over the question. Witch, after all, he thinks, and admires her for it. One of our own.

"I love this life, Clare. I love it all. The rain coming in off Howth on a January morning, the dogs on the green in summer, the old dogs frisking like pups, a pint after a long day, a freshly ironed shirt straight onto your back. I love fresh bread, fresh coffee, an apple from a tree hanging over someone's wall, coming down into Allihies on a June evening, the houses as bright as toytown up on the hill. A pint in Jimmy's with my pal Tony. I love white cotton sheets, fresh from the airing cupboard, or three days on the bed, the mark of the body on 'em. I love music, all kinds and every kind of music. I love hurling. I love mornings on a Greek island, the white of the houses, the deep blue shutters, the green shutters, that old dusty green, the old black grannies heading off to the bakery, mimosa, oleander, tamarisk, olive, the wind coming through all those, and the whoosh of the sea on the shingle down below. Books, Clare, the places books take you, old friends met on the street, old neighbours at funerals, young ones and young fellas giving each other the eye after school on a corner somewhere, the smell of earth after rain Clare, the smell of earth after rain!"

Clare looking away to sea, silently weeping.

"Ah Clare, Clare, it's all right, it's all right. Be worse if I didn't know, understand? When I was younger? I'd get this terrible grief come over me sometimes. Out of nowhere. Losing it all, the terrible pain of losing it all, the world going on without me, the beautiful world, the one and only, all this still happening and me not there to be in it, be part of it? I used to call it the nevers, you know? Never again this body turning under my hand, these eyes looking at me, the feel of my own strength on a long walk, anything, everything, never again, never again — and then the long, long never of never anything at all forever and ever? Oh Jesus, Clare, I'd be in bits for days. I still get flashes...

"You with me, Clare? I've a date, you see. Sell by date. Ah don't be like that, just my little joke. That changed things, you see? That and Ruth. Ah don't be so stricken, Clare, it's all right. Ruth was no saint, Clare, I'm not idealising her, she was human like us. But, she was everything to me, you see, and it's not the same without her. She's here and not here, every living minute of the day I'm talking to her but nobody notices because to them she's not there. So ... soon I'll be gone too. I know this, I've had a long time to get used to the idea. Today? Today is beautiful — this day next year, I won't be here. But I won't be in Ikaria, either, Clare, not in

Lesvos, not in all the places I'm not in today, right now. Do you get me? Poor Clare, do you understand a word I'm saying? Look at you, kidnapped and carried off to sea by a raving lunatic!"

"Oh Tom, Tom...."

"I'm afraid she won't be there", he said. "When the time comes. I'm afraid there won't be a 'there.'"

Blunt as that. Flat. Plain. Silence then.

"Get me a cigarette, would you?" he said after a while. "Sure they can't do me any harm."

Clare too proud of him to let herself weep any more.

They gave themselves to the morning after that, Tom all talked out, Clare absorbed in her helming.

"You don't look too good, Tom", she said, some time after noon.

"I don't feel too good", he said, "I think I'll go down for a bit. Call me if the wind gets any stronger, in case I don't notice."

Tom, who has always prided himself on communion with wind and weather, his bone-deep, keel-deep communion with the boat. His own bleak joke to himself, swallowing the pills, climbing heavily into the bunk: 'not dark yet, but it's getting there.'

When it came time for them to round to the east for Palma, the wind died. Tom shrugged, have to motor in, a pity, what can you do? They dropped all sail, tidied the boat. Halyard, Tom reminded himself, halyard. They motored in.

On the pontoon, the berth assigned over the radio, a familiar face. "Hola, Federico!" "Hola, Capitan Tom. Long time no see!" Staring frankly at Clare.

"Federico, my daughter Clare." Hand in the small of her back; "Clare, my old friend Federico." "Yes, yes of course, Tomas, your daughter. How do you do, Miss." Not believing a word of it. "I am not", she murmured. "His daughter", she added. Bending to hand him the bowline. A quick, complicit wink from Federico the unfooled, flash of a smile, carefully masked from Tom.

"I wouldn't mind", she says, sauntering back towards Tom.

"Wouldn't mind what?" he asks.

"Being your daughter", she says. "Not that your man believes you; he knew right away I was only along for the ride. Pick your jaw up, Tom, you'll only catch flies."

Walking to the chandlery a little later he stops her, gripping her arm, turns her to face him.

"Clare. Being serious for a minute, I wouldn't mind either. You being my daughter."

"I know, Tom love", she says. "I know."

They walk out the gate, arm in arm. A wave for Federico, back in his guard hut. Phone to his ear, he waves back. Phone she thinks. Phone. Hand in her shoulderbag, she switches on her mobile.

He hears the tone. Nothing wrong with Tom's hearing. At the chandlery door he says, offhand: "I won't be long. Go on, give him a call." Stops. Looking away.

"Ah Tom, Tom, you big fool. Do you ever listen to me at all? I told you, I've decided. All the way home, Tom, all the way home."

"Oh. Right. And if he doesn't like it?"

"He'd better like it." Said so fiercely that Tom, going through the door, is laughing his head off.

Emerging with a big coil of braided line, a bag of shackles, assorted bits and pieces.

"Expensive?" she asks, taking the bag.

"Money, Clare?" he says.

"Right", she says, biting her lip.

"Did you call him?"

"Yep."

"Was he there?"

"Yep."

"What is this, twenty questions? What did you say? What did he say?"

"Jesus, nosy! Keep your shirt on. I said…" ticking the points off on her fingers, "… One, that he better start looking for a house we both like; Two, that I really, really, really love him — no, that was one — anyway: Three, that I ran you to ground in Siracusa; Four, that you are a lovely, lovely man and you're not my father after all but no matter and that you have cancer; Five, that you're heading for home, that you're bringing the boat home and I'm signed on for the duration and that I'm in Palma and we're leaving, I said tomorrow, is that OK? Right, and Six, no, there's no six, oh there is, yeah — but it's none of your business. Private stuff."

All this in, more or less, one long breath. Striding along, crackling with energy.

"Clare? Clare? Did he get a word in anywhere at all, along the like? Donal?"

"Huh? What? Oh, oh yeah. He said that he's taken the liberty of lining up three houses for us to look at, that he figures Palma to Dublin would be about fourteen days, that right? That I'm to call him when we pass the Tuskar Rock, we should have a signal around there, and that he'll meet us in Howth, I said Howth, yes, and he's very, very sorry that you have cancer, a shame, such a good man you must be, judging by how I sound about you, and that he really, really loves me and misses me. I think that's all? Oh and some other stuff, too. Also none of your business. I hope he doesn't think he can make a habit of that."

Marching along, swinging her bag.

"A habit? Of what?"

"Taking liberties. We'll have to see about that. Here we are."

And up she hops.

34

Can't do it, Tom decides, looking up the mast. Can't do it any more. Clare showering, for an instant he thinks of her nude, water streaming ... get a grip, man, get a grip. Laughing as he strolls down to the gate. Not fooling Federico, who looks at him carefully, shakes his head. "You look ... different, Tomas; not good, huh?" "No, my friend, not good." "Ah, Tomas, Tomas, I am sorry to hear this."

They watch a boat come in, critically. "How is the music with you, Federico, my friend?" "Ah I play when I can, you know how it is?" "And how is Pilar?" "Pilar is very well, thank you for asking. Our second child will be born before Christmas." A happy young man, Tom sees this, and wishes mother and child well. Perhaps not so young after all.... He asks for a man to climb the mast, to fit the new staysail halyard. He asks for the number of our mutual friend Senor Delgado. He phones him at Federico's insistence from the airless little gate cabin. Waiting for the phone to be answered, he watches Federico through the window, abstracted, working out complicated chord shapes, his left hand fluttering from hip to shoulder. He asks Federico to arrange a taxi for four o'clock, and they shake hands, after a moment's hesitation on both their parts, with a certain formality. A look. He goes back to the boat.

"You're tired, Tom", she says, watching him climb down into the saloon, putting out a hand to steady him. He nods. "It's hot out there. You should sleep."

He pats her shoulder, heading past to the bunk. He says, "Have you any plans?" She says she's thinking of going for a stroll, maybe look at the Cathedral, "God, Tom, it looks huge, doesn't it?" "It's huge", he says. "I love the little lanes all around behind it, going away up from the water. The gardens...." And he's asleep, curled on his side, a hand flat under his face.

He'll be all right, she tells herself, he'll be all right.

Two minutes in the cathedral and she knows she can't handle it for long. Too vast, too overpowering. She searches out the altar of the Virgin, she lights two candles, tipping one slightly so that the wax runs down, so that the two candles fuse when she presses them together. She places the double candle in the bed of sand, then after some thought she lights three more, placing one beside what she thinks of as Tom's candle, two beside what she thinks of as hers. When she's done this she looks around furtively, afraid she's going to be … what, exactly? Found out, she thinks, surprised and puzzled. *Found out?*

She wanders into the maze of lanes, twisting and turning in the welcome shade. Taking her time. Stopping to look in, through gateway after gateway, at the exquisite little hidden gardens, the courtyard gardens of houses whose age she can only guess at. Each garden so different from the others that she thinks of intense, unspoken rivalries, the vying of one household with the next. Vanity and pride, she thinks, vanity, pride and beauty. And who am I to judge, she thinks, who made me the final authority on anything? So, peace. Looking in gateway after gateway, admiring the bougainvillea here, an artfully draped vine there, a cut-stone fountain, an intricate iron trellis, treasure of one kind or another in this house and that, soaking the quiet into herself, letting her feet wander where they will. In a kind of dream, a willed waking dream.

Wandering, she thinks, hazily, wandering … and she hears the hymn from childhood, sung by young voices, girl voices, far away but clear and distinct as if it were issuing through the stone back wall of the Cathedral, which she has just now, rounding a corner, encountered. 'Hail Queen of Heav'n, The Ocean Star, Guide of the Wanderer, Here below' — fading away now, then swelling back, but swelling too big a word for this soft return — 'Pray for The Wanderer, Pray for me. Pray for The Wanderer, Pray for me.' The strong girl voices, her own voice lost in the choir.

Coffee, she thinks, coming to, shaken. Coffee, strong. Now.

The taxi man wakes him, slapping the deck, loud and vigorous. "Senor Tomas, Senor Tomas, Taxi! Taxi!" Smoothly awake, clear-headed, refreshed. Sticks his head out the hatch, says "five minutes." "OK, Senor. I will be at the gate." Shower, scrub head energetically, speed up the old circ. Right then, slacks, shirt, reading glasses, briefcase, where's the damn briefcase? Ah! Ship's papers, passport, wallet. Anything else? Of course. Note for Clare.

'Bit of business in town', she reads, sunglasses perched on top of her head, head tilted to the hatch for light. 'Back around five, maybe six. Eating out tonight, my treat. Wash yourself, woman!!!'

Three exclamation marks, she thinks, sniffing her armpit. The cheek of him! Folding the note carefully, shoving it down into her bag.

She showers, taking her time. The luxury. She knows he won't mind — she takes one of his T-shirts from the neat pile in the forecabin locker, pulls it over her head, settles the hem below her hips, turning this way and that, as if before a mirror. She falls back on the saloon bunk, full length; she sleeps.

"Come on, Clare, come on! Rise and Shine! To rest is not to conquer!"

Insufferable! The noise! Bares her teeth to snarl at him, sees him piling bags on the table. What?

"Glad rags, Clare, glad rags! Come on then, see what Tom got you! Come on, sleepyhead!"

It's not much of a snarl, but she tries: "Have you been drinking, or what? What's all this anyway?" Awake, then, a sudden, inexplicable happiness rising her. A flash of quick gaiety. Up and at 'em, that's what you used to say, Mam! Up and at 'em. Rearing your imaginary cavalry horse. There were mornings, I swear, when I could see the sabre flashing, would leap to your side.

What am I thinking of? Here. Now. God, look at all those bags.

"Wait'll you see" — Tom beaming at her, stowing his briefcase under the chart table, tossing bags into the forecabin, vanishing into the shower. "Wait'll you see me. Go on, open yours, those are yours." He sticks his head around the door, the water already running. "Did you wash? Don't glare at me, you. You did? Try them on, then."

Still slightly dazed. Opens the first bag, the big one. Black linen suit. Fitted jacket, jet buttons, bolero cut. Pencil slim skirt to, mid-calf is it? Beautiful detailing, beautiful finish, my God. Next bag, black silk sleeveless top, cut high at the throat. She tosses it in the air, it floats. "All these for me?" "Yep." This small bag, then. Heavy. She unwraps the tissue, opens the box. Heavy silver bangle, big blue chunks of turquoise. She slips it on her wrist, the weight of it.

Doubt, then. "Tom? Tom!"

Puts her head out again. "Tom?" He's anticipated her: "Size? You're worried about size? Look in the red bag." Worn plastic bag. Inside, her black linen shift, the white, long-sleeved blouse with the high neck. Well aren't you the cunning old devil, she thinks. "Genius, aren't I?" he calls from the shower. "Who else would think of that, eh? Oh you should have seen their faces, in the shops. Couldn't figure me out at all. Especially the blue bag shop." "Blue bag? Oh, this one. Empty?" "No, ah would you look…" "Tom Harrington!" "Ah sure only for devilment. The poor young one was only scarlet, serving me. I'd say the Spanish lads wouldn't be big on buying the old scanty underwear."

"I'm going to shower again", she says, "have to now. Don't use all the hot water." Then, reproachfully, "Ah, Tom, you must have spent…"

"…Ah, Clare, Clare, money? Remember?"

The water helps wash away the sadness that came over her then.

"Well, look at you", she says.

Tom in cream linen, a high-button white shirt, silver and turquoise cuff-links. Pausing in the forecabin doorway to be admired.

"Not bad, eh?" he says. "Do I look great or what? The shirt? Tranchinos of Siracusa. Closed now. Pity. Had it cleaned and ironed while I was out. One of the great shirts of all time, this is. The suit's Oxfam from Malahide, by the way."

Clare choking back laughter.

"Can I watch you dress?" he asks.

"No. Out you go." Laughing and imperious.

She's shy, suddenly, when she steps carefully out on deck.

"Don't look at me like that, Tom, you'll make me cry. Don't make me cry, Tom, not now. Please."

Then, tentative: "Tom? The thing is, this suit is so exquisite…."

He holds up a hand. "Tom thinks of everything, never fear. Shoes, right? Suit like that, have to have the right shoes. Taxi."

"What?"

"That's why the taxi is waiting for us. I spotted a good place…."

I will not cry, she tells herself, I will not cry.

Then she says, "Tom? Am I a witch or what?"

Brings her hands out from behind her back, hands him the package. "Open it." Dark blue silk, goes perfectly with the shirt.

"The wide part, Tom, look on the back."

In perfect lettering, white thread, 'Tom and Clare, *Lon Dubh*. Siracusa, for Home.'

"I was always a dab hand at the embroidery, Tom."

"Ah Jesus, Clare! That's beautiful! See, there's the taxi, what did I tell you? Walk slowly, Clare, I want them all to be as jealous as hell. You could simper a bit? No? Ah sure God loves a trier."

Black suede, soft as good gloves. Four-inch heel. She spots them the minute they walk into the shop.

"That was quick", Tom says. "Give me the ones you're wearing, pop them into this bag here."

"What's with the bag, Tom?"

"Always handy to have a bag. You never know.... Those comfortable? Good. Now, here we are."

"Tom, this place has a doorman to open the door for the doorman!"

"Behave!"

Centuries of quiet. Scrubbed flagstone floors, dark beams in the white ceiling, dark with age. The hotel reception desk a carved table that might have come from a refectory or a Ducal palace. Maritime paintings, sparsely distributed, in simple gold frames. A broad stone staircase in back, heavy drapes to each side of it. Exquisite carpets here and there, making islands of colour on the otherwise bare floor.

Only one door, leading to the restaurant. The same air of elegant timelessness, tables for four, set a good distance apart. Three or four occupied. The walls here panelled in dark oak. The soft lustre of careful waxing.

"Don Tomas!" The head waiter, grave but friendly, showing them to their table.

"Don?" She muttered, sitting down. "Don Tomas?" "I may have given the impression", Tom said carefully, "that I am a person of a certain social importance. And substantial wealth, of course."

"Don't be smug, Tom. It doesn't suit you. The way that fella eyed me! Some place, Tom, some place. What was it, a palace?"

"Yep. Always wanted to try it, it just always seemed ... anyway", halting the approaching waiter with a gesture, "may I suggest the smoked fish paté with olives, for starters, then I think the grilled swordfish with a simple salad, or perhaps the Gambas de Gaudi, grilled prawns with peppers and olive oil, and then for the meat course, the pork fillet with manchego, you know, cheese? A good solid Rioja with that, I think. Hmm?"

The waiter has drifted alongside by now, is as dumbfounded as Clare by all this, nods enthusiastically in support.

"And you were never here before? I see. Prawns for me, I think. Never before, right?"

"You've got all that, waiter, have you? Good man. The swordfish for me. Now, a Castillio Diablo ninety-one, I think, and later the Marques ninety-four. The ninety-five, if the sommelier thinks it's better" — forestalling that functionary's advance by pointing the waiter at him. "Go."

"Tom, what the fuck…?"

"Now, Clare, language, language! The world isn't all that complicated, Clare, if you pay attention. I watch what you order in Ortigia, I observe what you linger over in the market in Carloforte; I watch what you choose to cook, I pop in here earlier to have a gander at the menu … voilá!"

Over the paté: "You see, Tom — Sandra, Cass, I need you to understand. It's not that she didn't have a good life. That scrapbook, I think she just had a certain fondness for you, that she wished you well? And she'd lost touch with the friends of her youth, you were the only one whose life she could follow, see what had become of you. I think in some way, I don't know, she knew that somewhere along the line she blew it. Her own life, I mean, not her life with you, not just her life with you; Oh, Tom, she could be very unhappy, you know? Months on end, then she'd just, just walk away from it. I think she felt that, well, that you stayed with 'The Path', you know? You see what I'm saying? Once only, I was in second year Law, that's a long time to have been thinking about it, once only I asked her straight out if you were my father. She just looked at me, no expression at all, shrugged and said 'Maybe, who knows?' Imagine! I didn't speak to her for six months, maybe more, then I just started speaking to her again. Like that. When you'd met Ruth, I don't know how long after, it's in the cuttings, I don't remember just now, I saw her one day looking at a photograph of the two of you. She showed it to me and said, 'Oh good man, Tom, lucky man, Tom.' No, not like that, more: 'Oh. Good man. Tom. Lucky man. Tom.' Like, a blessing. That make sense? She had a good life, Tom, better than most. Just, she had a feeling she'd blown something special somewhere along the line.

"I think she tried to help me not to do that, you know? To find, I don't know, my deepest instinct, and follow it, trust it?"

Over the swordfish, the prawns: "So, what's the plan, Tom, the route, from here to Ireland?"

"Eh, OK. Choices. Palma, down inside Ibiza, you could go to Alicante, then Almeria, Gib, then out into the Atlantic, up Portugal, around Finisterre, A Coruna people go into sometimes, La Coruna some people call it, either will do, then coastal through Biscay to Brittany, across from there, up the Irish Sea.

"Or, straight for the open sea, turn up north, stopover at a place called Nazaré that I like, Portugal, north of Lisbon, the entrance for Lisbon I mean. The Atlantic coast of Portugal beautiful, beautiful, white beaches miles long, we'd stay in close; then a bit of Galicia, good places to run into if there's a storm, Finisterre, out to about eleven West and straight for the Tuskar Rock. Big open sea run, you'd love it.

"You want to know which I prefer? One stop, Nazairé, then straight ahead.

"If you have the right winds, don't get into any trouble in Biscay, ten to twelve days I reckon.

"To be very honest, I have to say it's not the best time of the year for Biscay."

"Oh."

"But no need to commit to anything now. And there are variations inside these options, you know? OK? OK.

"It's a beautiful trip, Clare, this time of year you're running up out of summer into autumn, you feel it day by day, cold waters, crisp air, that snug feeling when you put on a woolly jumper in the afternoon? Makes you think of apples, robbing orchards when you were young, maybe first frost in the morning, that tingle on your skin when you look out the window. Running north out of the summer, out of the Med, you know? Heading home. The Atlantic. Running out into that."

Over the meat, Tom: "The poet Montague asked Beckett, near the end, 'How much of it (he meant life) was worth it, Sam?' — and Beckett said 'Very little'. I couldn't say that. I mean, Beckett might have been having his little joke, you know, but, me, I loved every minute of my life. Think about it, Clare, since we left Ortigia, was there a minute you'd give up, any single thing you'd change, anything at all? Wasn't it great, just being alive? Isn't it great, just being alive? Here, now?"

Clare, looking far away, nods, then says, coming back from wherever she's been: "I only slipped up once, you know? I was just thinking...."

"What? What are you on about?"

"In Ortigia, the Piazza di Duomo? Remember the lawyers? When I said 'I know how old you are, Tom', remember? Don't look at me like that, I heard your question. Questions.

"For a long time there, in my twenties, it was hard, you know? An act of will, mostly. Dour desire to endure, all that. And still, after a bad day in court, I still feel that sometimes. And I look around and see how people's lives are, not just my own; I see how desperate life is for so many people, you know? And I think this world is one big fuck-up. But more and more I think you just get one shot at it, life on earth I mean. Don't look like that, I'm not going all hippyish on you. Ha! I was right, look at you, that is what you were thinking, there's Sandra coming out in her. Am I right?

"Of course I'm right, Clare's always right. Oops, hear that? The wine talking. Never mind, where was I? Yeah. It's been a trip, man. Wouldn't have missed it for the world. You're a good man, Tom, you're a very good man."

"Some man for one man, eh?" Tom trying to lighten the tone, uncomfortable.

"Something else, man, something else.... See, in Ortigia, when I saw you with whatshername, all right, all right, Christine. That Christine, right? I knew you weren't my father and I could have walked away, you know? I mean, I could have been wrong, OK. Maybe the lawyer in me was whispering 'proof, Clare, proof', but I sort of knew. You looked up at me, and I saw, I don't know ... something. I have to figure out that something, you know?"

"What do you mean, you knew I wasn't...? what do you mean by that?"

"Look, I'm a bit uncomfortable about this, talking like this, OK. I just, *knew*. But I didn't realise that I knew then until after. Ah this is doing my head in. Dessert! A sugar hit! Please!"

Crema Catalana. "And now, brandy and cigars? The traditional...?"

"Oh yes, please."

The head waiter bringing the box, not raising an eyebrow when Clare beckons him, selects a long slim Panatella. Holding a small spirit lamp for her to light it. Smiling over her head at Tom.

"That fella's fond of me, you know?"

"He is", Tom said, "who wouldn't be?"

And the conversation floating on, and each of them thinking there's something not quite real about this, the night feels somehow unreal, and neither of them wanting to acknowledge this, not to say it out loud in case something terrible might be hovering out there, out there....

"Being in from the sea", Tom says, reaching for her hand. "Clare, look at me, it's OK; being in from the sea, after a journey? It feels unreal. Out of the only world there is into the bigger world, but not into the world yet. Always like this, it's OK. You'll see, it'll be like that in Dublin, too, when you get there, maybe worse because here at least has the comfort of being unfamiliar. Coming back to yourself."

"Ah, you old witch", she says, a candle sparkling in each eye as she leans across. "You old witch, Tom." In gaiety, in fun, but a cold shiver tremoring Tom's spine, a fleeting, pitiless mask appearing in her face, vanishing.

Then, leaning back again, stone cold sober: "What I saw, in Ortigia, I mean before you looked at me, you and Christine, what I saw was you were being warm and gentle and funny and companionable — and your heart wasn't in it. Your heart was away."

Not a challenge, more a reaching down and back for, well, the connection. That'll do for now, the connection.

Matter of fact, almost offhand: "Spot on, Clare, got it in one. Been like that since Ruth went. You know this. But this trip, all heart, Clare, all heart. And I thank you."

Do not cry, Clare, she tells herself, I'll fucking murder you if you cry now.

Tom picking the candle up. Tom putting the candle aside. Leaning across. Taking her face in both hands. Kissing her on the forehead. Tom murmuring, or she thinks he's murmuring, "Good woman yourself, good woman yourself. I do thank thee."

And what, Clare asks herself, shaken, the fuck was that? I'm hearing voices now? And then, yeah, so?

Like somebody cut the strings, she thinks then, I feel like somebody just cut the strings.

"Tom, I'm exhausted all of a sudden. I'm sorry."

"You are of course", he says, smiling at her, "you are of course. I told you, coming in off the sea…. Come on, get you to bed."

"In your dreams, pal, in your dreams" — one last hurrah for that joke. Tom, delighted, laughs out loud. So fond of him, she thinks, so fond of this man….

Tom hands his card to the head waiter as the man sweeps Clare's chair back with a flourish. The man nods, his free hand saying yes, yes, of course Don Tomas, understood, understood….

Smiling them away.

Drifting, drifting, out into the hall. Tom stops her, a hand light on her arm, turns her towards the stairs. A stout, uniformed woman, one hand on her belly, the other motioning towards the broad stone staircase. Huh? Tom hands her the bag he's brought with him.

"One last surprise, Clare, a little treat. Go on, enjoy. Big deep bath, Clare? Big, deep, soft, wide bed…"

"…But, but…"

Sighing: "…Clare, think of it like this, OK? Don Tomas, look at me, right, this man of a certain age appears here this afternoon? Are you listening, Clare? Pay attention, I'm trying to seduce you here. Appears in here in sun-bleached rags, you like the sun-bleached rags, Clare? He books a suite, excuse me, *the* suite, he makes a dinner reservation. Then this fabulously handsome man, right, that's me again now, appears in the evening with, forgive me, I have to say this, a stunningly beautiful young woman, clearly not his wife or daughter. You still with me, Clare? Clare? Pick up your jaw, Clare, it's making the staff uneasy. Can you imagine the delicious fun of all this for everyone here? And now, Clare, we're going to pull the rug out from under them, aren't we? I am going to bid you a courtly good night, maybe even a chaste peck on the cheek, you think? Maybe. And you are going to, what you have to do Clare is *ascend* this staircase *regally*. Alone. And it's going to do their heads in. Would you do it for that, Clare, for the devilment?"

Almost there, he thinks, coming round, coming round. Absent-minded, he signs for the waiter who's appeared at his side, palms the card to his back pocket.

"Come on, Clare. A gift, a surprise! I love giving surprises, it's been a lovely evening now. Up you go, whoa, what about my kiss? Up you go, Clare. Up into dreamland."

Looking back over her shoulder. Stopping on the landing, looking down.

Dying, she thinks, the wonder of it, who would ever think that man is dying. "Tom", she says suddenly, in a loud, firm voice, "Tom, thank you. For everything. You're a good man, Tom, I mean it. A good man."

"Go on, would you, bring a blush to me maiden cheek. Go on, sweet dreams. Take your time in the morning. No hurry, I'll be on the boat." And turns, head up, shoulders back, and strides across the echoing hall, and out through the doors, sweeping them wide with both hands. Out into the blessed night.

35

Clare woke, floating on air. Darkness, complete and utter.

Her eyes are open, but it's so dark, so dark. Floating, everything fresh and, lavender, what...? She sat up, feeling all round her. So many pillows, wow, some bed. Of course. The pleasant woman showing her in. The bed a white island on a deep blue carpet, the soft light from the bathroom beyond. All white, the room all white, some kind of picture, beams overhead, the lamps, tall, soft, on either side of the headboard. Wax, smelling of wax and ... of course, lavender. Pulling the drapes, big, heavy drapes....

Fool! Energy, jolting, out of bed, remembering to the right, the right. Remembering, nothing between bed and window, yes, heavy, heavy cloth, pull, both arms sweeping wide....

Blinded! Blinded. Eyes shut, then squint, then slowly open.

Looking down through the canopy of, yes, a fig tree, it's a fig, the leaves, down into the courtyard, cobbled, a well over there, wrought iron canopy. Cool, cool shade, walls, wooden doors painted red, the gateway opening to the lane, the heavy oak gates, studded in black, folded back against ... look up, sun, what time is it?

Janey, ten o'clock? Couldn't be, ten? Looks like.

Bathroom, piss, don't look in mirror yet, lotions and potions, my God the shower, you could hold a party ... better, whew, drank some wine last night, Clare. And then, remembering clearly, no. A bottle of white, a bottle of red, between us, I had a brandy. That wouldn't ... taste of cigar in my mouth, yuck! Teeth, look in mirror, ah not too bad, not too bad. Pick up his T-shirt off the floor.

Tom. At the bottom of the stairs. One hand half raised, smile, ah such a smile. Walking away.

The old dote, all the same. To think of it. The T-shirt packed in the bag.

To rest is not to conquer. Muttering. To rest is not to conquer. Gathering up her things. To rest is not to conquer. Finger brush hair, toilet bag, check. Glad for flat shoes, huh? Hot walking in this suit, carry jacket by nice broad tape loop here, good. Ready? Last look around. To rest is not to conquer. God, Tom, your Dad and you, I'd like to have seen....

Walking down the stirs, 'Ah shag it, who wants to conquer?' She hears him tell it. She freezes, part of her mind registering, 'Jesus Christ it's true, blood does run cold, feel that!' On the second step up from the bottom. Frozen. "I'll be on the boat. No hurry, I'll be on the boat". No, He wouldn't....

Out, scattering doormen, "Taxi! Taxi!"

Near the port now, come on, breathe, Clare, breathe. Come on! Turning in to the Marina, snagged, traffic jam. Money, shoving money at the driver, out, running, running now, panic, heads turning, the gate ahead. Federico. She slows. Federico. She stops, yards away. Federico. Oh dear Jesus, oh Mother of God no, no....

But of course, yes. Should have guessed. Should have known. You knew, girl, you knew.

I knew.

The empty berth.

She looks out to sea, looks around for a vantage point, somewhere higher, higher ... but no point, no point at all.

She can repeat it word for word, she can hear herself now repeating it word for word, such a memory I have ... "One of the best feelings in the world, you'll see. The town going about its business, the moon coming up, stars coming out ... slipping your lines, catching the ghost of a breeze, sail going up, drifting away down-channel, everything getting quieter, quieter, the sea calling...."

Rage, pure, blood-pounding, blind, deep rage.

You ... fucker Tom Harrington! You went without me! I said, didn't I? I said I'd bring her home with you, didn't I? Didn't I? Bringing it all back home, Tom, remember? Bastard! Mister go it alone. Mister fucking lone hero sailor. Mister oh yeah, could be a bit of a blow there coming up through Biscay but sure, a good boat, you know, good boat.... you left me! I'll swing for you, so help me, I'll swing for you, I'll ... what? What!

Federico, taking her arm, leading her gently away. Federico stopping, his eyes in shadow, can't see.... Handing her a package. Too bulky, she thinks, dispassionate now. Clear. Herself.

Too bulky. Weighing it in her hands. Big, padded envelope. Warm in the sun, that smell of hot paper. Too bulky....

Such a gentle touch, she thinks, notices, Federico leading her into his cabin, sitting her down at his desk. Steel there, too, sinew and muscle, more sensed than felt. He sits her down. He closes the door behind him, stepping outside. He stands there, his back to the cabin, his arms folded. He will murder anyone who disturbs her. He is perfectly prepared to.

She slides out the log. *Lon Dubh*. Gold letters on the blue cover. Faded blue. Coffee stain there in the corner, half moon. She turns to the last entry. Palma. Harrington, T., Capn., Hogan, C., Crew. End of voyage. All well. Today's date, then, and a crisp notation: 'Commenced new Log.'

Ah, Tom. Palma, towards Howth. Never give destination as an absolute, he'd said. Pushing your luck.

Papers, legal papers, she puts them aside after a glance. Fancy, headed paper, this Senor Delgado, whoever you are.

A Polaroid, themselves, brilliant and shining. Last night's finery. Ah, Federico, of course. She remembers now, him stopping them at the gate. But don't we look handsome, she murmurs, don't we look the business? Keep this, have it with me in Howth. Probably be pissing rain as usual. Remind him. Remind him the sun is shining in the south. Remind him....

Envelope. Janey, huh, envelopes inside envelopes. Oh, Tommy Earley. I must ... oh. Oh. Tommy Earley.

Coming to. Looking down, down past her hands. Her bag, neatly zipped. Well, of course. The box. Big cardboard box. Charts, pilot books ... Atlantic Pilot, Portugal and North Spain. Atl....

The white envelope in her hands. Her name crisply printed. A flourish under. A full stop.

Dread, a void of ice in her stomach. Specific as that, exactly that.

And you *knew*, girl, didn't you? You *knew*.

I did, I see that, I did. I knew.

Opinel on the desk, up against the window. She eases the blade out, twists the ring to lock the blade in place. Precise movements. Carefully, carefully she slits the envelope open. She takes out the folded sheets. She twists in her chair a little to keep the harsh sunlight off the pages.

My Dear Clare,

What else could I do? Could you have stood there and watched me sail away? No. You couldn't have borne it, and nor could I have.

Remember saying you'd thought of bailing when we reached Palma? Reached here, I mean. I thought you'd guessed, then, or intuited, or whatever it is you do. I was sorry, first, like I thought maybe you'd try to persuade me not to? Then I was glad you hadn't twigged.

I need you to think this through with me.

I have no family. I have cancer. I can't bear the thought of chemo and all that, wasting away, withering away. I'm afraid, Clare, I've been afraid all my life, it seems to me sometimes. On the bad days, you know? Anything brave I ever did, I did it to get past being afraid. Get past it, you see.

So this isn't brave, not really. And not just a notion that took hold of me.

I've done harm in this life, hurt people, wounded people. I am very sorry for that. I always tried to do what is best but — you know how it is.

I tried to do good, I hope I did some good.

I want you to tell no one. I'm sorry if that's a burden, but please, Clare, do that for me. Well, Donal obviously. You can tell Donal. Nobody else, Clare, not even Tommy. Tommy will know right enough, but you're a lawyer too, you know that you can guess all you like but without proof, a statement, evidence... So, please, no one. My business, you see. Not a gesture. Suicides kill other people, Clare, I know what I'm saying here. I'd have toughed it out to the end if it wasn't for being diagnosed. Seems no point to hanging around, you know? Get on with it.

I hope I'm not rambling, I thought this would be more — fluent? Is that what I thought? I never allowed for having to write a note, now see what you made me do?

West, Clare, that's the plan. Was always the plan, west out through the Gates, west out into the big ocean. Follow the sun, eh?

I've nothing to tell you, Clare. No wisdom to impart. We said everything there was to say, I think. I hope. Some trip, eh? Some team.

What I saw, in Siracusa that night? I saw you, Clare. Just that. You. Thank you for coming part of the way with me. Thank you for making it all so much clearer. That's what you did. I have learned so much from the women who have been my companions, my friends. Who came part of the way with me. From you.

Ruth, you see, this is all about Ruth really. When she went, well that's the point you see. She went, and I don't know where. I want to know where she went, you see, so that I can go there and be with her again. There's a line in a poem, "I made a bargain with that hair before time began." Haven't a clue what the guy meant by it, but I know what I mean by it. The connection, you see, Clare? When you make the connection, that's it. It stays made.

Remember I said, you asked me was I afraid, I said what I'm really afraid of is that Ruth isn't any where. That there is no where. When I got the diagnosis, when I'd had time to think it all through I mean, I decided there's only one way to find out. You see that?

The boat is yours, you've the papers there in the envelope. I did that yesterday, arranged it all with Delgado. Posted a copy to Tommy Earley just in case. You've another note for him there. Tell him nothing, remember. And there's a ticket home for you with this, too.

I'm dragging this out, aren't I? I suppose I'm putting it off. Fear, you see. My mind is made up, but I'm still afraid. Weird, huh?

What I'm going to do, Clare, so as you know: When I'm far enough out, I'll heave to. I'll make sure it's a sunny morning, never you fear. Heave to. Everything squared away. Hatch locked, she's a great boat, you know, she'll ride anything out until someone comes across her. I left money with Tommy, I mean I made arrangements. That'll pay the salvage. Someone's bound to come across her. Depends on how far I get, I suppose. So, remove the guardrail right? Sit on the deck, legs dangling over, the way I like to sometimes. Morphine and whiskey, eh, Clare? Very rock 'n' roll. Fall over eventually, you see. Down then, all the way down. And over.

You think I'm being cruel, telling you?

Maybe I know you better than you think.

What's the alternative, just disappear? Ah no.

So, there you have it. I didn't lie to you, I said I was taking the boat home. My best shot, Clare, all I have left of a shot at home. Taking the boat.

And now, you know how I love leaving harbour at night!

Take good care of yourself, do what's best always Thank you for coming the way with me to here.

Love,

Tom.

36

"I'll be back, OK, Federico?"
    "Yes, I will be here."
    Big blocks of noise and light and shade. With a long stride, carving through crowds, unswerving and undeflected. The cathedral a great cavern of light and air and shadow and stone. The side chapel. Carefully folding the notes from her purse, stuffing God alone knows how much into the slot. Weeping but straight backed. Taking candles in fistfuls, sticking them into the sand in clumps, in lines, in fucking *battalions* until every candle in the place, until the whole altar is a blaze of light and heat. The old women muttering, more drifting over by the minute, avid, enchanted, spellbound.
    The oldest one there, her authority earned by her years of suffering on this earth, shushing them with imperious gestures.
    Clare oblivious, tears pouring down her face. Radiant in her grief.
    Then Clare, proud Clare, unbowed, freelance, pagan, Buddhist, agnostic, rational Clare, begins to sing; softly at first, and then in a lifting, ringing voice, such a sweet voice too, they agree, the gathering crones; her voice ascending now into the vaults of stone and light, the deep blue sky above it all:

Hail, Queen of Heaven, the ocean star,
Guide of the Wanderer, here below;
Thrown on life's surge, we claim thy care:
Save us from peril and from woe.
Mother of Christ, star of the sea,
Pray for the Wanderer, pray for me.

This they know.

In their own tongue, one by one and in twos, then threes, they lift their voices with hers, shuffling inwards until they form a solid phalanx around her, the oldest one standing firm beside her, gripping her elbow, that deep voice immemorial as her ruined body:

Mother of Christ, star of the sea,
Pray for the Wanderer, pray for me.

Pray for the Wanderer, pray for me.